THE SAFEST PLACE

Born in Malaya in 1943, Fergus Linehan has been film critic and Arts Editor of *The Irish Times*. He has written extensively about the arts and is the author of plays, musicals and comedy material for radio and television. He lives in Dublin with his wife, the actress Rosaleen Linehan, and has a daughter, three sons and a grandson.

The Safest Place is his second novel.

THE
SAFEST PLACE

Fergus Linehan

Fergus Linehan

TOWN HOUSE, DUBLIN

First published in 1998 by

Town House and Country House
Trinity House, Charleston Rd
Ranelagh, Dublin 6

In association with Macmillan Publishers

ISBN: 1–86059–088–8

1 3 5 7 9 8 6 4 2

A CIP catalogue record for this book is available from
the British Library.

Phototypeset by Intype London Ltd
Printed and bound in Great Britain by
Mackays of Chatham plc, Chatham, Kent

*To Hugh, Evanna, Fergus
and Conor*

PROLOGUE

NEW YEAR 1942

For three nights now the two watchers had been waiting for the man they were going to kill. It was a road of small, cosy red-brick houses, each with a small porch and a bow window that looked out from a sitting room. The owners of these houses were grocers, clerks in Guinness's brewery, bus inspectors, printers, police sergeants.

Across the road from the house that the two were watching was a lane and, on the few occasions when anyone passed along the street, they would retreat a few paces down this lane, turn their backs and pretend to be in conversation. Eddie O'Sullivan, the younger of the two, didn't want to do it. Tall, with the long-boned awkwardness and pink cheeks of a typical Irish countryman, he betrayed his nervousness by shifting his weight constantly from foot to foot, taking little walks down the lane and back and smoking more than he had ever done before. The thought of the deed ahead weighed on him like a stone in his chest, depressing him and filling him with fears which he didn't dare to show.

On the first night they had waited for three hours, but their intended victim had not appeared. The second night seemed even longer, the empty road more drab, the winter cold more biting. O'Sullivan stamped his feet, but they still went numb, blew on his freezing fingers and pulled his trench coat around him. The boredom seemed to go on for ever and yet there was no respite from the thought of their mission.

The older man, McCaigue, was stocky and dark. For the most part he stood still, but when he did move it was confidently, with energy, even eagerness, as if he was a runner toeing the line at the start of a race. At ten o'clock he said: 'We'll give it one last try tomorrow night. If he doesn't appear then we'll have to think of another plan.'

Relief flooded through O'Sullivan. He wasn't going to back down – all his life, his background forbade that. But at the same time, he didn't want to kill this man, any man. Surely he wouldn't turn up now. Maybe he was away on some job down the country. And if a new plan was hatched maybe he, O'Sullivan, could get out of it some way.

The third night came. Again they took up their position in the freezing lane. A man appeared, out walking his dog. McCaigue put a hand to his cap, as if he was adjusting it, so that his face was hidden as the walker passed by. But O'Sullivan found himself staring directly into the stranger's eyes as he came up to them. The man looked at them curiously, as if wondering what they were doing out on such a cold night, but said nothing.

*

Inside his house, Detective Sergeant Paul O'Grady sat reading the *Irish Independent*, while his wife darned a pair of socks and his son Seán did his homework. A clock ticked, unnaturally loud in the silence of the room, while Seán's pen scratched on his exercise book.

The policeman read the war news and the popular cartoon feature, 'Curlie Wee and Gussie Goose', with equal lack of interest. He folded his paper carefully.

'I think I'll take a run up to the depot,' he told his wife.

''Tis nearly ten o'clock,' she said.

'So what.' It was a statement, not a question. Christmas and New Year meant he had been spending more time at home lately and this left him feeling cooped up and restless.

*

'Come on, you bastard, come on!' urged McCaigue outside, but no one came.

'There's no point in this,' said O'Sullivan. 'Let's go.'

McCaigue gave way. 'All right, all right,' he said. Then: 'Hold your horses, we'll give it another ten minutes.'

They had leant their bicycles against the footpath a few doors down. O'Sullivan had just got his and was getting ready to mount it when the front door of the house they were watching opened. The policeman came down the short path, wheeling his own big upright bike.

McCaigue didn't hesitate. Running across the road, he drew his revolver, holding it in front of him at arm's length. O'Sullivan dropped his bicycle, pulled his own gun and ran after him. What followed only took seconds, but it seemed to happen very slowly. When he'd go back on it in his mind subsequently it would be like a half-remembered nightmare, with bits missing and no sense to it.

O'Grady, on the footpath outside his house, stopped dead. The three men faced each other for an eternal moment, gazing stupidly, wordlessly. Then McCaigue fired, the revolver cracking thinly. The bullet hit O'Grady on the shoulder. He staggered, as if punched, but stayed on his feet. McCaigue fired again and this time O'Grady fell to the ground. O'Sullivan, his mouth open, gazed at him foolishly.

Then, incredibly, O'Grady staggered to his feet. He was gasping, glassy-eyed, like some huge ox that refused to die at the hands of a butcher. His lips were moving, he seemed to be trying to say something, but nothing came from his mouth except foam. This wasn't the way it was meant to happen. When someone was shot in the pictures they fell and that was it. It wasn't like this at all.

'Fire! Fire, fuck you!' screamed McCaigue at his companion.

Later, O'Sullivan had no memory of pulling the trigger. In dream-like slow motion, he heard his gun bark twice and felt the recoil in his hand. They were wild shots, passing harmlessly over the policeman's head, but O'Grady fell again and, as he did so, it was blood that came from his mouth and dribbled down the side of his chin.

From inside the house there came the sound of a woman's screaming. She screamed again and again, repetitively, unbrokenly, almost monotonously. Then the hall door burst open and she was running towards the fallen figure, still screaming.

McCaigue raised his pistol again at arm's length and pointed it at her.

'No!' shouted O'Sullivan, and knocked his hand aside. McCaigue didn't fire.

There were shouts, lights were going on along the road. Running feet were coming nearer. O'Sullivan turned and ran. As he went, he brushed against his bicycle, lying against the kerb, the wheels spinning around. McCaigue coolly mounted his own bicycle and pedalled off.

As O'Sullivan pounded down the road two men came running towards him, one in a woollen dressing gown. Seeing the revolver in his hand, they stopped as if transfixed. He ran past them, almost brushing against them as he went by. Through the empty suburban streets he ran, down sleeping avenues, past darkened shops, through areas of big houses where dogs barked at the sound of his footsteps. He ran and ran and ran until he could run no more.

PART ONE

WINTER 1941

(Six weeks earlier)

1

The melancholy of the afternoon. The rain had been falling without a break since morning and now, by half past three, what little November light there was was fading into night. The city was poor, wet, miserable. The inadequate street lights reflected on the wet roads, shop windows threw pools of yellow on the pavements. The air seemed thick with rank smells, turf smoke, horse dung, cheap tobacco, unwashed people.

In the Coliseum Theatre the first matinée of *Pull the Other One* was under way. This week's variety show was paired with a film – Gene Autrey in *Back in the Saddle*. On stage, Frankie Fox, the straight man, was feeding Dickie Delaney, 'Dublin's favourite funny man' according to the billing.

'I hear,' said Dickie, mustering what enthusiasm he could, 'I hear that Mrs Genocky from down the road was seen with ould Quilligan the butcher.'

'Seen with ould Quilligan?' repeated Frankie.

'Yeah, with ould Quilligan.'

'Quilligan, the butcher?'

'That's what I said, are you deaf or wha'?' He shouted at the audience. 'He's going a bit hard of hearing. Missin' in a few other departments too, if'n youse know what I mean.'

'She's a very nice person, Mrs Genocky,' said Frankie.

'Lovely,' said Dickie.

'Lovely.'

'Lovely.'

Sketches tended to run on at the matinées.

'I'd say she's getting somethin' extra, if'n you know what I mean,' said Frankie. 'From the butcher.'

'Oh God forgive you,' said Dickie. 'May the Lord forgive you, Francis. Getting an extra cut . . .' A single person in the audience laughed. 'Of meat, of meat!' he shouted. 'Oh God forgive you. Charity, charity now! I'm sure she's innocent.'

'Still,' said Frankie. 'Still, there's no smoke without fire.'

It was the lead into the punchline, so he said it very slowly, but not slowly enough for Dickie.

'No smoke without fire? No smoke without fire! Have you ever tried lighting the turf that's going these days? Who says there's no smoke without fire?'

The tiny audience tittered half-heartedly – a couple of women out shopping for the afternoon, three boys who were mitching from school and a smattering of milkmen, whose working hours meant they had to be in bed early.

*

In the Department of Supplies, all was quiet except for the steady scratching of pens and the somnolent tick of a clock. Mr Dolan, feeling his head nodding over the ledger into which he was entering details of rationing coupons, took out his pipe and lit it. A pungent cloud rolled across the room as he puffed, causing Mr Corrigan, who sat beside him, to cough and wave a disapproving hand. Dolan ignored him and went back to his work.

In his late thirties, Dolan looked older than he was, maybe because he had lost his hair at an early age, maybe because of a certain gravity of manner. He kept his counsel, never gave an opinion unless he was asked for it, never pushed himself forward. He was a shy man, who found intimacy of any sort difficult, but he occasionally made a dry comment whose wit wasn't always noticed by the people around him.

The sound of female shoes tip-tapped down a distant corridor. Mr Corrigan, a smallish man with thinning grey hair and a tight mouth, also toiling over a ledger, raised his head a little, surreptitiously. Was it the young one from Galway, pert, cheeky? Someone had commented on her legs. These modern skirts, women's legs were everywhere you turned. His lips pursed in disapproval, but at the same time he felt a familiar stirring between his own legs. He gulped silently, then forced himself back to his labours. Mr Crosby, head of the section, consulted his pocket watch briefly, sighed quietly at the thought of two more interminable hours and decided to visit another section head in another office.

*

In her lodging house Miss Nora Keating was making herself some tea. It was a commodity that was becoming increasingly scarce as the war went on, to the distress of the Irish, who drank more of it per head than nearly any other nation in the world. Miss Keating, however, heaped four full spoons into the pot. She liked it, as the saying went, strong enough to trot a mouse across it. Rationing rarely worried her. She had a chest of tea that she kept locked up in a back room, a 'gift' from a smuggler in Northern Ireland.

As the kettle boiled, she went on with the job of placing a tiny square of margarine, evil-tasting bright yellow stuff, on each of the plates which her lodgers would use for their evening meal. The pretence was that it was butter, and butter was rationed, so she measured each piece with mathematical exactitude, knowing the ill feeling that would result if one piece was a fraction bigger than the others. But her belief in equal shares did not extend to herself. When she had finished doling out the margarine, she went into the pantry and, from a hiding place behind a large plate, pulled out half a pound of fine creamery butter and a snowy coloured loaf. White bread was a luxury that other people longed for as they chewed the gritty, grainy wartime loaves. Miss Keating had got the bread from her grocer, a man who owed her a favour.

She spread the salty, creamy butter thickly on the bread and smeared it generously with home-made jam. She poured herself a cup of strong bogwater-coloured fluid. She was a well-rounded woman, tall, with full breasts and a strong, handsome face. On her head was a bun of gleaming black hair in which she took great pride, though, truth to tell, she had taken to touching it up from a bottle. Her dress too was black, as were her shoes and stockings, alleviated only by a large silver brooch, by the whiteness of her face and the twin spots of rouge on her cheeks.

*

In the Kennedys' house, next door to Miss Keating's, Kitty Maher, the maid, knelt in front of the fireplace in the upstairs sitting room. The sods of turf were heavy and still damp, though they had been in the house for a week. It was said that fuel merchants turned hoses on them to make them heavier. A few lumps of coal, from the rapidly dwindling supply in the coal hole under the steps leading up to the hall door, were placed strategically among the turf, together with sticks and paper. But it, too, was poor stuff, almost impossible to light and apt to spit gritty pieces into your face as you knelt trying to kindle it.

Kitty looked dispiritedly at the smoking mass in the fireplace. She thought of getting the bellows, but it was three flights of stairs below in the basement kitchen. Taking a deep breath she blew and blew again into the grate. Her pretty pink-cheeked face went red with the exertion, and she pushed back her dark brown, curling hair, as it fell over her face. A thin, anaemic-looking flame flickered among the fuel.

'That'll have to do,' she said to herself.

*

Conor Kennedy came out of school with his friend, Clancy. Two nine-year-olds, schoolbags on their backs, caps on their heads. Conor was tall and growing. His wrists stuck out from the sleeves of his navy gabardine raincoat. Clancy was small, plump, soft. He'd grow into a fat man. They were bosom friends, despite the fact that, since they lived on opposite sides of the river, they didn't see each other much outside of school hours.

'Do you remember when your man, the little fella, is doing the drill and he's always turning the wrong way? He turns left when all the others turn right, and right when the others turn left, and each time he gets a bang on the side of the head from the rifle of the fella beside him, kchoo!' Conor staggered like the little fat chap in the picture.

They were talking about *Rookies*, 'the gassest picture I ever saw,' according to Clancy. Conor could never remember which one was Abbot and which Costello. The little one *ought* to be Bud Abbot, that was a funny name and the other fella that was always with him wasn't really funny, but maybe the names were the other way round.

'Which one is the fat guy?' he asked.

'I *told* you,' said Clancy, with the exasperation of an expert faced with a mere amateur. 'Lou Costello is the little fat guy. Do you remember that one where they're sailors? *In the Navy.*' Clancy knew that Conor hadn't seen *In the Navy*.

'I didn't see that,' admitted Conor, though Clancy had described it so often and in such detail that he almost felt he had.

'The gassest picture I ever saw,' said Clancy. 'I'm a ba-a-a-a-ad boy!' He imitated Costello's catchphrase.

Clancy went to the pictures twice a week, sometimes three times. He was an only child, doted on by his mother, his father something in an insurance office. He'd seen everything in town, sometimes twice. On Fridays, when the programme changed in the cinemas, he was always given a shilling and went straight from school, usually to the Corinthian, a picture house known as 'The Ranch' because it showed so many cowboy films. On Saturdays he went to the matinée at the Drumcondra Grand, near where he lived, often to something he had already seen in town. There, he told Conor, he lived the fast life, smoking cigarettes with girls. His mother would sometimes take him to something at night as well, a glamour Conor had never known, Betty Grable in *Down Argentine Way* or Bing Crosby in *Rhythm on the River*. Lousy pictures, said Clancy, full of kissing.

'See ya, pardner,' said Clancy, tipping a single finger to his cap and heading towards home.

'Adios, amigo,' said Conor, heading in the opposite direction.

But he had only gone a few paces when he heard his friend again.

'Go for your guns!'

'Kchh! Kchh!' Conor spun round, drawing index fingers and thumbs from imaginary holsters and firing simultaneously.

'Got you, you're dead!' said Clancy.

'No, I'm not. I got you. Kchh! Kchh!' He fired again, ducking in behind a lamppost as he did so.

'They got me!' said Clancy, staggering, falling, staggering again, then falling onto the pavement, oblivious to the wet. But, just as he was about to die, he raised his gun and fired again, three times, 'Kchh! Kchh! Kchh!'

'Aaah!' shouted Conor, about to die too. Looking at the dirty pavement on which the rain ran in rivulets, however, he decided against it.

'I have to go for my tram,' he said.

A flat cart, drawn by a scraggy horse, rumbled past. 'Hey! Roy Rogers!' shouted a ragged-looking man who was driving it to Conor. He raised an imaginary rifle. 'Bang! You're dead!' The cart clattered on.

Conor ignored him, but felt himself blushing hotly. Roy Rogers! He *hated* Roy Rogers. He was even worse than Gene Autrey, singing all the time. In some pictures he even drove around in a big American car. A car! In a cowboy picture! You'd never see Hopalong Cassidy driving a car.

The rain had slackened to a drizzle, with a promise of more to come. Conor walked down the hill towards Nelson's Pillar, from which his tram left. Down-at-heel city, shoddy city, mean city. A few people passed by: a couple of soldiers in coarse, ill-fitting uniforms, Woodbines hanging from greasy lips; a tough-looking woman in a hat with a lot of rouge on her cheeks; a couple of old shawlies, grey hair, dirty clothes, smelling of drink. In a doorway a barefoot boy of about his own age was selling the evening papers. 'Hegggulumwail! Heggulumwail!' he bawled, meaning '*Herald* and *Mail*.' His feet were caked in mud, there were holes in the elbows of his thin jacket, which was sizes too big for him, his face was smudged with dirt, and he shivered uncontrollably in the chill air.

The trams came in to their terminus at the Pillar, like rattling ships coming into port. Bang, rumble, whirr, they rolled along the shining tracks, over the cobblestones, crossing the points, seeming to tack and yaw before coming to a halt. A small knot of people, women in head scarves, men in hats, their shoulders hunched against the rain, were waiting. Long rods protruded from the trams onto the electric lines above, like the unlikely sexual organs of unlikely insects, and from these occasionally would come a blue flash. The incoming passengers got off, the rods were lowered off the wires with the help of a rope attached to them and the drivers and conductors got out for a smoke and some tramway chat, the drivers taking with them the brass steering tiller, like a large key. Then they would go to the compartment at the far end from the one in which they had come in, fix on the tillers and head off once again towards the suburbs from which they had come.

The lights were on as he boarded it. He made his way upstairs and up through the damp, tobacco-saturated tram to the front seats. He rubbed himself a porthole in the steamed-up glass of the window in front of him. Ding-ding, went the conductor's bell and they started, the tram clattering through the town, over the canal bridge and down the long straight street past the big church with the green dome, where he went to mass every Sunday and where his mother spent what seemed like hours, involved in prayers and novenas and missions for the safe return of his father, missing in action.

He tried to think of his father, but already the face was fading from his memory. There was a photograph beside his mother's bed and others in some albums, small black and white prints of a smiling man in bathing togs, holding a baby who, he was told, was himself. He could remember strong arms lifting him up, an adult smell of whiskey or beer or one of those unpleasant things grown-ups drank. He could remember someone faceless, sitting on the side of his bed and a voice saying: 'Who's the best boy in the whole of . . .?' and him completing the sentence ' . . . Ireland!'

The tram halted at a row of shops and he got off, though it was a couple of stops before his house. He wanted to see what comics they had in the newsagents. He was surreptitiously examining *Our Boys*, a magazine got out by the Christian Brothers, when the girl behind the counter saw him. Conor didn't like *Our Boys* much; though he didn't realise it, its air of self-righteousness made it less attractive than its English counterparts.

'Are you buying that?' asked the shop girl.

'I'm just looking at it,' he said.

'This isn't a library,' she said sniffily and he put it down. It was a different matter when they'd come in here after mass on Sundays, he to get his *Champion* with its tales of Rockfist Rogan, hero of the RAF, his mother to buy the Sunday paper and her ladies' magazine. Then they were as friendly as could be. Putting down *Our Boys*, he left and walked on up the road home.

As he went in the front gate a young man was coming out of the house next door, wheeling a bicycle. He was in his early twenties, with an agreeable, humorous face. He wore a shabby mackintosh, a tweed cap on his head, and his trousers were tucked into his socks.

He grinned, wagged his head and lifted a finger to Conor, in the friendly way of country people. 'How're you?'

'Hello,' said Conor gravely.

The young man took a run, swung nimbly onto his bike and headed across the road and towards town. Conor went into his home. It was a tall narrow house, a basement just below ground level and three other stories. He went in by the lower front entrance, under the steps that led up to the hall door. Kitty was in the dark kitchen with its black stone flags and big black range, inadequately lit by an underpowered light bulb.

'Where's my mother?' he asked her. To her face he called his mother 'Mummy', but was always slightly ashamed of a usage that was so English, so seemingly posh and stuck-up compared to the more usual and plebeian Irish 'Mammy'.

'She's gone into town with Mrs McCarthy,' said Kitty, giving him a large mug of creamy milk and a thick slice of brown wartime bread, spread with butter and 'mixed fruit' jam, pink glutinous stuff that tasted of no fruit he had ever known.

Kitty busied herself round the kitchen, putting a pot of potatoes on the range that she would boil later when the gas came on, and placing crockery, knives and forks on a tray with much crashing and banging. As ever, she shone with a spotless cleanliness, as if she had just stepped out of a bath.

'Kitty?'

'What is it, love?'

'Kitty, that house across the road. I don't believe it's haunted.' The house was old and grey, with filthy net curtains and a small overgrown front garden. Nobody ever seemed to go in or out of it.

'Oh don't you, now? Well, I can tell you different, 'cause I found out what happened there. But maybe you wouldn't like to hear.' Kitty lived in a world of ghosts and ghouls and banshees, where every empty or unusual house hinted at unspeakable horrors, which for the lack of any facts she was quite prepared to invent.

'I don't care whether you tell me or not,' said Conor with a bravery he didn't feel.

'All right. I won't tell you then,' she said, teasing.

He paused but, as she knew it would, curiosity got the better of him. 'What was the story, then?' he asked, trying to sound nonchalant.

'In that house, that house across the road,' said Kitty, speaking very slowly and solemnly, 'there lived a very old man. A man who, when he was young, done a terrible crime.'

'What crime?'

'He killed a child, a boy, a boy of about your age.'

'Why?'

'Why?' She paused, nonplussed for a moment. 'He choked him, while he was robbing him.'

'Ah go on!' said Conor, trying to sustain his disbelief. But Kitty was carried away by her own invention.

'The boy's dead body was found, but the police never worked out who done the murder. No one knew who done it, except one man, and that man was the murderer hisself. Years went by and the man got old, and the older he got the more he used think of that terrible thing he done. He shut himself up in his house, that house across the road . . .' Conor felt the hair at the back of his head prickle, ' . . . and he never went out no more.

'One night,' Kitty went on, 'he was lying in his bed and he couldn't sleep. He couldn't sleep this particular night, do you know why?'

'Why?'

'Because it was twenty years to the day since he done that terrible murder. And as he lay in the bed, trying to sleep . . . Suddenly! What did he hear?'

'What?' said Conor, a tremble in his voice.

'He heard footsteps, a child's footsteps, outside the door, coming nearer. Nearer they came and nearer and then, very slowly, the door started to open . . .' Big pause. 'That man was found hanging from the rafters next day!'

Kitty stopped, triumphantly. Conor could hear the grandfather clock in the hall upstairs ticking.

'What did he see?'

'No one knows,' said Kitty. 'But they say that every year on that day, if you go by the house, though there's no one there, you can hear those footsteps, footsteps like a boy's, and then a terrible scream, the scream of the man that's hanging hisself.'

'Arrah go on, I don't believe it,' said Conor.

'It's true, they told me down in Brannigan's shop. Everyone round here knows it.'

'You just made it up,' said Conor, but he knew with a sinking feeling that when he was alone in bed that night the choking boy, the footsteps and the scream would terrify him.

The door opened and his brother Barry came in. He was in good form.

'Hello, Con, Kitty. Guess what? I'm on the seconds next week.' Barry's life was divided between rugby football and a succession of girlfriends, with his studies as a law student coming a bad third.

'Will you play soldiers, Barry?' asked Conor. His brother made up great games with Conor's toy soldiers. Air raids in which they dropped marbles, and shelling with his toy cannon that fired pencil stubs.

'Sorry,' said Barry, 'I have some study to do. Later, later maybe,' and he left the room at speed.

'Are you finished your milk?' asked Kitty. 'Your mammy says you're to do your homework straight away and not be putting it off.'

'Okey doke,' said Conor, taking his schoolbag and heading upstairs to the dining room, where he would work. 'Kchh! Kchh!' Already he was riding the range again.

He could hear Barry singing above him in the sitting room. The radio came on, a dance tune, a foxtrot, and he could hear the footsteps as Barry twirled an imaginary partner to the music.

He unbuckled his schoolbag and got out his exercise books, unscrewed the ink bottle that was kept on the mantelpiece and placed it beside them. Blotting paper, his arithmetic book, with its pages of sums, and then a pen with a scratchy nib and a well-chewed end. 'A.M.D.G.' he wrote laboriously at the top, *Ad maiorem Dei gloriam* – To the greater glory of God. Then 'Arithmetic.' Then his name and class 'Conor Kennedy, Rudiments.' Father Curran, the maths master, was a louser the amount of homework he gave. Twenty sums! And he still had to do his English and his Irish. Still, Curran was decent enough. Not as bad anyway as O'Cathain, the lay master who taught them Irish. Small, rimless glasses and a tight mouth, given to sarcasm and sending you out for nothing at all. He was frightened of O'Cathain, who according to school legend had an ungovernable temper. Broke a fella's wrist once with the strap. The fella's da had complained to the rector and O'Cathain had nearly got the sack. Clancy swore it was true. The guy had left the school the next day.

Sixty-seven multiplied by twenty-three, eighteen into three hundred and ninety-one. He scratched away, the ink getting on his fingers. On the opposite page Curran had written, about yesterday's homework: 'Good, but untidy work.'

Barry was singing again in the next room, '*You are the promised breath of springtime that makes the lonely winter seem long*,' bursting into a bellow when he got to the bit that went: '*Some day my happy arms will hold you, And some day I'll know that moment divine, When all the things you are, are mine.*'

2

The offices, factories and shops disgorged their workers and they hurried home, huddled against the soft rain. The streets filled, queues formed for trams and buses, the roadways became crammed with bicycles. Crowds hurried along the pavements, drab in brown and grey and blue, shoulders up, hats pulled down, umbrellas high, anxious to get out of the persistent, soaking wetness. The pubs filled, too, with smoking men, standing on bare boards, their wet clothes steaming from the rain, while they drank black pints of Guinness or half-ones of whiskey, and discussed football, ways of getting round the rationing, and the war, always the war.

Corrigan and Dolan left the Department of Supplies and went back to their digs, as always, by separate ways. Some nights, after work, Dolan liked to go to the pub across the road from the office and have a single pint of stout before cycling back to the digs. He would sit there, sometimes joining in a conversation with some of the lads from the office, but refusing to buy or be bought a drink, more often reading the *Evening Mail* or just gazing silently into the creamy head of his pint. On Mondays, though, it was impossible. That was the night the landlady, Miss Keating, went to play cards with her friends and she particularly liked to have everything tidied away before seven o'clock. Woe betide you if you were late. By the time you got back, even if only half an hour after you should have, the table would be cleared and you'd go to bed that night on an empty stomach.

Carefully he put on his heavy overcoat and tweed cap, and secured the bottoms of his immaculately creased trousers with a pair of bicycle clips. His shoes, as always, shone from their morning polish. Out in the shed at the back he selected his bicycle from the dozens that were stacked there. Like his clothes it was carefully maintained – scrubbed, well oiled and in perfect working order. Taking it into the road, he clipped on the light, which he had removed and taken into the office with him that morning, mounted carefully and pedalled away, another anonymous figure in the hundreds making their way homewards.

Corrigan took his raincoat off the hook in the office and slid his arms into the sleeves. A Homburg hat, a pair of woollen gloves that made his small hands look big and awkward, and a rolled umbrella.

'Good night, Mr Corrigan!'

It was the young Galway one, with another of the secretaries, teasing, her eyes dancing. He murmured a strangulated reply and wondered was he blushing; he felt as if he was.

The two girls swung off down the corridor, heads together, and as they did he heard a burst of giggling. Could they be laughing at him?

Corrigan went out onto the street and headed for the tram stop. No after-work drinks for him. He was a Pioneer and wore the little pin with the Sacred Heart on it in his lapel, to show that he had renounced all alcoholic liquors to make up to God and His Holy Mother for the sins that were committed as a result of excessive drinking. He passed a big city church. It was

Monday, and if he didn't get home in time there'd be no tea in the digs, but maybe he'd have time for a quick one.

Corrigan was a pious man – he went into the church at lunch hour and after work; he'd been known to hand out little cards with devotional prayers on them, invoking Our Lady of Lourdes and various saints; he carried rosary beads and wore a brown scapular under his shirt; he was a member of the Society for the Abolition of Evil Literature and had on several occasions spoken vehemently and bitterly about the appalling effects, particularly on the young, of filthy books and moving picture shows. He should have been a priest, they said.

On the same tram, downstairs, Frankie Fox sat, gazing unseeing at the steamed-up window. He didn't usually go back to Miss Keating's for the evening meal, but there was just about time between the early and late evening shows and tonight he couldn't face the pub next to the Coliseum, where the rest of the cast of *Pull the Other One* would foregather. The pain in his stomach was there again, as it seemed to be more and more these days, a dull knot that would occasionally stab him agonisingly. A half-one of whiskey, he knew, would bring him temporary relief, but the aftermath would be even worse, a night of suffering, belching and retching through the long hours. He chewed on a couple of the chalky indigestion tablets which he always carried with him.

He was a small unprepossessing man, overweight, with lank, thinning, grey hair. His nose seemed too big for his face but, especially when he was feeling well, his large brown eyes and smiling mouth had a humour and a friendliness that was instantly attractive. Among the drably dressed tram travellers he stood out because of his lurid American tie, on which was painted a desert sunset. A long-ago present from a fellow variety artist, it was by now stained and grubby, but it was the mark of his trade, a sign that he belonged to the colourful, glamorous world of showbiz.

Truth to tell, neither he nor his world was particularly glamorous, though in austere, lacklustre wartime Dublin it almost passed for such, for want of anything better. But for Frankie it was and always had been the Golden Way, the rainbow along which one could travel, where, no matter what, one might some day find the crock of gold that would make everything worthwhile.

To the dispassionate onlooker Frankie might have seemed little enough, a small town comedian, playing second fiddle to the leading comic in a third-rate cine-variety theatre. But to Frankie himself the very fact of being where he was seemed a miracle. To be part of that rackety, shabby yet adventurous body of people, the pros, the variety artists. Even after all these years, to be accepted as one of them made him proud. Jimmy O'Dea knew him by name and greeted him in the street. So did Jimmy Campbell, the immaculately clad conductor of the orchestra in the Theatre Royal. Frankie had even played the Royal on a couple of occasions, even though he'd hardly had a thing to do. Still.

He had a magic in him, somewhere. It was what had released him from the grim slums in which he had grown up. Living ten and more to a room, the straw mattresses alive with bed bugs, the stinking slop bucket in the corner, the ragged clothes. Rats that ran over your feet on the dark, creaking, dangerous old stairs. His drunken, brutish father who would beat his mother, himself and his brothers and sisters night after night. Cold, hunger, hunger, hunger.

The old story, nothing new about it. But in the filthy hallways, where the children gathered to play games, he was the one who led the way. He could out-sing everyone, dance, do Charlie Chaplin only great, or other fellas you'd see on the pictures. Above all, he could make people laugh, adults as well as children. Take off everyone who lived in the tenement, all the local characters. He learned to turn aside anger, and the blows that were never far away, with a quip or a trick.

'He should be on the stage,' said the ould ones in the street. 'He's a right turn.' And that's where he went. First at concert parties, then in an amateur pantomime that was got up in the church hall. He stole the show, although he had only a small part. The following year it was different, *Aladdin*. He was Wishy Washy, the undoubted star. He even wrote some material for himself, including a take-off of 'Underneath the Arches', and then, to show how versatile he was, sang a straight number, 'My Prayer', that brought down the house. It was so successful they even put on variety shows in the hall when the panto finished its run. In many ways those were his greatest years. They roared, they cheered. He had only to come on stage and they'd start to laugh. That was when he started his catchphrase: 'Where's me hat?' A sketch set in a pub. He'd come in, drunk, put his hat on a chair, do some business with a pint of porter, staggering, weaving, just avoiding spilling it, then sit down on his hat.

'Where's me hat?' People would shout that at him when he'd pass in the street. He worked it into everything he did and it always got the best laugh of the night.

A fella came from the *Evening Mail* and did a write-up on one of the shows. 'Variety Follies at the Laurence O'Toole Hall is a bit of a mixed bag, but it has some very promising talent on display, which makes it all worthwhile. Most promising of all is the more than useful principal comedian, Frankie Fox, who has the power to develop laughs. This young man has the ability to tread the professional boards, if he ever so wishes . . .'

Someone must have seen that, because he got the call to appear in a show that was being put on. Cecil Sheridan was in it, Peggy Dell at the piano and Bing Kelly. He'd made several attempts before to get a part in such things but without luck, so someone must have read the bit in the *Mail*. The money was only dire, five bob a week, the same as he was getting as a messenger boy. But it was his breakthrough, his big chance. He could remember the pure, undiluted joy of that day.

In a way, that was as good as it got. He was given a few minor spots in shows. He did all right, but the world of the pros was different. The audiences seemed harder to please, what made them roar in the Laurence O'Toole Hall could only raise a titter. The other comics gave you nothing on stage, they were prickly about their status and jealous of anybody else's success – in fact they often seemed to hate each other. One time he thought he'd done really well, got real good laughs, only to find the next night that his number had been cut. The show was running too long, he'd been told, but he knew it was because the leading man didn't like anybody else taking the limelight.

It wasn't all bad, of course. He was accepted quickly into the freemasonry of the stage and well liked. When it didn't come to questions of precedence, the variety artists were great company, warm, friendly, generous and ever ready to help out a mate in need. It was like being a member of another family, a larger, warmer one than he had ever known. Even if there were disappointments, professionally, it was good to belong to it. There were nights of magic, when everything seemed to go right on stage and other nights filled with fun and drink after and between shows.

And there was Magser. All those years together. Good ould Magser with the fag never out of her mouth, hair all untidy, gathering up costumes, sewing, packing, putting up sets like a man, fixing the lights, in the corner with the script during the show. They did everything together, panto, variety, tours down the country where you'd rig up a stage on barrels in some little hall, and there'd be a show and a play about something like Our Lady of Lourdes and a raffle as well.

'Why the hell don't you marry her?' someone had asked him once.

'Ah, I'm not the marrying kind,' he'd said. 'Don't get me wrong now, when I say I'm not the marrying kind I don't mean like Jimmy Blue.' Jimmy Blue sang John McCormack numbers like 'Ireland Mother Ireland' and 'The Fairy Tree' and was said to wear women's dresses when at home.

No, he wasn't like Jimmy. Himself and Magser had done it a few times. They were only human after all, though she always made him promise to go to confession afterwards. 'Is she pregnant?' That was the first question the priests always used to ask. No, of course she wasn't. 'Well, thank God for that,' they'd usually say. He hadn't the heart to tell them they took precautions. They got hot and bothered enough about it already, that would only drive them demented altogether.

But marriage, kids? No, they'd both seen how tough it was for those in the profession. Some day, maybe.

Then, quite suddenly, Mags got sick. Gaunt, hollow-eyed, unable to breathe. He'd go and see her in hospital. He'd cry afterwards in the corridor. Then, one day when he went, there was a strange man there, a brother whom he'd never met.

'She's dead,' Magser's brother had said, abruptly, just like that. He'd burst into tears. The brother had said nothing.

That was years ago now. He'd gone on in the business, what else could he do? He was rarely out of work. The war had caused something of a boom in the Irish variety theatres. Previously they had been filled with touring acts, mostly English, but since these could no longer come local talent had filled the vacancies, new stars had been made. Frankie didn't drink excessively, he didn't make trouble and he was no threat to anybody. But he was starting to get on, there were younger comedians coming up these days, whom the audiences seemed to want. He had to take what he was offered. For the past three years he'd been straight man to Dickie Delaney, the meanest little bastard in Dublin.

He still dreamed of making it big, getting his own show. If he could get some new material, rework the hat sketch maybe, do some new parodies – he'd started on one last week. Then all he'd need would be the chance to perform them on stage. That was the problem. When would he ever get the chance? Dickie wouldn't let another comic do a single in one of his shows in a hundred years.

'Fares, please.' The conductor was standing beside him. 'How're yeh, Frankie,' he said, recognising him. 'Where's me hat? Wha'?'

'Oh, hello, Tom.' Frankie had the performer's knack of remembering names and faces. 'How's the form?'

'Game ball. Are you still working with Dickie Delaney?'

'Yeah.'

'That man must have a filthy mind.'

'Not at all,' said Frankie. 'His material is as clean as a whistle, every time.'

'That's what I mean,' said the conductor. 'He must have a filthy mind to keep it that clean.'

Frankie laughed loudly. He'd remember that one next time he was in the pub.

He saw Corrigan for the first time as they got off the tram together.

'How're yeh,' said Frankie without much enthusiasm.

'Heh, heh, heh.' Corrigan had a dry humourless giggle which appeared when he was ill at ease. 'Good evening.'

'Jaysus, do you think it'll ever stop raining?' asked Frankie.

'It's very wet,' said Corrigan, his pursed lips managing to show without comment his disapproval of the use of the Holy Name.

'And it'd freeze the bollocks off you.' Though he had the naturally exuberant speech of the Dubliner, Frankie was not usually greatly given to bad language, but Corrigan's evident disapproval made him want to discomfit this bloody Holy Joe.

'Heh, heh, heh, it's very cold.' Corrigan looked out of the corner of his eye at the little man. A foul mouth, he thought, is the sign of a foul mind. Someone had said that, who was it? A priest probably. You could take a pledge against bad language, the same as you could against drink, with a little pin that you wore in your lapel. For an instant he thought of suggesting it to Frankie, but immediately decided it wouldn't be a good idea. The two men walked along the footpath in silence.

Mean-minded little shite, thought Frankie. These stage people, thought Corrigan, what could you expect? They had the morals of barnyard animals, he'd always heard.

'Well, here we are,' said Frankie as they reached the gate. 'All set for another sumptuous repast from Nora Keating, the Carmen Miranda of Rathmines.'

*

Dolan, Corrigan and Frankie sat down to eat. Thinly sliced grey bread, the tiny pats of butter on each plate, a teapot from which emerged the palest of fluid. Miss Keating came into the room, followed by the young man whom Conor had seen earlier with his bicycle. Miss Keating's bearing, as usual, was regal, stately, her back straight, her head back, one hand to her throat.

'We have a new guest,' she said. 'This is Mr O'Sullivan.'

The young man who followed her in was in his early twenties and could have passed for even younger. He was tall and gangling and held himself badly. A shock of fair brown hair that needed cutting curled around the back of his neck. Even when it was trimmed it always seemed to defy the efforts of the comb and, as he never used hair oil, it flew away in all directions. Though not outstandingly good-looking – his jaw was too long, his nose a little too large for that – he had clear blue eyes and a benign, open expression whose friendliness attracted people at once. He was without guile.

'Eddie O'Sullivan,' he said, beaming around at the company.

'Mr Corrigan, Mr Dolan, Mr Fox,' said Miss Keating graciously. Then her face changed into something approaching a snarl. Turning round she bellowed out of the room. 'Nellie! What's keeping you?'

A sound of somebody galloping up the stairs from the basement announced Nellie, Miss Keating's slatternly maid. Lank, greasy hair, nails bitten to the quick, rumpled clothes.

In her hands she carried a tray with plates, on each of which a pale fried egg swam in a pool of grease.

Frankie looked at her. 'It's Dorothy Lamour,' he said.

Nellie put her face an inch from his. 'Hehhhhh!' A single-noted high-pitched wail came out her mouth. She was laughing, showing a mouthful of decayed teeth.

Frankie recoiled from her bad breath. 'Where's me gas mask? Did you ever think of going to the dentist about them teeth, Nellie?' he asked.

'I'd be in mortal terror, sir,' she said.

'That will do, Nellie,' said Miss Keating disapprovingly.

'Yes'm.' Nellie, who was terrified of her mistress, left the room and clattered down the stairs, again at full tilt.

'Enjoy your meal, gentlemen,' Miss Keating said majestically and followed the maid out.

Corrigan crossed himself ostentatiously and bowed his head. 'Bless us, O Lord, and these Thy gifts, which of Thy bounty we are about to receive, through Christ Our Lord, Amen.' He blessed himself again with a flourish, while the others awkwardly muttered 'Amen.'

Frankie spread some of his butter thinly on a slice of bread and looked at his egg with distaste, knowing what it would do to his digestion. He bit into his bread and made a face.

'Pah! God Almighty! She's been mixing the butter with

margarine again,' he said. 'The ration is small enough without jumbling it with this muck. What's it made of, axle-grease?'

'Eat it with your egg,' said Dolan. 'It doesn't seem so bad that way.'

'I don't fancy an egg this evening,' said Frankie, his stomach heaving faintly as the oily smell hit his nostrils. 'Anyone want mine?'

'Not me, thanks,' said Dolan. Corrigan said nothing, chewing his food slowly and thoroughly, his elbows close to his sides as he held his knife and fork.

'I wouldn't mind, if no one else wants it,' said the new young man.

'Here you go, son.' Frankie pushed the plate over towards him. 'What did you say your business was?'

He paused for a moment. 'I'm a traveller,' he said, 'a commercial traveller.'

'Oh? For what?'

'Sweets, confectionery.'

'Who do you work for?' asked Dolan.

'Mooney's.' Mooney's was a small firm in the south that made cheap sweets. 'What do you do yourself?'

'Mr Dolan and I are in the civil service, Mr O'Sullivan,' said Corrigan, joining the conversation for the first time. 'The Department of Supplies.'

'Eddie, call me Eddie.'

'Jack Dolan, and this of course is Frankie Fox.'

'What do you work at, Frankie?' asked Eddie.

'Me? I'm on the stage,' said Frankie, in the grand accent he sometimes used when talking to strangers.

'An actor?' Eddie was suitably impressed. 'I love plays. We

get Anew McMaster down home every year. Did you ever see that one, *The Merchant of Venice*?'

'*The Merchant*,' said Frankie, 'ah yes. I know it well of course.'

'What are you in now?'

'I'm doing the show at the Coliseum,' said Frankie.

'Variety,' said Corrigan. 'He's a comedian.'

'A comedian? I never saw a comedian in my life, except in the pictures. What do you think of Abbot and Costello? God, they're gas men!'

'Not bad,' said Frankie, 'but not up to the greats really. Chaplin, of course, he's the top, but Max Miller, George Formby, Arthur Askey . . .'

'I think Jimmy O'Dea is as good as any of them,' said Dolan.

'Jimmy? Of course,' said Frankie, 'and a decent skin, too.'

Eddie was impressed. 'Do you know Jimmy O'Dea?'

'Oh yes, known him for years. Worked with him a lot, you know.'

'Gor!' Eddie was wide-eyed. 'And what do you think of that one on the radio – ITMA?'

'Not bad, not bad,' said Frankie.

'God, I think it's a panic. "Can I do you now, sir?" "I thangk yow!" Do you like it, Mr Corrigan?'

Corrigan's lips pursed. English vulgarity of the worst sort!

'I never listen to the wireless,' he said, 'except to hear the news.'

'Do you not like music?'

'Irish music, yes. Not this modern jazz band stuff that you hear everywhere now. What's wrong with our own music, the finest in the world?' asked Mr Corrigan.

'I like Irish music,' said Eddie, 'but I like some of the modern stuff too.'

'Bless 'em all, bless 'em all,' Frankie sang, 'the long and the short and the tall. Bless de Valera and Sean McEntee, who give us brown bread and a half ounce of tea.'

'That's not Irish music,' said Corrigan disapprovingly.

'Of course it's Irish,' said Frankie. 'What do you like, Dolan?'

Dolan considered the question, as he did every question, carefully.

'I like John McCormack,' he said eventually.

'Ah yes,' said Corrigan. That was more like it. A papal count. Sang at the great Eucharistic Congress in Dublin in the thirties. ' "Panis Angelicus",' he said, 'and "Bless This House".'

'Bless thees house oh Lorrd we pray . . .' sang Frankie through his nose, in a fair parody of the great tenor. Eddie laughed.

'Did you ever hear Jimmy Blue?' asked Frankie. 'Some people think he's as good as McCormack.'

'Never heard of him. Is he in your show?'

'Sometimes, not this week. You must come along and see it. I'll get you a couple of briefs.'

'A couple of what?'

'Briefs, complimentaries.' He turned to Corrigan and Dolan. 'I'll get them for you too,' he said.

'That'd be smashing,' said Eddie.

'How about next Saturday?'

'Great, thanks very much.'

'Does that suit you men?' he asked the other two.

'Yes, Saturday would be fine,' said Dolan.

'Heh, heh, heh,' tittered Corrigan, 'a lot to do.' A snapshot of chorus girls kicking bare legs flashed across his mind, and the phrase, 'an occasion of sin'.

'I'm busy on Saturday,' he said.

'Some novena or something, is it?' asked Frankie. He joined his hands in prayer, putting his head to one side and rolling his eyes, so that he looked like some particularly revolting statue of an unlikely martyr. Eddie burst out laughing.

'There's no need to make fun of prayer,' said Corrigan crossly. 'I don't find that particularly funny.'

Frankie pulled a face. 'Sorry, sorry,' he said, 'no offence.'

Corrigan cut into his egg, sending the soft yellow yolk squirting across his plate.

'Eddie,' said Frankie, changing the subject, 'do you have any samples?'

'Samples?' asked Eddie blankly.

'Samples, from the job. Any ould sweets or bars or anything?'

'Oh,' said Eddie hesitantly. 'I . . . er, yes I do, sometimes. I don't have any at the moment.'

'Well, next time you have some, give us a few, will you? I'm not a great man for the sweets meself, but some of the girls in the show do love them.'

'Sure, yes, if I get any.'

'If?' asked Frankie. 'Sure how can you be a commercial traveller if you don't have samples?'

'I er, I do have them, but,' Eddie paused, 'but, you know, they go stale, the chocolates.'

'I don't mind that,' said Frankie. 'Don't throw them out.'

'Where are you from, Eddie?' asked Dolan.

'Me?' He paused. 'From Waterford.'

'That seems more like a Tipperary accent to me,' said Dolan, who had a fine ear for the niceties of regional speech.

'Me, me father was from Tipp,' said Eddie.

'What part of Waterford? The county or the town?'

'The town.'

'You'd probably know Gerry Foley then.'

'Er, no.'

'You don't?' Dolan raised an eyebrow. 'I thought everyone in Waterford knew him.'

'Ah well, I know *of* him,' said Eddie. 'My da knows him.'

'A great full forward,' said Dolan. 'One of the best I've ever seen.'

'Well, I'd better get back if I'm to catch the late show,' said Frankie, rising. But before he could get to his feet, Corrigan was blessing himself again and intoning.

'We give Thee thanks, oh Almighty God, for these and all Thy gifts, which of Thy bounty we have received, through Christ Our Lord . . .'

'Amen!' said Frankie cutting in. 'Well, some of us have to work. I suppose you'll be off now, Corrigan, dancing the night away.'

'Heh, heh, heh,' went Corrigan. 'No, no, I have a meeting.'

'The Society against Dirty Books, is it?' asked Frankie, twinkling.

'The Society for the Abolition of Evil Literature.'

'Sounds like a laugh a minute,' said Frankie in an all-too-audible aside as he left.

Eddie, who was new to Dublin, gazed after Frankie, wide-eyed.

'The vulgarity of that man would sicken you,' said Corrigan.

'Ah, he's all right,' said Dolan. 'I'm going for a walk. Do you want to come?' he asked Eddie.

'Er, no, not tonight, thanks.'

'Perhaps you'd like to attend a meeting of the society?' suggested Corrigan. 'You'd be very welcome. It's quite informal and we need all the help we can get.'

'Not tonight, I'm afraid,' said Eddie.

'Ah well, perhaps you'll come another night. There's a great flood of filth coming in from pagan England that's got to be stopped if this country isn't to drown. Unfortunately, people are careless about it.' This was directed sideways at Dolan, who had steadfastly refused to be recruited.

'Anything in the news today?' asked Dolan.

'Not much,' said Eddie. 'They're still fighting in North Africa.'

'The English aren't bet yet.'

'Rommel will finish them off soon,' said Eddie, with an enthusiasm that surprised the others. 'The English are nearly done for, even though they've more men. He'll destroy them, he's a genius, and anyway the English are cowards.'

'I'd hardly say that,' said Dolan.

'What about the Black and Tans? Was there ever anything more cowardly than that? Attacking civilians, burning and murdering innocent people.'

'The scum of the British slums,' said Corrigan. 'A degenerate race.'

Dolan said nothing, thinking of his two brothers in the British army, serving God knew where.

'Well, they won't be here much longer,' said Eddie. 'By the time this is over they'll be out of the Six Counties too.'

'They will, they will,' said Corrigan, 'with the help of God.'

'God will have nothing to do with it,' said Eddie fiercely. ''Tis the men of the IRA'll do the job.'

'Nothing happens without God's will,' said Corrigan. 'You should know that.'

'Well, whatever,' said Eddie. 'Anyway God will be on our side.'

'God is not an Englishman,' said Corrigan.

'Yes,' said Eddie and then, as if he'd given away too much, he said, 'See you,' and left the room.

3

The rain had cleared at last by the time Miss Keating's lodgers finished their modest meal. The wet pavements glistened, the suburban streets were empty in this quiet city while everywhere else, it seemed, the world was alive with the march of armies, the drone of bombers, and the thud of artillery.

Dolan put on his coat and headed out on one of the long solitary walks he took on such evenings. Brought up on a farm, where physical labour was part of everyday life, he felt restless without some form of exercise. On Sundays there was hurling, and when there was a stretch in the evenings he could go up to the Phoenix Park and puck around a ball with some others. The sweet smack of the hurl on the *sliotar* and the wide spaces of the big park lifted the drabness of the city off his shoulders and made him feel ten years younger. In the spring and summer, they would cycle out to the Feather Bed, a hard push up the hills to the Dublin mountains, where one of the men in the office owned a bank of turf. There in the long evenings they would spend a few hours cutting turf, which would later be brought back down to Dublin in a hired horse-drawn cart, or even pulled along behind the bike on a little trolley. He loved it up there, sending the big chocolate-brown sods flying in the air or stacking them in pyramids to dry, the high sky clear above him, the purple and brown of the hills, the heady air and the song-bursts of skylarks. Afterwards, too, the free-wheeling ride home down the hills and the few pints, tired and content.

At this time of year, though, it was too dark and too wet for that, so he walked briskly for long distances through the silent avenues. Sometimes his walks took him down as far as the river, nearly empty now of the ships that used to crowd it, or towards the old part where the city had begun, through dark cobbled streets, bordered by squalid slums and poor small pubs, where ragged men drank porter and laughed and sang and quarrelled.

As he walked, he thought of the meal he had just had and the young man who had joined the company. There was something there, something not quite right, and he thought he knew what it was . . .

*

In a small church hall the Society for the Abolition of Evil Literature was preparing to hold a meeting. Mrs McGuire, chairman, founder and leading light of the society, was a widow who led a life dedicated to prayer, fasting and the relentless pursuit of anything that smacked in the slightest way of sensuality. She was a small, trim woman, with the boundless energy of the self-righteous. With her were her two chief acolytes, Miss Johnson and Miss O'Neill, and they were joined by Mr Corrigan and a nervous young man named Seamus McGill.

They began with prayers. After a decade of the rosary, they said additional prayers for those whose souls were in mortal danger because of pornography, for the Pope and for the conversion of Russia. Corrigan's thoughts, never long at rest, turned towards a poster he had seen for a film starring Betty Grable. 'In the name of the Fawther and of the Son and of The Holy Ghost, Awmen,' intoned Mrs McGuire, ending the prayers with all the solemnity of a cardinal celebrating high mass. She blessed herself slowly and they sat in a circle on kitchen chairs.

'It seems,' said Mrs McGuire, looking round disapprovingly, 'that, once again, we have a disappointing turnout. I thought that at our last meeting we agreed to search for new members.' She eyed the others accusingly. 'No success, Mr Corrigan?'

'There's a new young man in the digs, who I've hopes for,' said Corrigan. 'He expressed an interest. I'll work on him.'

'Do. We need greater involvement in our work from The Youth. Who else, after all, is at greater risk from the torrent of filth that is threatening to drown the world? I know, we all know, that the good holy people of Ireland do not want their country overrun by the dirt of so-called intellectuals and Jewboys and, indeed, of some who are nearer to home. It is only a question of doing the work, of letting them know what we are doing, and they will join our society in numbers. Am I not correct?'

'Yes, oh yes.' Miss O'Neill nodded her grey head in total agreement.

'Indeed,' agreed the others.

'Has anyone anything to report?' asked Mrs McGuire, fixing the others with a baleful stare. A deep silence fell as the other members of the group gazed bashfully at the floor. Their chairman sighed, disappointed as ever in the failure of her acolytes to match her own zeal.

She took from a paper bag a copy of the *Evening Mail*. 'I'm surprised,' she said triumphantly, 'that none of ye noticed this.'

The *Evening Mail*? The others looked amazed, for outside the religious press itself there could be few more harmless publications than that rather dreary journal, with its heavily censored war reports, its accounts of minor court cases and its letters to the editor column.

'What's in it?' asked Miss Johnson, alive with curiosity.

''Tis an advertisement, a vile advertisement, for Clery's. Not at all what one might expect from a Catholic firrum. Modesty forbids me from showing it to the gentlemen present. See, ladies.' She unfolded the paper so that Corrigan and McGill could not see it. The two women craned forward.

'Where is it?' asked Miss Johnson.

'There,' said Mrs McGuire, grimly.

'I don't see anything,' said Miss Johnson.

'There . . . there!' said Mrs McGuire with irritation. 'The underwear ad.'

In her agitation she half let the newspaper drop and Corrigan got a glimpse of a number of small, badly executed drawings of women in corsets. The corsets covered them from their armpits down to the tops of their legs, from where suspender attachments held up their stockings. They had all probably seen them dozens of times before without noticing the slightest eroticism about them, so stiffly posed, tiny and poorly printed were they.

'Disgraceful,' said Miss O'Neill.

'This is a particularly grave case,' said Mrs McGuire, 'when one thinks that this is a paper that goes into Catholic homes, that is read by women and young people, many of them who would usually read little else.'

'Tch, tch, tch.' Mr Corrigan clicked his tongue in disapproval, while surreptitiously trying to get another glimpse of the offending drawings.

'It proves what I've always said,' went on Mrs McGuire, warming to a familiar theme, 'that even in holy Catholic Ireland, the forces of immorality, the devil himself is ceaselessly striving to corrupt and deprave souls, to pull them down into hell, to degrade and, and . . .' She searched for a word.

'Prostitute them,' offered Miss Johnson.

'What? Yes . . . no . . . debase them!' said Mrs McGuire. 'Yes, debase and drag down the pure and the innocent.'

'God save us!' said Seamus McGill.

'Again, we can expect little or nothing from the so-called Censorship Board,' said Mrs McGuire, 'but I feel sure that the archbishop will take an interest.'

'The archbishop?' asked Miss Johnson, 'take an interest in ads for corsets?' and immediately wished she had bitten her tongue.

Mrs McGuire fixed her with a basilisk glare. 'Just what do you mean by that?' she asked.

'Just, just . . . I'm sure the archbishop is so busy. Too busy to be, to be tying himself up with corsets, corset ads, to be . . .' Her voice trailed away miserably.

'His Grace,' said Mrs McGuire, speaking as if she were a close personal friend, 'is a very holy man, who at great personal cost to his health works morning, noon and night. He is never too busy for any detail of what goes on in the diocese, least of all those that deal with faith and morals. Now, is there any other business?'

And so the meeting wound its dreary way on until it was time for another burst of prayer, followed by a final admonition from the little group's leader, to go out in search of new recruits, not to mention the pornography which they knew lurked somewhere in virtually every column of print and every picture in the land.

*

Eddie O'Sullivan made his way into town on his bicycle. Though hardly ablaze with lights, Dublin was one of the few European cities left that did not enforce a black-out. The yellowy-lit trams rumbled past, street lamps threw a dim shine on the pavements and houses and pubs added their quotas.

As he approached the city centre more people were to be seen, queuing outside the many cinemas, going in and out of the pubs or hurrying for the theatres. *Applesauce No. 6* at the Theatre Royal, *Lovers Meeting* at the Abbey and, celebrating the theatre's seventieth anniversary, Michael Mac Liammoir in Shaw's *Caesar and Cleopatra* at the Gaiety.

Eddie cycled up to one of the big pubs on the riverside quays, dismounted and propped his bicycle against the pavement edge. A beggar, filthy in rags, his breath stinking of stale drink, stumbled over to him, hand outstretched.

'Give us a penny, sor, for the love of God.'

Eddie ignored him and went into the pub.

'Fuck you anyway,' said the beggar loudly, spitting a gob onto the footpath.

Inside, the pub was full and noisy with men. They sat on stools along the bar, at the tables placed against the opposite wall or just stood, most of them drinking black pints of stout or amber half-ones of whiskey.

Eddie edged his way to the bar and tried to catch the eye of one of the barmen. A short bald man stood beside him, drinking large gins, the only one in the pub doing so, it seemed. He wore a camel-hair overcoat and what remained of his hair, around his ears, shone with brilliantine. From his conversation to a taller, cadaverous-looking companion, it seemed he was a bookie, just back from attending Limerick races.

Eddie held up a hand. 'A pint,' he said to the fresh-faced barman, a country lad like himself.

'One pint,' confirmed the barman.

'Any man from the North here?' asked Eddie.

'What?' asked the barman blankly.

'Not yet.' It was a second barman, drawing pints of Guinness and letting them settle in a row of glasses. 'He said he'd be along.'

The bookie's eyes darted sideways, suddenly full of interest, but he gave no other indication of having heard.

'Right,' said Eddie. Taking his pint, he found an unoccupied table for two against the wall, and settled down to wait. From his pocket he fished out a copy of the day's paper and started to read.

*

In the digs, Miss Keating sat in her own small parlour at the back of the house. A bright fire burned in the grate, beside her on a small table stood a glass of port and she sat in a comfortable armchair, looking at the cartoons in *Dublin Opinion*.

A flunkey in tails and a powdered wig was addressing a rotund moustachioed member of the gentry.

'My lord, your carriage awaits without,' the flunky was saying.

'Without what?' asked his lordship.

'Without petrol.'

At the bottom of the page an ad proclaimed: 'Pour yourself a pair of stockings. That's all there is to it – just smooth on a pair of the most flimsy gossamer-like silk stockings you ever saw . . . Made in two real stocking shades, Grape Mist and Gold Mist – Miner's Liquid Stockings.'

Miss Keating smiled slightly and looked down at her own legs, clad in sheer silk, ending neatly in a pair of highly polished high-heeled shoes. She still had very good legs, she had been told that, for a woman of her age.

The door burst open without warning. It was Nellie, ungainly as ever. Uncertainty about how to behave and terror of Miss Keating made her talk, as usual, at the top of her voice.

'Ma'am, ma'am,' she shouted, 'there's a man at the door.'

'Did you ever hear of knocking before you came into a room?' asked Miss Keating icily.

'Jaysus, I'm sorry, ma'am,' she said. 'But, ma'am, ma'am, there's a man at the door.'

'I can hear you, I'm not deaf,' said Miss Keating, rising.

She headed up the hall towards the front door. Nellie followed, like some eager but unattractive mongrel dog after its master.

'That will do, Nellie,' said Miss Keating.

'Wha'?'

'That will do. Go to your room.'

Nellie still hesitated.

'Go!' said Miss Keating angrily and the unfortunate girl turned and clumped noisily off down into the basement, where the miserable room she inhabited was situated.

Miss Keating went to the hall door, pausing only to touch her hair as she passed her reflection in the mirror over the hall table. A small man in a dirty coat waited on the top step outside the hall door.

'Yes, what is it, my man?' she asked grandly.

'Miss Keating? I've a delivery for you.'

Miss Keating put her head out the door and looked up and down the street. There was nothing to be seen but a horse, tethered to a flat cart, which stood in the street outside.

'All right,' she said, 'how much?'

'Three sacks.'

'Put them in under the steps, I'll let you in.'

She went downstairs to the basement and opened the door under the steps leading up to the main entrance. The man was waiting for her with the first of the sacks on his back.

'In here,' she indicated where some fuel still remained, and he emptied the sack of black high-quality coal onto it. The other two followed, some bank notes changed hands, and he was gone into the night without speaking further.

In her squalid room Nellie heard the rush of coal out of the sacks. She wondered what was going on, but was afraid to look.

*

Eddie had become so immersed in his newspaper that at first he did not notice the man standing beside him in the pub. He was smallish, with a squat, powerful build, dark, curling hair, narrow eyes and a tight mouth.

'A bad day,' said the man in a Belfast accent. 'Do you think it'll clear up at all?'

Eddie looked up. It was McCaigue.

He gave the countersign: 'I'm sure it'll get better, with the help of God.'

McCaigue shook his hand and sat down beside him.

'How are things?' asked Eddie.

'All right,' said McCaigue noncommittally.

'Any news?'

'Keep your voice down,' said McCaigue, though Eddie hadn't raised it.

'What'll you have?'

'I don't drink,' said McCaigue.

'A mineral?'

'All right.'

'Lemonade? Orange?'

'It doesn't matter. Anything.'

Eddie went to the bar and ordered himself another pint and a brightly coloured fizzy orange-flavoured drink for his companion. McCaigue kept his eyes steadily on him as he did so.

Eddie felt the hair prickling on the back of his neck. He'd never met the Belfast man before, but his reputation had gone before him. He was one of the IRA's hard men, wanted in the North for half a dozen killings, it was said. He'd been in the celebrated raid on the RUC barracks in Tyrone that had ended in calamity for the Movement, but McCaigue had got away with a bullet in his shoulder, back across the border to safety. It was said he was one of those who earlier that year had tortured Stephen Hayes, the IRA chief-of-staff suspected of being a police spy, who had escaped his interrogators before they could execute him and walked barefoot into a Dublin police station, still protesting his innocence.

Eddie brought back the drinks to the table.

'Everything all right?' asked McCaigue, ignoring his orange.

'Yes. They have me staying in . . .'

'I know where you're staying,' McCaigue interrupted. 'Just say as little as possible. You never know who might overhear.'

Eddie looked round the bar. No one seemed to be paying any attention to them. He said nothing.

'There's a job coming up,' said McCaigue, lowering his voice so that Eddie could only just hear him.

'When?'

'Soon. There's some preliminary work to be done.'

'What is it?'

McCaigue looked round again, carefully. 'We have to take someone out,' he said. 'You too.'

Eddie felt a sinking in the pit of his stomach. He had always known in his heart of hearts that it could come to this, but never really faced up to it. His only previous operation for the cause, the raid on the bank in Tipperary for which he was now on the run, had been different. It had been exhilarating. Bursting in, waving guns, the terrified bank clerks. Someone might have got shot, but it would have been different, it wouldn't have been in – he paused even at the thought – cold blood. Stuffing the money into sacks, bursting out into the street, someone firing a shot in the air. A man on the street applauding them: 'Up the IRA.' Into the waiting car, careering through the town. Looking back at the streets filling with people, including a policeman, looking after them helplessly. Then the excitement of the head-long drive through the country roads, the sheer delight in what they had done, cheering, waving fists at each other, holding up the stuffed sacks of banknotes in wonder. Then into the remote farmhouse and hiding the car in the empty haybarn.

Go to Dublin, they'd told him, to this address. Lie low for a bit, we'll be in touch. He hadn't thought it would take such a short time till they contacted him again.

'It'll take a bit of time,' said McCaigue. 'Someone will get on to you. Slán.'

And he was gone, his drink untouched.

Eddie looked after him with admiration. Here was a man who'd done it all for Ireland, short of making the ultimate sacrifice. To work with him would be a privilege. Then he thought again. Killing someone. Call it what you will, that's what it was, and the old sense of foreboding returned. No, if it had to be done, it had to be done, he'd taken an oath and, whoever it was, he was sure there must be a good reason for it. The great men of the past, the Fenians, the 1916 men, they hadn't held back when it was necessary, nor must he.

Slowly he finished his pint, left the pub and cycled back towards the digs.

'Come on. Let's go to the Dolphin and get a steak,' the cadaverous man said to the bookie.

'I'll be with you in a minute,' replied the other. 'I just have to make a quick phone call.'

4

The night went on and, one by one, the lights went out in the two tall adjoining houses. The streets were totally empty now and still the rain came down, softly, relentlessly. In other cities, searchlights stabbed the skies, bombers droned overhead, there were explosions and burning buildings and people cowered in air raid shelters, but Dublin was quiet, quiet almost as the dead.

Inside the darkened bedrooms some slept, but others were still awake, or half awake, for the night had not yet reached that last, exhausted phase when even the sick and the insomniac drift into an uneasy slumber before another day begins.

Frankie Fox lay trying to ignore the dull pain throbbing in the pit of his stomach. Jaysus, it was bad tonight! He'd go, he'd have to go to the doctor tomorrow, it had been going on too long. He'd told himself that before, but he never went. He had a mistrust of doctors, you never knew what they might try to do to you. Supposing they said an operation. He couldn't face the knife. Or they might stick him into hospital. He might never get out again and when he did he'd be out of work. He might never get another job. The thought of returning to the slums where he had been born caused another jab from his stomach. He grimaced and pulled his knees up into the foetal position in an effort to relieve the pain.

There was wind trapped in his chest. That's what it felt like. It would be better if he could fart or belch, but nothing would come. It held him like a vice. Maybe it was a heart attack. How did you know? Jaysus, the cramps!

He thought of getting up, but he was cold already and the idea of padding over the bare linoleum of his room, up the cold stairs and into the freezing bathroom, where a window had stuck open months before and never been fixed, was almost worse than the pain.

If he went to the doctor, what would it cost? It could take every penny he'd saved. God knows it wasn't much, but he was relying on it to give him a little comfort when he was too old to work. He'd seen what could happen to old variety pros. Old Ben Griffiths that did the skin act, playing the goose or the cat in the pantos year after year. He remembered visiting Ben in the ward of one of those hospitals, a grim place full of dribbling, crippled, mad old men and the sour smells of senility. It had been a mercy for Ben to die and not to be stuck any longer in that terrible kip of a place. Frankie had vowed to himself that he'd never finish up like that. Get a few bob together. Even if he could never afford a house, he could stay in digs somewhere. Over the years he had scratched together two hundred and fifty pounds. Not much, but better than nothing. He'd go up to Harry Mushatt, who had the chemist shop in Francis Street, the fellow with all the cures. Harry would give him a stomach bottle.

To take his mind off his pain he tried to think of something else. He thought of Kay Nelligan, a number-singer in the Coliseum shows, for whom he harboured a secret passion. She was so pretty, so young! If he was twenty years younger, perhaps. What do you mean, twenty? Thirty years younger. No, even then she'd never have looked at him. There were young fellas mad about her, big handsome young chaps, hanging round the stage door looking for dates. Still, he could watch her, even if he could do nothing else.

His stomach bit at him again. He forced himself out of the bed, struggled into his old raincoat, in the dark, and with freezing feet headed for the bathroom. There were a few tablets in the coat pocket, dusty with bits of fluff, and he chewed them thankfully, but they made little difference. There had been a time when they gave him relief, but less and less so of late.

*

In his room, which he shared with Dolan, Corrigan was in bed with Betty Grable. She had come to him just before he went to sleep, wiggling her backside and looking flauntingly over one shoulder in that way she had. He had tried to get her to go away by reciting a prayer to the Little Flower, the symbol of purity, but Betty had obstinately refused to leave, pushing herself against him and suggesting all sorts of lewd carry-on.

He tried to remember an exciting football match to drive the bad thoughts out of his head. The priest at school always suggested that as a cure, but he had scant interest in football and could only think of a few miserable occasions when he had been forced to take part himself. A more practical bar to the consummation of his solitary passion had been that he wasn't sure whether Dolan, in the bed at the other side of the room, was asleep yet. But now the deep rhythmic snoring of his roommate made it all too clear that the coast was clear for him to have his way with Betty. Once more he attempted to fight the urges that were rising in him so powerfully. If he got out of bed, he thought, and went to the lavatory, the cold would quieten him down. He was just about to put out an exploratory foot from under the bedclothes when he heard footsteps on the landing outside. Someone else was going and he would have to wait.

As he lay there another imaginary figure stood beside him and the film star. It was Miss Keating, and she was clad only in underwear from Clery's. From the look on her face it was clear she had only one thing on her mind – she wished to partake of a three in the bed romp. Corrigan surrendered, turned on his stomach and with the minimum of movement, so the creaking bedsprings would not disturb the sleeping Dolan, started to massage himself . . .

*

In her bed the real Miss Keating slept soundly, dreaming of her lost love. In her dreams she was young again, in her early twenties. She had been a beauty then, she dreamed, admired and desired by men. Mick Collins himself had flirted with her, and many of the other great ones of the Troubles, fighting Ireland's fight, had a fancy of her. She had carried messages for the Boys, hidden them while they were on the run, endured raids and heart-stopping escapes.

But it had been Phil Hurley who had won her heart. Phil, one of the bravest of the brave. He it was who had led the ambush in Saggart when ten Black and Tans had been shot. He had held her in his arms and kissed her with deep, sweet kisses, swearing to marry her when it was all over. She dreamed again, too, in a haunted far-off way, of the day when word had come through that there had been a shoot-out in the Liberties, that he was taken prisoner and badly wounded. She remembered when they told her that he was dead, tortured to death, or so the story went. The wake, his poor body laid out, the Tans bawling drunk outside the window, the priest who berated them for their lack of respect and the foul language they had used back to him. She remembered the shadowy men who came bearing messages from the leaders of the cause, who could not come themselves as they were wanted by the British. 'A hero . . .' 'He has joined Pearse and Tone, Emmett and the Fenians, all the great men who died for Ireland.' 'He shall not be forgotten.' It all seemed such a short time ago, but it wasn't. Phil was dead more than twenty years.

After that the fight had gone on and she had played her part. In the civil war, she had taken the republican side, the die-hards, for she could not accept that less-than-fully-free Free State, with its Oath of Allegiance to the hated English crown and the Six Counties still under the Union Jack. She was a tragic, romantic figure to her fellow-republicans who knew no better, one who had loved and lost and suffered for Ireland. It would somehow have lessened her in their eyes if she had ever married, which may have been why she never did so. It wasn't for lack of offers, anyway.

Then de Valera had founded his Fianna Fáil party, gone into the hated Free State parliament and split the republican cause again, leaving a rump IRA to carry on the armed struggle. Like many another she had dropped out of politics, whether through disillusion or just weariness. But she knew most of the men who had become government ministers when Dev had come to power in the 1930s and wasn't above using her acquaintanceships with them, of varying intimacy, when it suited her purposes.

What they didn't know was that in her heart she was still a

supporter of the old Sinn Féin way of things. She may have taken no part in the meetings, the speeches, the tussles between the IRA and the Garda Special Branch, but she was prepared to help where she could, in this instance by providing a safe house for anyone from the Movement who wanted to stay hidden from the law. It was an allegiance which, so far, had escaped the notice of the authorities.

She turned over in her bed and her half memories of a heroic past merged with a confused dream involving the local butcher, black-market tea and smugglers from Northern Ireland.

*

Days, weeks went by uneventfully. In the wider world the Russian campaign went on ferociously. The tide was turning against Germany, but few enough people in Ireland recognised the signs. Eddie, increasingly bored and discontented, waited for word from McCaigue, but none came. Though he claimed to be a commercial traveller, the others in the digs did not seem to notice that he never travelled anywhere, out all day as they were at their work. To pass the time the young man offered to dig the garden, an offer graciously agreed to by Miss Keating who never refused anything that was not going to cost her money.

There was, in truth, little enough to do at that time of the year. The potatoes were already planted, in neat drills, deeply dug and well manured by an unemployed man whom Miss Keating had got in for the purpose. There was a small weed-covered patch down at the bottom of the garden that he had neglected to do, thereby giving Miss Keating the chance to cheat him of half of what she had promised to pay, and here Eddie dug and weeded, though it was the wrong season to do so.

Next door, in the parallel garden, Conor had found a broken airgun, left behind by someone who had rented the house before the Kennedys, and he was storming a German pill box – actually a little summer-house that stood halfway down the narrow strip at the back of the house.

He had secret, ambiguous feelings about the Germans. On the one hand they had shot down his missing father, on the other there was a glamour about them, their uniforms, their weapons, which was undeniably attractive, despite the bestial Nazis who featured so prominently in his comics and the hatred of them that was so often expressed by his family. Once, when he had gone with his mother to look at a house they were thinking of renting, they had opened a cupboard and hanging there was a full Luftwaffe uniform. He had never discovered how it came to be there, something to do with those pro-German people about whom his mother spoke darkly from time to time. They had not rented the house. Again, at the birthday party of a boy from his class, he had met and got along famously with a son of the German diplomatic representative to Ireland. They had played happily together all afternoon and made an arrangement to meet again some time. But when his mother heard about it, she had firmly said he was never to see him again.

Yet his brother Barry, who pretended to republican leanings, which was the fashionable thing to do among students, had once said you had to admit that there were good Germans, too. It was an argument angrily resisted by his mother.

He crept along with his back to the wall, 'rifle' at the ready. He was a commando, carrying out a raid on the French coast.

The Gerry gunners were peering through a slit in the pill box, a heavy machine gun at the ready. As he raised his own gun to fire Eddie stuck his head over the wall.

'How're you, young fella,' he said. 'Playing cowboys and Indians?'

'Yes,' said Conor, bashful as always when interrupted in his fantasies. There was a little rockery against the wall and he stood up on it, so that he could see over into the next garden.

'Do you not go to school?' asked Eddie.

'Of course I do,' said Conor.

Eddie grinned. 'How come you're not there today?'

'We got a half day. It's the feast of Saint Francis Xavier.'

'Do you play hurling?'

'No, football.'

'What position?'

'Second row forward.'

'That's not football, that's rugby.'

'Rugby is football. That's what we call it, anyway.'

'Why don't you play an Irish game?'

This was a new one on Conor. The male members of his family had always played rugby.

'Rugby *is* an Irish game,' he said.

'No it's not. It's a British garrison game.'

'Well,' said Conor, 'how come my uncle played rugby for Ireland, before the war?'

'Well, you should play hurling. 'Tis a great game.'

'So's rugby.'

Eddie laughed again. 'Maybe. Tell us, what else do you like to do?'

'I like to go to the pictures.'

'What kind of pictures do you like – cowboys?'

'Yes and funny ones.'

'I like them too,' said Eddie. 'Did you ever see your men, Abbot and Costello?'

'Yes, they're great.'

'The little fat fella is a gas ticket. I can never remember which one is he?'

'Lou Costello,' said Conor.

'Did you ever see the one where they're in the army? God, that was the greatest laugh.'

'*Rookies*,' said Conor, with the air of an expert. 'Did you ever see the one where they're in the navy? It's called *In the Navy*.'

'No,' said Eddie, 'I must have missed that one.'

'That's their best, that I've seen anyway,' lied Conor.

'What's it about?'

'Well, they're on a battleship, in the navy,' said Conor lamely.

'Is that right?' said Eddie. 'I wonder would they ever bring it back? I'll watch out for it. What's your name anyway?'

'Conor, what's yours?'

'Eddie. Tell us, Conor, where did you get the gun?'

'This old rifle?' said Conor off-handedly. 'Oh, it was just in the house when we came to live here.'

He didn't mention that, since the first time his mother had seen him playing with it in the garden, he was strictly forbidden to touch it. He had tried to explain that it was broken and harmless, but she would have none of it and confiscated it forthwith. He had sneaked it out of a cupboard where she thought it was safely hidden.

'It isn't a rifle,' said Eddie. ''Tis an air gun. It fires pellets. Do you mind if I have a look?'

Conor took a guilty peek in the direction of his house. No one seemed to be watching. He handed over the gun.

Eddie examined the gun expertly, peering down the sights, breaking it open and looking carefully into the breach and the barrel.

''Tis in a right mess,' he said. 'It needs a clean and an oil, and probably a new spring.' He handed it back to the little boy.

'Could you shoot someone with it?' asked Conor. 'If it was mended, I mean.'

'Ah no, it only shoots pellets. It's not powerful, it'd just sting you. It'd give you a fright though.'

'Kchh, kchh!' Conor fired a couple of imaginary rounds at him.

'Never point a gun at someone,' said Eddie virtuously. 'Did you never hear that? Show me.' He took back the little gun. 'And when you carry it, carry it like this.' He broke it open and held it in the crook of his arm. 'Here.'

'Is that what soldiers do?' asked Conor.

'I suppose so, yes. It's what they should do.'

'Are you a soldier?'

'No, not really.'

'My friend's da is in the LDF.'

'Is that a fact? How about your own father?'

'He's a flyer.'

'A flyer? You mean in the RAF?'

'Yes, he's missing in action.'

'I'm sorry to hear that.'

'We're all saying prayers he'll turn up safe.'

'I'm sure ye are. I hope he'll be okay.'

'O'Sullivan!'

Eddie turned round. It was McCaigue.

'Who's this?' asked McCaigue, nodding towards Conor.

'This is Conor, a ferocious gunman,' said Eddie. 'He lives next door.'

'Is that right?' McCaigue's face broke into a rare grin. He was fond of children. 'He looks a desperate character right enough,' he said.

'He's shot a heap of Indians,' said Eddie. 'So how are you?' he asked.

'Okay. Let's have a word,' said McCaigue.

'Sorry,' said Eddie to Conor, 'I've got to go. I'll see you round.'

'Come on in,' he said to McCaigue.

'Right,' said McCaigue. 'So long, Conor . . .' He pointed at the air gun and laughed. 'Don't shoot anyone I wouldn't shoot with that,' he said.

The two men walked back into the house. 'Who's there? Is it safe?' asked McCaigue.

'No one. They're all out at work except the maid and the landlady.'

'Still,' said McCaigue.

'We can talk in my room. Come on, no one will hear a word.'

Eddie sat on his bed, his legs swinging, while McCaigue paced the floor.

'How's things?' asked Eddie.

McCaigue shook his head angrily. 'Not good. Hogan, O'Mahony and Keogh was all lifted last week.'

'Jaysus,' said Eddie. Hogan and Keogh had been on the bank raid with him.

65

'There's an informer at work, more than one maybe. I'd swear it,' said McCaigue. 'Jesus, when we find the bastards.'

'Would they know about me? The Clonmel job?'

'Probably. They'll have been well worked over by now. Keep your head down.'

'That's what I'm doing. It isn't easy.'

'Isn't easy. Isn't easy?' McCaigue looked round contemptuously. 'Haven't you got a good roof over your heard and a bed to sleep in and food in your mouth? What about men that are sleeping in old barns, aye and out in the fields and in the woods, hunted like animals. What do you mean, isn't easy?'

'I didn't mean it that way,' said Eddie. 'I know, I know what you're saying, but there's nothing to do here. Just waiting round day after day. 'Tis driving me mad.'

'You'll have plenty to do soon enough,' said McCaigue.

'What's the job, anyway? Can you not tell me?'

There was a long pause. McCaigue looked at him intently. 'You know what happens to informers,' he said.

'Who are you calling an informer? I'm no informer!' said Eddie hotly.

'Who said you were?' Another long stare. 'We're going to plug someone.'

'I know that, you told me that already. Who?'

'You'll find out soon enough. Here, I have a delivery for you.'

From under his raincoat he took out a brown paper parcel and handed it over. Eddie untied the string that bound it. Inside was a bundle of oily webbing wrapped around a revolver. He felt it in his hand, weighing it, examining it.

'Where will you keep it?' asked McCaigue.

'Under the floorboards?' suggested Eddie.

'No, not in the house.'

'In the garden then. I'll bury it in the garden.'

'All right. Be sure it doesn't get damp.'

'Sure.'

'And cover it up well. Flatten the earth.'

'I will. What's the job?'

McCaigue paused again. 'I can't tell you yet,' he said. 'Orders. You're to hang on here and keep your head down. It won't be much longer. And keep your eyes and ears open, you never know who the hell's looking out for you. Slán.' And he was gone again.

*

That night Frankie Fox was home for tea again. It was scrambled eggs, or rather a pale yellow mess made from egg powder, a cheap substitute which Miss Keating had discovered from one of her many contacts. It tasted like sawdust and the bread was worse than ever.

'I hear they're making it even browner,' Frankie said, 'and the brewers has agreed to reduce the amount of alcohol in the beer. As I said in the show tonight: "It gives me great pleasure to stand up here tonight and play for you. In fact on these rations, it gives me great pleasure to stand up."'

Eddie roared with laughter. Frankie was in good form. In spite of, or maybe because of the meagreness of their diet and its monotony, and also the fact that he'd been staying off the jar, his stomach had been behaving itself of late. In fact, he had half started to kid himself it was on the mend.

'Did yiz hear the latest about Jack Doyle and Movita?' he asked the others. Doyle, the boxer and his Mexican film star wife were a colourful pair who stood out like neon signs in the murk of wartime Dublin.

'On top of the Donnybrook tram. A fella I know saw the whole thing,' lied Frankie. 'The pair of them got on, legless, and the next thing this almighty row starts. The language, the cursin', they turned the air blue.'

Corrigan, who had been listening with displeasure, winced visibly.

'The next thing,' Frankie went on, 'he ups and hits her a box that sends her flyin' out of the seat. Now she's only a little thing but she jumps up, takes off one of her high-heeled shoes and she goes for him. Bejaysus, she bets him all round the tram! He's got a dirty big shiner of a black eye at the end of it and he's as meek as a lamb! The Mexican spitfire, wha'?'

'And him a heavyweight boxer,' said Eddie in wonder. 'They do say, you know, that he could have been world champion if only he'd trained.'

'He ruined himself with drink and women,' said Dolan. 'And then there were all them hooky fights where they say he took a dive.'

'Doesn't he sing too?' asked Eddie. 'He's meant to have a good voice.'

'Yes,' said Frankie. 'They used to say he could box like Joe Louis and sing like John McCormack, but the truth of the matter was that he could sing like Joe Louis and box like John McCormack.'

Their laughter was interrupted by an irate Corrigan.

'That fella,' he spluttered, 'what else would you expect from the sweepings of the gutters of Cork? And that film actress of his, that Movita one, do you know she's a divorced woman?'

'Is that a fact?' asked Frankie in pretended amazement.

'She is, she is. So what is that only a bigamous marriage? They should both be locked up.'

He lapsed into an angry silence, chewing his bread vigorously and taking long drinks of tea. Frankie leaned back so that Corrigan could not see him, and pulled a comical face. Eddie tried not to laugh and had to pretend to be coughing.

'I fail to see anything particularly funny about it,' said Corrigan.

Frankie changed the subject. 'Listen, I got you the briefs, the free tickets for tomorrow night. One each.'

'Thank you very much,' said Dolan.

'God, I don't know if I can . . .' Eddie thought of McCaigue's order to lie low.

'Come on, it's a great show,' said Frankie. 'Call off whatever you're doing. And there's a good film on this week too, Errol Flynn in *The Sea Hawk*.'

Oh the hell with it, thought Eddie, who could spot him if he just went out one night? No one would notice him in the middle of a crowd. 'Ah sure, I suppose I could go, thanks,' he said.

'Right, and how about you, Mr Corrigan?' asked Frankie.

'No,' said Corrigan. 'I have an appointment. I'm going to another film,' he lied, trying to make it sound as if he had another, interesting life.

'A date?' asked Frankie. 'Sure why don't you bring her along to the Coliseum?'

'No, it's er, it's not a, it's not with a young woman. Just someone I arranged to go to another film with. Excuse me now.' He got up. 'Er, thank you anyway, very kind.' He left the room.

'Begob, what's he up to?' asked Frankie with a twinkle at the

others. 'Would you say he has a little mot tucked away somewhere? Someone from the Society for Dirty Books?'

5

When Eddie and Dolan arrived the next night, a long queue had formed outside the Coliseum, drawn by the popular swashbuckling Errol Flynn film. Eddie felt important, but also uncomfortably in the limelight when they went to the head of the line, as Frankie had told them, and informed one of the uniformed commissionaires that they were Mr Fox's friends.

'*Mister* Fox? Frankie, is it?' said the commissionaire jovially. 'Some people are getting very tony.' He went to the box office and was back in a moment with two tickets. 'There yiz are,' he said. 'Enjoy the show and tell Mr Fox I'll have a pint next time I see him.'

The Coliseum was a handsome, if rather run-down old theatre, built in the days of music hall but long converted for cine-variety. It held over a thousand people and tonight there wasn't a spare seat. The stalls, to which they were ushered, the boxes at the sides, the circle, the bare wooden gods were all packed. People came and went, even in the middle of the film, for it was a continuous programme. They talked loudly, ate sweets and smoked incessantly, so that a great cloud of fug hung over the whole place, penetrating the clothes and hair and the mouths of the audience. They were a comfortable crowd, who knew they were going to like what they were going to get. They were not rich, but apart from a few ragged characters in the gods, they were well off enough. Husbands and wives, young men and girls, either out on dates or in single groups. Everyone was good-humoured, though some of the older people might throw an occasional disapproving eye at the rowdy groups of young men, who whistled and shouted or gave thunderous belches that drew titters from the girls. To Eddie it seemed a place of glamour and sophistication.

The evening began with a newsreel, which showed Mr de Valera reviewing troops of the Irish army. When he appeared on the screen the whole cinema clapped – even Eddie, whose views on Dev were less than favourable. He felt ashamed to be applauding someone who had locked up so many of his comrades, but didn't want to draw attention to himself, so he brought his hands together making as little sound as possible. Dolan, on the other hand, applauded vigorously, for he belonged to that majority of Irish people for whom the Chief could do no wrong, incorruptible leader of his nation, international statesman and world-class mathematician that he was.

There was a trailer for *The Carson City Kid*, followed by the main feature in which Errol Flynn fenced his way round the Spanish Main in the cause of Good Queen Bess. Eddie loved it, even if its depiction of the English as the good fellas was, as everyone knew, less than truthful. But he was prepared to forget such inaccuracies for the duration of the film, caught up as he was in the excitement of the action.

But it was the live show that really thrilled him. He had seen travelling fit-up companies at home, but compared to this they were poor tatty outfits playing in draughty, badly lit tents. Though the Coliseum show was second-rate, even by the standards of Dublin, to his eye it seemed dazzling.

The organist, Gerald La Tour (alias Gerry Kelly), rose from the pit and led off the show with a selection of popular hits. And then, enter The Coliseum Girls, arms linked and legs kicking, all twelve of them. 'Girls how are you!' thought Dolan. As they danced they grinned, showing large teeth, the lights shining on over-rouged cheeks and their muscular legs moving almost in unison. After their first number they picked up hoops garlanded with paper flowers and did a routine involving much swinging of arms as they sang 'You're Getting to Be a Habit with Me'. For Eddie they were the like of something you'd see in a film.

They were followed by Dickie Delaney, with Frankie Fox in close attendance, and Eddie applauded vigorously, digging Dolan in the ribs with his elbow. They were dressed as a pair of charwomen, and entered with much clanking of buckets and sloshing of mops.

'This'll be good,' said Eddie to Dolan.

The sketch, though, was nothing more than a string of gags.

'Have you heard about the cannibal who ate the priest?'

'Wha' about him?'

'It was his first taste of Christianity.'

Eddie roared at it all, but was surprised at how little Frankie Fox had to do, just kneeling there with the bucket and cloth while the other fella told the funny bits of all the jokes. Still, maybe he'd have more later.

Any disappointment he might have felt, however, was alleviated by the arrival of Kay Nelligan, the numbers singer, announced as 'The Ace Number One Glamour Girl of Dublin Theatreland'. She was a pretty girl, young, slight, with brown hair piled up on her head, and a knowing face. She wore a blue evening dress with pads that hid the thinness of her shoulders, in front of which she held up her hands, palms towards the audience, moving them in rhythm with the music, like you'd see the Andrews Sisters or some of them doing in the pictures.

'Jaysus, she's a smasher,' said Eddie.

Dolan grinned and sucked his empty pipe, for even in the atmosphere of the Coliseum, he knew it would generate too much smoke.

She sang 'Sweet Embraceable You'. Her voice was too thin to be remarkable and the American accent she tried for kept slipping into her native Dublin, but she had large dark eyes, which she could use to effect, creating a sexual magnetism that drew the men in the audience, who all felt she was looking directly and slightly mockingly at them.

Eddie clapped his hands off. She was the most beautiful thing he had ever seen in his life. She was indeed a glamour girl, lovely enough to win the Dawn Beauty competition. Like something from Hollywood. Eddie went on clapping after everyone else had finished, to the amusement of those sitting near by.

'I think you're smitten,' smiled Dolan.

'Begor,' said Eddie, 'I think I am.'

For the rest of the show he could think of little else as he sat through an Apache dance by Flynn and O'Brien and Bing Crosby songs from 'Bing' Kelly. Then it was time for the highlight of the night, Dickie Delaney's single spot, the last item before the Coliseum girls re-entered as sailors in 'Anchors Aweigh' and were joined by the company for a final bow. Dickie would do his famous character Paddy MacMud from Ballymacspud, a gormless countryman at large in the big city, which was always guaranteed huge laughs.

But something was wrong. There was a pause. The orchestra had started to play, then it died away. A gurrier at the back of the house gave a piercing whistle. Everyone laughed, but it was the wrong sort of laugh, unplanned, embarrassed, a feeling of unease about it.

Then, not Dickie, but Frankie Fox appeared.

'Where's me hat?' he bellowed.

No one laughed.

Frankie had gone to Dickie with an idea he had for a solo spot for himself, a parody he had written. He had the lyric with him as a matter of fact, he had said. Dickie had taken the song and promised to have a look at it, but weeks had passed and Frankie had heard no more of it. Taking his courage in his hands, he had called into Dickie's dressing room and raised the subject a second time a few weeks later.

Dickie was putting on slap at the time. He hardly paused. 'It'd never work,' he said.

'Let me try it out, at one of the matinées,' Frankie had pleaded.

'I tell you, it's no fucking good. There isn't a laugh in it. It'd die the death,' said Dickie, throwing the dog-eared sheet of paper back. 'And while we're on the subject, would you for God's sake ever come in quicker on your cues. You're killing me tag lines.'

That had decided it. Frankie made up his mind he'd slip it in some night. It was a winner, he knew it, and even if Dickie hit the roof there would be nothing he could do about it if the number had been a hit, or so Frankie thought. He was a fool, fooling no one except himself, but ill health, frustration with the tiny parts he played and just plain boredom made him press ahead with his plan. He made up his mind he'd put in his number on the night Eddie and Dolan came to the show. He had been blowing so much to them about the world of show business, dropping names, Jimmy O'Dea, Noel Purcell, Jack Hilton, even Gracie Fields, who he implied was a pal, that he knew that when they saw the very minor part he played in the Coliseum show they would be sadly disillusioned. That night, then, he had stood in the wings and before Dickie could enter – he always took his time about making his entrance, letting the orchestra fill in for him – Frankie was on the stage.

Harry Harmond, the conductor, looked up startled.

'It's okay,' said Frankie. 'Give us "South of the Border".'

Harry looked around the pit at the musicians, some of whom were laughing.

'What's the matter, maestro?' asked Frankie. 'Forgotten your music?'

Harry shrugged and struck up the tune.

Out of the corner of his eye Frankie could see Dickie in the wings. He was glaring at him, with a mouth on him like a rat trap.

'South of the Border, down Monaghan way,' sang Frankie, in an absurd posh accent. 'I had a leg of ham, a pound of Spam and some eggs that day. The customs men told me I really must stay South of the Border, down Monaghan way . . .'

There were a few titters, not real laughs, the sort that came from the kind of people that would laugh at anything. But the real laughers, the ones who made the difference between a great house and a bad one, stayed silent.

Frankie soldiered on with his song about smuggling. Surely, he thought, they'll break up when I get to the bit 'She sighed when I whispered bananas, but bananas never came.' He had thought that was pretty good himself when he had written it, but even there the reception was cool.

And then, gradually, more and more, they did start to laugh. Uneasily, Frankie became aware that there was something happening behind him. Dickie Delaney had come on stage and was miming to Frankie's words. He was wearing an enormous, waxed false moustache, which kept sliding to one side. The audience roared. Frankie soldiered on, his words becoming less and less relevant. With a huge facial effort Dickie got his moustache straight on his face again. It started to slide off the other side of his upper lip. His face was a mask of panic. The audience howled. A man in the row in front of Eddie and Dolan started to beat his hand helplessly on the arm of his seat. Frankie came towards the end of his song. Very slowly, with great relish, Dickie started to eat his moustache, swallowing it with a great gulp as the song ended and exiting to thunderous applause.

Frankie stumbled off the stage, but was no sooner in the wings than he was pushed on again by Dickie. The audience continued to applaud, but it soon abated.

'Where's Dickie?' roared one of the gurriers.

Dickie came on again, wearing the moustache, and once more the whole theatre erupted.

Dickie smirked and bowed, smirked and bowed. Then he called to the wings, 'Come on,' and Frankie was shoved out again.

'Give him a big hand,' said Dickie. The applause dropped. 'Ah now fair dues, fair dues. Sure God love him he was doin' his best.'

The orchestra struck up 'Anchors Aweigh' and the girls, dressed as sailors, went into the final routine.

'Listen, you no-talent little bollocks,' said Dickie to Frankie in the wings, loudly so that everyone could hear. 'If you try to pull a stunt like that again you'll be out on your ear quicker than you can give a cue, which is not very quick I admit.' This last was addressed to the rest of the company. 'I'd have fired you out long ago if'n I wasn't sorry for you. "Where's me hat?" ' He imitated Frankie cruelly and accurately. 'Don't give me any of that shite in future either. Nobody wants to hear it.'

The show ended, to be followed immediately by *The Sea Hawk* again, the last showing of the night. Some of the audience left, to be replaced from those queuing outside, happy enough to see the film by itself, even though the stage shows were over for the evening. Eddie and Dolan left their seats. Frankie had invited them to 'come round' after the show and go for a drink, but Dolan had his doubts whether he'd want to see them after the 'South of the Border' debacle. Eddie, his mind full of Kay still, would not be deflected, however.

'Sure 'twasn't that bad,' he said. 'It all ended in a great laugh, didn't it?'

The pair went in through the stage door, awkward visitors in an alien world, and were sent to Frankie's dressing room. Up a couple of flights of stone steps and along a corridor with the dressing room doors off it. The place smelled of an odd mixture, Jeyes Fluid and grease paint mingled with the sharp onion-like smell of female sweat. As they went along they passed a half open door and caught a glimpse of a roomful of women in various stages of undress. They seemed quite unselfconscious about it, though the two men were embarrassed. Kay was deep in laughing conversation with her pal Vera, one of the younger Coliseum Girls. She looked around and for a split second Eddie caught her eye. He felt himself blushing and then he was past the door.

Frankie shared his dressing room with Bing Kelly and Tommy Flynn of Flynn and O'Brien. He sat morosely, slumped in front of a mirror, dressed only in trousers and a vest that was grey from lack of washing. His stomach was playing up again.

'Ah, how're yeh?' he said listlessly.

'It was a great show,' said Eddie.

'Yes, you were great,' said Dolan insincerely.

'Did you think so?' asked Frankie, in a tone that implied he didn't think so himself.

'And you were great too,' said Eddie to Bing Kelly.

Bing adjusted his bow tie and took his pipe from his mouth – he played the same role on and off stage. 'Thanks, old man,' he said. 'You were a great house.'

Eddie was puzzled. What did he mean, how could they be a house?

Little Tommy Flynn got up to leave. 'Better be on me way,' he said. 'May will be waiting below for me.'

'Are you coming for a pint, Frankie?' asked Bing.

From next door came the voice of Dickie Delaney. He was entertaining guests in his dressing room. 'South of the Border, down Monaghan way . . .' he sang in a perfect imitation of Frankie. There was an explosion of laughter from his room.

'Bastard!' said Frankie. 'Okay, see you in Curran's in five minutes, lads,' he said to Eddie and Dolan.

Curran's was the pub next door to the Coliseum. One end of the bar was sacrosanct to the theatre crowd and when the two men came in there was already a good few of them in, as it was the end of the week and pay night. The musicians had got away first, 'cause they didn't have to change costumes, and many of them were already into their second pints. They were soon joined by the ladies of the chorus, who looked fast and garish away from the lighting of the stage. Eddie and Dolan stood at the bar, a little bit away from them, feeling out of it as the exotic group chattered and laughed. The conversation seemed to be all about people and past shows of which they had never heard.

'Joe Bell, there was a character,' Harry Harmond was saying. 'Remember old Joe? He was doing a show in the fit-ups, I can't remember which one. Anyway he had to come on as Napoleon in a sketch and they didn't have a proper costume, so he makes his entrance wearing a pair of old wellington boots, an ancient pair of tails with the elbows out of it and on his head an old Homburg hat that he'd squashed into what he thought was something like what Napoleon used to wear. Well, the audience, even though they were only from the arse end of nowhere, burst out laughing at the sight of him. He drew himself up: "Go on, laugh, you peasants," says he. "Just wait till you see Josephine!" '

In the general laughter Kay came in, with Vera, and threw a brief sidelong glance in Eddie's direction. Then it was the turn of Frankie to appear, looking grey in the face.

'I'll have a Jameson, a large one,' he said to the barman.

'Are you sure, Frankie?' asked the young curate, who had heard all about Frankie's stomach problems from Frankie himself.

'Just give it to me, Billy, will you?' The barman shrugged and poured him the large one. 'What'll yiz have, lads?' Frankie asked the pair.

'No, no,' said Dolan, 'this is mine. And two more pints,' he called.

'It was a great show, honestly,' said Eddie.

Frankie swallowed his drink at a gulp. 'Except for a certain bastard that won't let anyone else have a spot.' He saw Kay and Vera. 'How are yiz, girls?' he said. 'What's your poison?' They came over to the bar.

'I'll have a gin and orange,' said Vera, bold as you please.

Eddie was amazed. Where he came from women would never drink the likes of that. 'I thought you were great,' he said to Kay. 'You have a wonderful voice.'

'I *told* you he fancied you,' said Vera to her. She grinned up at Eddie. 'Not bad for a country fella,' she said.

Eddie felt himself blushing to the roots of his hair.

'Will you quit it!' said Kay, laughing back. 'You're desperate! You couldn't bring her anywhere,' she told the others.

'Same again and two gin and oranges,' Frankie told the barman.

'Right enough, that was a shitty thing Dickie done on you,' said Kay to him.

The whiskey was beginning to go well with Frankie. 'What else would you expect from a little shite like that that wouldn't give you the steam off his,' he paused, 'tea.'

At this moment Dickie came into Curran's. With him was the bookie who had been drinking in the bar where Eddie had first met McCaigue and a handsome but tough-looking woman, who wore a fox fur round her shoulders and a hat with a wisp of veil. She was Dickie's current girlfriend, the latest of a long line, for though he was married, his wife was never seen. The official story was that she was an invalid, though some said you could see her out around Drimnagh any day of the week.

Dickie was in fine form, greeting all the rest of the cast with unaccustomed warmth. 'Whatever everyone is having, Billy,' he told the barman. The others were amazed: this was something unprecedented. They crowded up to the bar, ordering drinks. 'Except for "Where's Me Hat" over there,' said Dickie.

'Ah come on, Dickie,' said Bing Kelly. 'Have a heart.'

Dickie's face went hard as stone. 'What?' he said. 'What? He fucks around me spot, he wrecks the show, and I'm expected to buy him drink now.'

'Jaysus,' said the girlfriend, 'some people have a neck.'

'Where's me hat? Where's me hat?' Again Dickie did his cruel impersonation. 'What's that meant to mean anyway? Where's me hat? Where's your professionalism? The last time he got a laugh was when the midwife first saw him.'

The girlfriend gave a too-loud shriek of mirth. The rest of the company looked uncomfortable, but no one spoke up for Frankie, who slumped over the bar.

'I think I'm doing enough by not fecking him out on his ear, let alone buying him drink. He should be buying *me* drink.'

'Give him whatever he wants,' Frankie told the barman, in a low voice.

'What?' said Dickie loudly, pretending not to hear. 'What did you say?'

'What'll you have to drink?' asked Frankie.

'Huh!' Dickie snorted. 'Give me a brandy, Billy, and none of that Portuguese muck.'

'I've got just the stuff, Mr Delaney,' said the barman, reaching under the counter for a hidden bottle of all-too-rare Hennessy's.

Dickie took the glass and carefully added a splash of soda from the siphon which was placed beside it. 'Cheers,' he said to the rest of the company, pointedly ignoring Frankie.

'Cheers, Dickie,' they more or less chorused weakly.

Dickie turned to his companions. 'I took that little gurrier in out of the goodness of my heart, when he hadn't a backside to his trousers,' he said. 'Amn't I right?' he asked Frankie.

Frankie said nothing.

'Are you deaf? I asked you a question. Didn't I take you in and give you a job when no one else would? Well?'

'Yes, Dickie,' said Frankie miserably.

'God knows, it wasn't for anything he could add to the show,' Dickie told the others. 'Am I right or am I wrong?' he asked Frankie again.

'I'm sorry,' said Frankie.

'What? You're what?'

'Cut that out!'

Everyone turned. It was Eddie who had spoken.

'And who the hell do you think you are?' asked Dickie coldly.

'I'm a friend of his, and there's no need to be going on and on at him. He was only doing his best.' He was making a show of himself, he knew it. Everyone was looking at him, the very last thing he wanted, but he couldn't help himself.

Dickie's girlfriend drew in her breath. 'Little fart!' she said. 'Mind your own business.'

'Are you some sort of expert?' said Dickie menacingly. But underneath he felt uneasy. There was something about the steady angry eyes of the young man that was unsettling.

The bookie, who had stayed silent until then, leant over and whispered something in his ear.

Dickie gazed at Eddie again. 'Look, son,' he said, 'I've no row with you. Leave it at that. Come on.' He turned to his girlfriend and the bookie. 'Our table will be gone at the Red Bank.' He turned to the company, with a beatific smile. 'Where's me hat?' he said. They roared as he left.

Frankie slumped over the bar, looking sicker by the minute. He was getting drunk, too, for he was not used to drinking whiskey.

'Gi's another one, Billy,' he slurred.

'Maybe you've had enough, Frankie,' said the barman.

'Yes, come on, Frankie, take it easy,' said Kay.

'That bastard,' said Frankie, 'that, that hoor's get!'

'You'd never think he was like that when you'd see him on the stage,' said Eddie. 'You'd think he was the greatest bit of gas.'

Bing pulled on his pipe. 'Still, it wasn't a very bright stunt to try.'

Frankie said nothing. He didn't need to be told that he'd messed himself up, probably for good and all. Dickie Delaney wasn't the type who would forgive and forget, that was for sure. Befuddled as he was by drink, he still knew that he'd be out of a job as soon as a replacement could be found.

'Gi's another one, Billy,' he repeated.

The barman sighed and poured another whiskey, a small one this time.

'You could be on the films,' Eddie was saying meanwhile to Kay Nelligan.

'Oh yeah!' she mocked, though she was pleased.

'You could, no bother. I seen a lot worse than you. Are you long on the stage?'

'Forever. Me and Vera started – when was it, Vera?'

'When we were nine,' replied Vera.

'Yeah, nine. The Harmony Twins they called us, song and dance, though of course we're no more like twins than yourself and your pal.'

'He's a great laugh, isn't he?' said Vera in a piercing aside, indicating the silent Dolan.

'The strong silent type, are you, mister?' laughed Kay.

'Still waters run deep,' said Dolan, making his first contribution to the conversation.

'My God, he can talk,' said Vera. Dolan just grinned.

'Do you ever get the chance to go out of an evening?' Eddie asked Kay.

'Why? Are you looking for a date?'

'I wouldn't mind.'

'Well, get in the queue.'

He had never known women like this before, who spoke up brashly, were cheeky and said exactly what they thought.

'Do you like dancing, or do you see too much of it at work?' he asked.

'I don't mind. Ballroom is different.'

'Maybe we could go out some night after the show.'

'Maybe we could and maybe we couldn't.'

'We could make a foursome,' said Vera. 'The two of us and yourself and Gabby Hayes here.' Vera, though she had a good figure, was frankly plain, but she never let it hinder her unending interest in the opposite sex, no matter what their age or appearance.

'Sorry,' said Dolan. 'I'm afraid I'm not the dancing type.'

'Foiled again,' said Vera merrily.

'You don't know what you're missing,' said Kay.

At this point Frankie slumped off his bar stool, bringing a pint of stout crashing onto the floor with him.

'Oh Jaysus!' said Vera as it splashed over her.

Billy was out from behind the bar in a second, lifting up the drunken comedian.

'Come on, Frankie, me ould son,' he said, 'time to go home.'

Frankie muttered something incomprehensible.

'Okay, I'll take him,' said Eddie, putting Frankie's arm round his shoulder. 'Okay, Frankie?' he asked.

Grey in the face, Frankie looked at him like a wounded dog. Dolan moved to the other side and the two half carried him from the pub.

'We'd better get him home,' said Dolan, pointing to a nearby tram stop. Somehow or other they got him across the road and leant him against a lamppost. He started to moan, wordlessly, stupidly.

Kay came out of the pub and followed them.

'You forgot this,' she said to Eddie, holding out his cap, which had fallen on the pub floor.

At this point a tram arrived, pulling up in a blaze of light.

'I'll get him home,' said Dolan.

'Are you sure?'

'Yes, no bother,' he said. He looked at Eddie and Kay. 'Go on with you, we'll be all right.'

'Is that Frankie Fox?' asked the conductor, helping him up the steps and into the tram. He winked at Dolan. 'Come on, Frankie, me ould flower,' he said, 'time to go home to bye-byes.' The tram pulled away, clanking.

Eddie looked at Kay. 'Can I see you home?' he asked.

'It's a bit early for that,' she said.

'Will we go back to the pub?'

'No, I'm sick of them. We'll go somewhere else.'

They walked up O'Connell street, full of people as the cinemas disgorged the late crowds.

'Let's go in here,' she said, and they went into another pub, jam-packed. This time she had a mineral, while he had another stout.

'Quit looking at me,' she said.

'I can't help it. I've never seen anyone as beautiful as you before.'

'Cut that out! Actin' the maggot!'

'I mean it.'

She was used to compliments, well used to them, but there was something about him, the intensity of his gaze, the openness of his face, that attracted her powerfully.

'You certainly know how to pitch a line,' she said.

'What?' He didn't know what she meant.

'I'll bet you've said that to dozens of girls.'

'I've never said it to anyone else in my life.'

'Oh I'm sure,' she said scornfully, but she knew he was telling the truth. 'Where do you come from?'

'I'm not from Dublin.'

'Tell me something I don't know.'

'I'm from Tipperary.'

'What do you work at?'

'I'm a commercial traveller. For Mooney's, the sweet people.'

'Do you get any samples?'

'I do, I'll bring you some. Can I see you again?'

'Well . . . anyway, you can see me to me bus,' she said.

There was a long queue for the bus. While they waited, almost without thinking, she slipped her arm into his. When the bus did come he jumped aboard with her.

'Hey, where do you think you're going?' she asked.

'I'll see you to your door.'

'This is the last bus, you won't be able to get back into town.'

'What matter, I'll walk.'

'You're daft,' she laughed.

The bus was packed and they had to stand, crammed close to each other. When they reached Kay's stop they got off and walked to her house.

'Do you have brothers and sisters?' he asked.

'Six. Four sisters and two brothers. I'm the eldest, but.'

'Daddy's pet.'

'I am like hell. If he sees me now with you I'll get what for.'

'Is he in the show business?'

'Him, are you kidding? He hates it.'

'Where did you get all the talent from then?'

'Me granny was a singer and me mammy used to do a bit too, amateur. She's mad on it. She had me going to classes and all since I could walk. Here's me house.' It was a neat little Corporation semi-detached, one of the newly built ones.

They stood outside, awkwardly, looking at each. Well, she thought, he's certainly different. She was used to fellas she'd be fighting off, all hands, down some lane trying to get under her skirt.

'When will I see you again?' he asked.

'You know where to find me,' she said. 'Sometimes I've a few hours off. We could go to the pictures.'

'I thought you'd be sick of them.'

'Me? I never get to see them. There's no time between the shows.'

Silence fell between them again. He gazed at her as if she would vanish if he took his eyes off her.

'Stop it,' she said. 'I'd better go. You can kiss me good night if you like.' She turned her face up to him, like she'd seen them doing so often in the films.

He kissed her, very gently, awkwardly. Not like the fellas would nearly strangle you, trying to stick their tongues down your throat. Her lips seemed amazingly soft to him.

'Good night.' She went down the little path to the front door and opened it with her key. Before she went in she turned and smiled. She had a large mouth and beautiful teeth and had, she knew, a dazzling smile. He was dazzled.

'See you.'

He walked home. She lived on the north side, well out from town. How long would it take to get back to the digs? An hour, two hours? He didn't care. There was a spring in his step that made him pace out at high speed. He had the feeling of something important starting. He felt drunk with love, pacing along, arms swinging. Only when he got back to the city centre did he remember that he was on the run and meant to keep out of sight. He took side streets and walked in the shadows, but even then felt so full of energy that he could not restrain himself from striding out, so that his footsteps rang out on the empty pavements.

*

Meanwhile Dolan had been taking Frankie back to the digs. The heat and the closeness of the tram had awakened the little comedian from his torpor and he started to sing. 'Pardon me, boy,' he sang in his posh version of his rich Dublin accent, 'is that the Chattanooga chew chew?'

People in the tram turned around and looked at him, mostly in disapproval. A couple of young ones giggled. Dolan, sitting beside him, looked embarrassed.

'Hey, Frankie, put a sock in it,' said the conductor.

'*Meet me at the station at a quarter to four,*' sang Frankie, louder than ever.

'Can you not get him to shut up?' the conductor asked Dolan. 'Come on, Frankie, there's a good man, a bit less noise.'

'Oh Jaysus, I feel terrible,' said Frankie. Leaning over the aisle he was copiously sick on the conductor's shoes.

People scattered.

'Ah Jaysus Christ!' said the conductor. 'You dirty divil! Get off, get off the car!' He rang the bell and they came to a stop. 'No messin'. Off!'

'Sorry,' said Dolan, half carrying Frankie down the steps of the tram. 'He had too much to drink,' he added foolishly.

'Dirty divil!' repeated the furious conductor. 'Hey, Lar, give us that paper of yours,' he shouted up the tram to the driver.

'I'm not finished with it yet,' said the driver.

'I don't care whether you are or not,' said the conductor, going up and taking it. 'This town is full of savages, savages! God, the smell of it!' and he threw the newspaper on top of the vomit.

Fortunately they were only a couple of stops from their own so, half carrying Frankie, Dolan was able to make it to the front door of the digs.

'Come on,' he said, 'the best place for you is bed.'

'Sorry,' said Frankie, who had gone the colour of lard, 'sorry.'

With difficulty they got up the front steps of the digs and Dolan opened the hall door. As if she had been expecting them, Miss Keating was in the hall, rigid with disapproval.

'Oh dear, oh dear,' said Frankie.

Dolan felt like a schoolboy who had been caught out. He grinned weakly. 'A bit of an accident.'

'I made it perfectly clear,' said Mrs Keating, 'when you came here. No drunkenness, and no women callers.'

'Where's the women callers?' asked Frankie, faintly, sick though he was.

'I think I'd better get him up to bed,' said Dolan.

'I'll see about this tomorrow,' said Miss Keating. 'Take him away.' She waved her hand like a queen dismissing some disgraced courtier.

Dolan manoeuvred Frankie up the stairs somehow and into his cold, dismal room. He lowered him onto the bed, where the little man lay, hunched up. He took off Frankie's shoes.

'Will you be okay?' he asked.

'Ahhh,' said Frankie incoherently.

'Yes, well, cover yourself up and get a night's sleep.' He left the room.

Frankie didn't know how long he lay there. Then it came again, an over-powering nausea. He managed somehow to make it to the wash basin which stood on a stand beside the window and was sick again. Despite the chill of the night he was sweating. He fell on his knees but somehow crawled back to the bed. He pulled the blankets over him and lay there moaning, still fully dressed. The night closed in on him.

Next morning Miss Keating went to his room, waving away

Nellie, who usually did a cursory tidying of it. A whey-faced Frankie had left early, without breakfast, as he had a rehearsal and knew full well that retribution would be awaiting him if he was a minute late.

Miss Keating's nose wrinkled in disgust at the sour, metallic smell of vomit, alcohol and something worse which filled the bedroom. Despite the chill of the winter morning she threw open the window to let in the air. She looked around at the clothes, thrown higgledy-piggledy on the floor, a used shirt, a pair of socks which had not been washed for months, a pair of trousers with a hole in them. Steeling herself, she peered into the wash basin and felt her gorge rise. She turned away quickly, but not before she had noticed the blood which mingled with the vomit in it. He'd have to go, she decided, and the sooner the better.

She went to the bed, a mass of grey sheets and blankets whose twisted mass testified to Frankie's tossing and turning through the night. She pulled them back and was just about to go when she felt something, a small bump under the mattress. Most people would not have noticed it, and certainly not Nellie, whose half-hearted making of the bed hardly disturbed it. But Miss Keating was one of those people who missed nothing. A worn shirt collar, a button that had fallen off, the movement of an ornament or an ashtray six inches from its usual resting place, the emptying of a bottle by so much as a couple of drops, these and a thousand other minute details fell under her eagle eye every day. Putting her hand under the mattress she pulled out a wallet, greasy with age.

Her eyes widened as she saw it was stuffed with bank notes, Frankie's hidden savings. Ten, twenty, fifty, a hundred, two hundred, two hundred and fifty pounds. Her fingers flipped over the notes with all the dexterity of a concert pianist in full flow.

She paused. For a moment she considered pocketing the lot, but then decided against it, not from any qualms of conscience, for that was not something that ever worried her unduly, but for fear of being caught – Nellie, after all, knew she was in the room. She thought for a moment. She'd let Fox stay after all, disgusting though he was. She would bide her time and keep her eyes open.

6

Detective Sergeant Paul O'Grady of the Special Branch rode his bicycle carefully along the street, avoiding the slippery wet cobblestones and the tram lines that could trap the wheels. It was a big bike, a heavy upright bone-shaker, and it needed to be, for its rider was a big man. He was in his early forties, well over six feet, and was massively built with a thick neck, accentuated by the short-back-and-sides haircut of a policeman. There was something bull-like about him, a feeling of great physical strength, further accentuated by the grim set of his face, the unblinking way he met anyone's gaze, and because he never smiled.

He had been a boxing champion, winning a police tournament and fighting for an Irish amateur title at the National Stadium, where he had narrowly failed against a quicker, more skilful opponent. When the animal gangs had gone out looking for trouble in the city he had taken them on fearlessly with boot and fist and truncheon, making himself a reputation for scattering the most famous of their fighters. He had received a fearsome cut across the eyebrow from a docker who had set a razor blade into the peak of his cap. He had had to have fifteen stitches and still had the scar, but his assailant had ended up in hospital with a fractured skull.

A few years later he had been transferred to the Special Branch, which was regarded as a promotion. Those who resented this, and he was not generally well liked, hinted it was due to political pull, the fact that he had a brother who was a Fianna Fáil county councillor. But the truth of the matter was that he was highly regarded by his superiors for his unswerving commitment to duty and for his devotion to the force.

He had gone about his duties in S-Branch with enthusiasm, investigating subversive activities, and tracking the movements of IRA members and sympathisers. He had followed them round and sat on the doorsteps of their friends and families so that they found it hard to move without being seen. Most of all he had made himself a name as an interrogator, skilfully covering the extreme brutality he practised on suspects, so that all but the very toughest cracked. Yet it had not been possible to make any charge of wrongful behaviour against him stick. He had taken part in a number of operations which had nipped vital IRA schemes in the bud and, more important, in interrogations, after which several republicans had been induced to turn informer. The IRA was no longer the potent force it had been a few years before. Too many failed operations, too many of its members locked up. To O'Grady's superiors he was a coming man, marked for promotion. To his opponents he was one of a number of specially hated enemies.

The road was busy with traffic, so he had to keep his eye on the other cyclists, the trams and the occasional horse and cart. Otherwise he might have seen the pedestrian who started visibly as he went past. It was McCaigue, who had been scouring the city for him for the past month.

After the first instant of shock McCaigue quickly turned his back and pretended to look in a shop window. As soon as O'Grady had gone past, however, he peered down the road after him. The detective stuck out an arm, signalling he was turning right, and then he was gone.

If McCaigue had but known, O'Grady was nearly home. He lived a scant ten-minute cycle from where they had passed and was actually on his way back for tea. It was a route he took nearly every day on his bicycle at around the same time, unless he got a lift in a police car. He had had threats made to him, the word was about that the Boys were out to get him, but that was months ago. The continuing success against the IRA, the repeated failures of the organisation, had made him incautious. The way things were, he thought, they'd soon be beaten. A few more of the bastards plugged or locked up in the Curragh and they would no longer be capable of keeping going. It was just a matter of unrelenting pressure, giving it to them twice as hard as they could give it to us.

Meanwhile McCaigue was hurrying to Miss Keating's, which was not far away either. Eddie came down to the hall when he was called and brought the other man up to his room. There was a newspaper on the bed and a book, a detective story. He seemed remarkably cheerful.

'So, what have you been up to?' asked McCaigue.

'Not much.'

'That's not what I'm hearing.'

'What do you mean?'

'I hear you're going out with some young one.'

'Who told you that?'

'Never mind. Cut it out.'

'What?'

'Cut it out. You're a Volunteer of Óglaigh na hÉireann. You

have a job to do. Time enough for running round with girls when that's done.'

'What job? I've done nothing but sit around here for the past month.'

'Well, that's your job. To keep your head down and be ready when the call comes. It won't be much longer. Is she safe?'

'Who?'

'Who do you think? This female, whoever she is. Does she come from a republican family?'

'I never even thought to ask her.'

'Listen, boy, don't you be smart with me. You've sworn an oath, I'm your commander. I don't have to tell you what happens those who disobey orders.'

'Who's disobeying orders?'

'Just watch it. And get rid of that girl, there's no future in it.'

Eddie made no reply. He had no intention of getting rid of that girl, even if the whole Army Council of the IRA decreed it.

McCaigue pulled a newspaper cutting from his pocket. 'Do you know who this is?' It was a smudged, badly printed photograph, the head and shoulders of a man in a boxing singlet.

'No, who is it?' Eddie asked.

'That is Detective Sergeant Paul O'Grady.'

'Is he the one?'

'That's him. It was because of him Johnny Lawlor was shot dead. He was the one got Dunleavy to turn informer and he set up Johnny Lawlor.'

'How did he do it? How did he get Dunleavy to turn?'

'Bet him till he cracked. Every day for three weeks, they worked him over. Teams of them under O'Grady. They took it in relays to torture him. Oh, they're experts, you know. Never touch a man's face, so it won't show, and concentrate on the body and the left side, so he'll still be able to sign a confession when they've finished with him. The others are bad but O'Grady's the worst. He's a sadist, he enjoys his work.'

'Were you ever done over yourself?' asked Eddie.

'Never mind.' But Eddie knew he had been. Tortured and been tortured. Killed and probably would be killed.

'What do you want me to do?' Eddie asked.

'We've been trying to find this hoor for the past month without success. Today I saw him by sheer chance, cycling along the main road from town, not five minutes' walk from here. I want you to hang around the spot with your own bike and, if you spot him, follow him. See where he goes, maybe we can discover where he lives. Take the picture, memorise his face.'

'It's not a very good picture,' said Eddie, squinting at the blurred image.

'You can't miss him. He's a huge fella with a big bullet head on him. Rides an extra big bike. He has S-Branch man written all over him.'

'I'll give it a go,' said Eddie.

'If you find out anything go to Doogan's. Say to the barman there that . . . that you think Cavan will win the All-Ireland next year. Leave the rest to me. Where's the weapon?'

'I buried it in the garden like I said. It's safe there.'

'All right. I'll be in touch with you. Don't do anything stupid. Slán.' And he was gone.

Eddie went out into the garden and looked at the spot where he had buried the gun. He half thought of digging it up to make sure it was all right, but just then Conor put his head over the wall.

'Hello, Eddie,' he said.

'How're you, Conor. Hold on a minute, I've got something for you.'

He went back into the house and re-emerged with the airgun. It was cleaned, oiled and gleaming.

'Can it shoot?' asked Conor.

'Yes, I managed to fix the spring and cleaned it up. 'Twas in a fierce mess. Here, I got a box of pellets too.' He placed one in the breach and handed it to the boy.

Conor took aim down the garden and fired. The gun gave a cracking sound and recoiled with a jump.

'It jerked,' he said.

'That's not how you do it,' said Eddie. 'You've got to keep it tucked in against your shoulder. Here, I'll show you.'

There was an old can lying in one of the flower beds. He placed it on the wall between the two gardens, put another pellet in the breach, took aim and fired. With a clank the can fell off the wall.

'Gimme another go,' said Conor.

'Right. Here, jump over the wall.' He stood behind the boy. 'Now, in against your shoulder. Firmly, not too tight. Now, do you see that little V – that's the sights. See the little tit on the end of the barrel? Close one eye, squint along the barrel. Get it so the bit at the end is right in the middle of the V. Now squeeze the trigger. Don't pull it, squeeze it gently.'

Again the airgun cracked. Again the can went flying. Conor was entranced.

'Here, let me try again,' Eddie said.

A mangy cat sat on a wall two gardens down, sunning itself in the weak winter light. As it sat, it licked its patchy fur with a pink tongue. Paying especial attention to its loins, it delved into the unspeakable reaches of its body. Eddie took swift aim and fired. With a yowl the cat jumped a foot in the air and fled. Conor roared with laughter.

'Will it die?' he asked, anxious on second thoughts.

'Not at all,' said Eddie. 'It just gave him a bit of a sting. Here, have another few shots, you.'

The little boy took the gun again and practised shooting for a while.

'I've got to go,' said Eddie. 'Take good care of it now. Keep it clean, look along the barrel and make sure there's no dust there, give it a polish with an old oily rag. See you soon.'

'Thanks a million, Eddie,' said Conor. He climbed back into his own garden and looked around guiltily, knowing he'd be in trouble if anyone saw him with the gun. He'd love to show it to Barry and tell him how the man next door had taught him to shoot, but knew that his brother would spill the beans to their mother, sooner or later. He would just have to satisfy himself by boasting about it to Clancy. This was better than all those films that his pal was going on about always.

He crept along the garden wall with his back to it, like he'd seen them doing so often in the films, then let himself in the back door very quietly and went upstairs to Barry's room. His mother had hidden the gun behind a big cardboard box of old clothes that was kept on the top shelf of a cupboard there and he'd been scared she would go back some day while Eddie had it. But she had never done so. He had to pull a chair over to the cupboard to reach up and put it back in its hiding place. He felt relieved that it was there again.

He pulled the chair back to where it had been and was about

to leave the room again when he noticed papers on the table where Barry allegedly did his work. His older brother had been roughing out a letter and having difficulty with it. Conor read it avidly.

'My darling Mairéad,' Barry had begun, then crossed it out and written 'Dearest Mairéad,' then settled for 'Dear Mairéad.'

'I have been unable to sleep' – 'unable to sleep' was crossed out and replaced with 'unable to think of anything else' – 'since we danced together at the hop in Eighty-Six last week. I wanted to see you home but you were gone before I got a chance to ask. Your friend said you had to go for the last tram. All I can think about is your beautiful blue eyes, your soft lips, your lovely red hair . . .' After this Barry had written the word 'legs' but thought better of it obviously. There were doodles next, little drawings of aeroplanes and rugby balls, then he had apparently abandoned the letter altogether and decided to break into verse.

> Oh sweet Mairéad,
> I wish you'd stayed,
> So I could see you home,
> I'd speak of love,
> Of heaven above . . .

Dissatisfied with this line he'd written beside it 'Shove? Glove? Dove?' and then gone on:

> As through the night we'd roam.
> Your lovely hair,
> Your face so fair,
> Your eyes so big and blue,

At this point inspiration had begun to run out, for the doodles

increased. 'What am I going to do?' 'I'd love to go with you.'
Then 'lips, hips.' Then 'From Guess Who?' at which point the
whole enterprise had obviously been abandoned.

Conor read it with open eyes. This was obviously love, that
mysterious thing they were always going on about in the pictures
and in those soppy magazines for women. It was not that he
wasn't attracted to girls, though he would never, ever admit it,
to an adult anyway. Sometimes he thought, secretly, that he
would like to kiss Nancy Hughes, whose mother was one of his
mother's friends. She was very pretty, but he would never, ever
let on. Anyway, it was out of the question. She was two years
older than him and treated him as if he were a baby.

'What do you think you're doing, fellow me lad?'

Guilty, he twirled around, blushing, to see Kitty.

'Nothing,' he said, 'just messing around.'

'Yes, well, your brother wouldn't want you in his room,'
said Kitty, who had read Barry's effusions herself with amused
contempt when she had gone to make the bed that morning.
'Come on, I'll give you a cup of milk.'

*

Eddie cycled along the road to town, where McCaigue had seen
the Special Branch man. He kept his eyes skinned, but there was
no sign of their quarry. He decided to pedal in as far as the
canal and then back again and to repeat the operation three or
four times. That was about the most he could do. There was a
police station not far away and he didn't want to be spotted.
He had been told that he was still a wanted man. The police
had called at his home in Tipperary. They'd asked his father
questions about his movements at the time of the bank raid and

had done the same at his Uncle Pat's. How had they known? An informer, probably, the Movement was riddled with them.

He was glad enough to have something to do during the afternoon at last, though that was no longer a problem in the evenings and on many mornings, too. Every night after the show he called for Kay. To the rest of the Coliseum artists he was now known as her boyfriend. Sometimes in the mornings, too, they met, when she wasn't rehearsing.

They spent blissful times walking round the city, drinking coffee in Bewley's or Mitchell's of Grafton Street, where a trio of ladies played music ('too posh' they decided). They walked along the quays, looking at the bookshops, wandering into the shabby joints where they auctioned second-hand furniture and knick-knacks. One memorable day they went even further, all the way to the Phoenix Park, where great walls of turf were piled along either side of the long road that bisected it, fuel for the Emergency. They went to the zoo and saw a baby lion, the wonder of Dublin. The keeper had seen Kay in a show and she was allowed to hold the cub for a moment. In the years to come she would remember that day and remember it again and again.

They were gone so long that Kay was almost late for her matinée and Dickie Delaney threatened her with the sack.

'I knew he didn't mean it, but,' she told Eddie later. 'I think he fancies me.'

'Dickie Delaney?' said Eddie, horrified. 'He's an ould fella, he must be forty.'

'Yeah, dirty divil,' said Kay, laughing.

Some days they wandered around the shops, Henry Street, Mary Street, Grafton Street, George's Street. He would patiently stand by as she looked at dresses. 'Isn't that only beautiful? Do you think that would suit me?'

He wished a thousand times that he could buy her things, shower her with presents, but he had little money, close to none at all. When he was going on the run, his Uncle Pat had taken him aside and given him ten pounds, a small fortune it seemed to him. But that was months ago and it had dwindled to nothing, even though his rent to Miss Keating was being paid in some shadowy way. Even being careful, he had to bring Kay to the pictures and dancing and he had to buy her the occasional drink or sweets. She offered to pay for their outings sometimes but he refused with horror. He had considered asking McCaigue for a loan, but thought better of it after their last meeting.

Sometimes she asked him about his job. He answered haltingly, saying the pay was bad and he wanted to get out of it. Once, in desperation, he bought half a dozen bars of chocolate and gave them to her, saying they were samples. She was no fool. She looked at him quizzically, but said no more. Perhaps she had guessed what he was really at, for he had been schooled in the jargon of the republican movement and was given to spouting about British perfidy, Irish freedom and the joys of martyrdom.

But this had lost much of its savour for him. His mind was full of her, every hour of the day and night, so that he no longer cared about anything else. It was the joy of love, made doubly sweet because it was love returned.

Compared to him, gauche and inexperienced as he was, Kay was no blushing virgin. The theatrical world lived up to its racy image. There had been fellas, plenty of them, and like all fellas they were always trying it on. Once, in one of the old dressing-rooms in the Coliseum, the ones that were no longer used, she let a fella go all the way. He had been nice, an English guy, a novelty dancer who'd been in Ireland when the war had begun and who had stayed on. She'd only done it, really, she told herself, because Vera was always going on about doing it. It had been okay, but a bit uncomfortable on the dirty old floor. It wasn't a bit like she had always imagined it would be, romantic like. To hear her pal talk you'd think it was the greatest thing since fried bread, but at the time all she could think of was the smell of the dust and his hair oil. In the pictures it looked so different, with the music playing and the long, long kisses, and of course they never showed them doing the dirty thing.

There had been others since, too, but the only serious one had been Tommy Hardy, the footballer. Vera thought he was only gorgeous and so did a lot of the other girls in the show. Kay and he had done a bit of a line, gone out together for a few weeks. He was always mauling at her, trying to stick his hand up her skirt or his tongue down her throat or feeling her. One night at a party she'd done it with him in one of the bedrooms but he was langers drunk, so there wasn't much romance about that either. Then she found out that he was taking out Peggy Duignan, one of the Coliseum girls, on the QT, at the same time as her. Well, she wasn't so keen on him that she'd put up with that. She gave him his marching orders, football hero or no football hero.

Vera thought she should just have given him a warning, but then Vera would do anything for a man. And in the end wasn't it the right thing to have done? Didn't it turn out that not only was Tommy going out with both her and Peggy, he was playing round with half the women in Dublin, some of them old enough to be his mother.

Still, she'd always dreamed of romance, of falling in love, marrying that one man, Mr Special. Like the big clinch at the finish of the film, with the music swelling and the words 'The End'. After that it would be happy ever after, in so far as she thought about it at all, babies, a happy home and bliss in the arms of Mr Right. Who he'd be she couldn't even guess, though she took it for granted he'd be handsome and probably quite rich, well, comfortable anyway. Not in a million years would she have thought it would be someone like Eddie, a culchie without a tosser to his name. She had her doubts that he even had a job and, if he did, it must be pretty tiny. He had a good sense of humour, he could make you laugh, but sometimes he'd go on with all that wrap-the-green-flag-round-me-boys nonsense. You'd have to bite your tongue not to make some wisecrack about it.

Yet it was love, whatever had caused it. It was like that song, 'What is this thing called love?' It wasn't even that he was a smasher, just good-looking. Straight. She was sure he wouldn't lie to you. At first she thought he was okay, nothing special, but now she was doting about him. She wanted to be with him all the time, to put her hand in his as they walked the streets, to feel his arm round her shoulder at the pictures, to look and look and look into his eyes, to hold him and kiss him.

The sweetest hour was at the end of the evening, when he would see her home at the end of the show. She was going to ask him in for a cup of tea, but thought she'd leave it till after Christmas. She didn't want her mother quizzing her about him and her da running him down and all her young sisters giggling and screaming. Instead, they would go down a lane that ran at the back of her house and, with her back against the wall, oblivious of rain and dark and cold, kiss and hug and murmur to each other. It was there, on a night when the snow was falling, that she first told him that she loved him and there, as he trembled, she placed his hand upon her breast while she undid his clothes and, opening herself to him, put him inside her. And as they felt the warmth of each other, the cold ceased to exist and a great river of fire and a surge of joy that she had never known ran through her.

Afterwards, when they looked down, they saw that the snow was nearly up to their ankles. Laughing, they went round to her front gate and kissed goodnight. When he left, she stood looking after him, until he went round the corner at the end of the street.

He stumbled homewards on the long walk through the empty streets in a daze of happiness, and walked round a corner slap into a young policeman.

'Here, watch out!' said the policeman, a pink-cheeked youth with a west of Ireland accent.

'Sorry,' said Eddie.

'Where are you going at this hour of night?'

'I . . . I was seeing my girlfriend home and I missed the last bus, Guard.'

'Where do you live?'

Eddie gave a false address.

'You're a long way off base,' said the police youth. 'Tell me, can you prove this story about your girlfriend?'

'Er . . . no.'

The young guard laughed. 'Well, I can. You've got lipstick

all over your face. Go on, off with you,' he said, adopting the manner he had heard older members of the force use.

Eddie went homewards, sweating.

Christmas came near and work began on the panto. It was the highlight of the variety year, even though the Coliseum's show was a truncated affair of a little over an hour, designed to fit in with the film that would be showing. This year it was to be *Cinderella* and Kay was sore that she had not been given the title role. Instead, they were bringing in Mamie Dwyer, better known as an opera singer.

'Cinderella me eye!' said Kay. 'She's old enough to be me mother. She should be one of the Ugly Sisters.'

Kay had been given the minor role of Buttons with the sop of a spot of her own, but things weren't helped by the behaviour of Mamie, who made it all too clear that she regarded pantomime as a sad come-down and her appearance at the Coliseum as slumming.

'Who does she think she is, Deanna Durbin?' asked Kay.

Meanwhile Eddie kept his daily vigil on the road where McCaigue had seen the Special Branch man. But there was no sign of O'Grady, who had in fact been out of town, guarding a government minister who lived in the south.

The days passed in what seemed interminable boredom for Eddie, the nights in a dream of love. He had heard no more from McCaigue and sometimes he would imagine that the other man had been captured or shot and that he would somehow escape having to obey his orders. Sometimes, too, he would think about leaving the Movement or of giving himself up. But he knew that either course would bring down retribution on his head. Tommy Power had tried that and been accused of informing. They brought him up the Wicklow Mountains and shot him dead.

Often, too, he dreamed of getting away, going to America and starting life afresh. It couldn't be done now, of course, but the war wouldn't last for ever. He talked about it to Kay and she seized on the idea even more enthusiastically than he did. It was, then, a far off land, a paradise glimpsed through films, where riches and happiness seemed to be there for the taking. She brought in an old copy of the *Saturday Evening Post* that someone with a relative out there had been sent and they pored over it in wonderment. The cars! The clothes! The houses, with their amazing machines, vacuum cleaners, clothes washers, huge refrigerators packed with an amazing profusion of exotic foods.

'Those must be millionaires' houses,' said Eddie.

'Not a bit of it,' said Kay. 'Did you never see the Andy Hardy pictures? They have all those things and they're just ordinary people.'

'I could get a job easy there,' he said. 'I have cousins, they have a bar in New Jersey. They'd see us right till we got started.'

'Once you got your foot in nothing would stop you,' Kay said.

'What about you, singing like that? Sure you'd be famous in no time.'

'Get off!'

'You would, you'd end up in Hollywood likely.'

'Oh yeah!'

He grinned. 'You'd probably divorce me out there. They all do that all the time.'

'You'd have to marry me first.'

They looked at each other for a long moment.

'I'll marry you the first moment I can,' he said seriously.

'I love you,' she said and kissed him, right in the middle of the street. A passing messenger boy on a bicycle whistled loudly at them.

'Mind your own business you!' Kay shouted after him, but she was laughing.

That night she told her pal, as a deadly secret, that she was engaged to Eddie.

'Where's the ring?' asked Vera.

'He's getting it later,' Kay explained. 'The job isn't going well, he has no money.'

'And you the one always said you were going to marry a rich guy.'

'I can't help it,' said Kay. 'I'm mad about him.'

By the time Eddie arrived to collect her after the show that night the whole company knew and were congratulating him. Kay was fit to be tied.

'I told you to keep your mouth shut,' she told Vera. 'It's not official. Jaysus, if my parents find out, I'll gut you!'

'Keep your hair on,' said Vera, 'I won't tell your parents. Anyway why keep it a big secret, it's good news, isn't it?'

Later on in the pub, though, Vera said: 'I think she's making a big mistake. He hasn't a bean, nor any prospects as far as I can see. I don't know what she sees in him.'

'Ah, he's good-looking, in a country kind of way,' said one of the Coliseum Girls, who was drinking a hot port.

'He's all right,' said Vera, 'nothing special. When you think she could have had Tommy Hardy, the footballer.'

The Coliseum Girl said nothing, having had Tommy Hardy herself, several times.

Next day Eddie was cycling on the long road towards town. His thoughts, as always, were on Kay, a mixture of love, longing and worry about the future, when he saw a big figure cycling towards him on the other side of the road. They passed in a second, but one furtive glance, even allowing for the rotten quality of the newspaper picture he had been given, made him realise that this was his man. Pulling on his brakes, he steered into the footpath.

For an instant he paused, an instant he was to remember later. If in that moment he had shrugged his shoulders and gone on his way, no one would ever have been the wiser and his life would have changed utterly. Instead – for what reason? – he made a U-turn on the road and followed the other cyclist, about fifty yards behind. Obeying orders? An instinct, long bred in him, to do what he was told? A loyalty to the cause to which he had pledged himself completely, as had so many others? Whatever it was that made him do it, it set off a chain of events that would change the rest of his life.

O'Grady cycled carefully down the road, unaware that he was being followed. At the same place as McCaigue had seen him he stuck out his arm in deliberate fashion and turned right. Eddie followed, trying to stay neither too near nor too far behind. The shops on the street where they had passed gave way to large solid houses and these in turn to roads of little red-brick ones, built some time around the turn of the century. Outside one of these O'Grady swung his leg over the crossbar, while his bike was still moving, and came to a halt. Eddie kept pedalling, hoping the other man would not look around as he came nearer, but O'Grady paid no attention to him. He was hungry and thinking of his meal. As Eddie pedalled by, the policeman walked up the short pathway that led to the front door of his house. Eddie did not dare to look closely, but noted that there was a lamppost, already lit in the gloom of the winter afternoon, on the pavement in front of the house.

That night he went to Doogan's pub and told the young barman there that he thought Cavan would win the All-Ireland football next year. The barman made no reply and for three days nothing happened, so that Eddie began to wonder if his message had got through. But on the third day McCaigue turned up and made Eddie take him to O'Grady's house.

McCaigue was pleased. 'Good man,' he said. 'You done well.'

'What now?' asked Eddie.

'We'll have to wait a while,' said McCaigue.

'Why?'

'It's too near Christmas. I have to go home. I've fixed it to see my wife and kids.'

Somehow Eddie had never seen McCaigue as having a family. 'Is that safe?' he asked.

'No,' said McCaigue, 'but we've worked out something.'

'What about me? I wouldn't mind going home for Christmas.'

'No, better not.'

'Well, if you can go.'

'Never mind me. Your job is to stay and keep an eye on things. Word is they're still watching your home. We don't want you pulled in now. I'll see you after Christmas.'

7

Christmas 1941 and the war seemed as if it would never end. For Eddie it was to be the most miserable one he had ever spent. He had told Kay that he was going home, just for a day, and the others in the digs that he was staying in town and spending Christmas Day with cousins. He was the only one of them who was not leaving Dublin, except for Frankie Fox who had been invited to the home of Tommy Flynn and May O'Brien, the dancers, and their large family. Corrigan and Dolan were going back to their homes in the country and even the unfortunate Nellie was being given one of her very rare days off and departing to places unknown. Miss Keating knew that Eddie was going nowhere, but was less than helpful.

'You can't expect me to do anything, Mr O'Sullivan,' she said, when Eddie told her that he'd be staying on. 'I'll be going to friends on Christmas Day.'

'I know that, ma'am,' said Eddie. 'I just thought I'd let you know.'

'There'll be nobody in the house, it's most inconvenient. Is there no one you could go to?'

'I'm afraid not.'

She sighed heavily. It was one thing to provide a safe house for someone on the run, another to be put out like this, especially at this time of year. 'I suppose I'll have to leave something for you to eat.'

'Thanks very much, ma'am.'

'Don't expect too much now. It's impossible to get anything for the Christmas the way things are.'

'Anything at all will do, thanks.'

*

Next door the Kennedys were preparing for Christmas too. A turkey had come from Conor's Uncle Fred's farm, a fine plump bird, though it would have to be plucked and cleaned and the sinews drawn from its legs. There was a ham, too, ordered from Donahue's, the butcher's, and there would also be a Christmas pudding and a Christmas cake. This was smaller than Mrs Kennedy would have liked, but, she told her friends, she was lucky to get any stuff to make it at all, the way things were. Her grocer, with all the graciousness of a duke distributing largesse to the worthy poor, had provided her with two pounds of currants, at the scandalous price of seven shillings, but half of the bag was made up of little gritty stones and bits of twig.

Conor's older sister, Maeve, and her boyfriend had taken him to the pictures to see *Pardon My Sarong*, not one of Abbot and Costello's best, according to Clancy, who thought there was too much old singing and dancing. Still, he had said, there were good scary bits in it, with the pair of them on this voodoo island being chased by bad guys. Conor went to it with some misgivings, the thought of zombies causing butterflies in his stomach, but Maeve, who knew all about his night terrors, told him it would be nothing, all just a joke, and she was right. Though he had had a few anxious moments, they were more than made up for by how funny it was.

'We were mortified,' Maeve told her mother, smiling. 'He

was laughing so loud the whole cinema turned round to look at him, and he kept kicking the seat of the man in front.'

Clancy had told Conor long ago that the whole Santa Claus thing was a madey-up for babies. There was no such person, it was just your father sneaking in with presents on Christmas night. As he had no father, Conor wondered whether he'd get anything, but at his mother's prompting he had written a letter anyway, and they had put it up the chimney. He still half believed in it and, anyhow, even if it was done by grown-ups, you got the present at the end of it, didn't you? Besides, if you said you didn't believe in it you might get nothing at all.

'And what's your name, little boy?' the Santy in Pims' department store asked Conor, when his mother took him there with her friend, Mrs Hughes, and her little girl, Nancy.

'Conor.'

'And are you a good little boy?'

'What a silly question,' said Nancy.

'Yes,' said Conor, half strangled with shyness.

'And what would you like for Christmas, Conor?'

'A cowboy suit.'

'Do yiz hear that, fairies?' Santy shouted into the red papier mâché chimney beside him. 'A cowboy suit for Conor. And here's another present for you.' He reached into a barrel marked 'Boys' and gave him a slender parcel, wrapped in bright paper, the 'free gift' that came with admission.

'This one's for you,' he said shortly to Nancy, giving her a parcel from the 'Girls' barrel.

Nancy shook it suspiciously. 'If you ask me, it's really bad value,' she said to Conor loudly as they left.

'Jaysus, kids today,' said Santy, half under his breath, which smelt of whiskey.

They tore open their free gifts. Nancy's was a small doll made in the Far East.

'Pooh!' said Nancy, who had a cupboard at home full of magnificent dolls. 'I hate her.' Ostentatiously, she put her on a counter covered with boxes of gloves and left her there.

'What did you get?' Nancy asked Conor.

He tore open the paper. It was a sheet of cardboard. You cut along the dotted lines and, when you glued the bits together, they made a tank.

'Cheap and shoddy,' said Nancy.

Conor agreed, but secretly he was thrilled and couldn't wait to get home and make the tank. When he did it was a bit of a disappointment, for he was not a boy who was naturally good with his hands. The tank leant drunkenly to one side and there was a bit at the back where the glue wouldn't hold, so it kept bursting apart. He enlisted Barry's help, though, and now at least it held together.

*

The British were making a push in North Africa, the battle for Wake Island waged ferociously in the Pacific and Hong Kong had been bombed continuously for twelve hours, but the lead story in the Irish papers was that the Pope sent Christmas greetings to Ireland and that a dispensation from fast and abstinence had been give to the faithful for the duration of the war.

Even with the constraints of the Emergency, Dublin came to life for Christmas. There were shortages, to be sure, but despite everything, 'the safest place in Europe', as one of the papers called it, spent its third Christmas of the war with its lights burning and its gates open. There was food and drink in plenty for those who could afford it and the more expensive hotels had bookings of parties from Britain and Northern Ireland, 'anxious to spend an unrationed Christmas'. (A crowd of black marketeers and draft-dodging bowsies, according to Frankie Fox.) Extra supplies of tobacco were made available and shopkeepers pulled out hidden stocks for the holiday, though there were still some things that were hard to get.

Dickie Delaney did a thriving blackmarket trade from his dressing room in the Coliseum. He had established a relationship with a guard on the Dublin-to-Belfast train, and as a result had a locked cupboard there, which he kept stocked with all sorts of things that were in short supply.

'I can get you lovely scented soap, silk stockings, make-up,' he'd tell the women in the cast, while for the men there were cigarettes, Bushmills whiskey, even on one occasion a consignment of bananas, something which the younger generation had never even tasted. Customers would appear at the theatre, most of them not even in the business, and Dickie, as if doing them personal favours, would pass over the goods at exorbitant prices. The Coliseum crowd grumbled about it, even threatened from time to time to report Dickie to the authorities, but in the end found it more convenient to keep quiet and, when they could afford it, buy goods at Dickie's blackmarket prices.

Eddie's main worry, besides which the thought of Christmas Day spent on his own paled into insignificance, was how he was going to get a present for Kay. His money was, by now, almost at an end. It was Frankie Fox who saved his bacon.

'How's the job going?' he had asked one day.

'Not great. The war, you know, shortage of supplies.'

'Yeah? Are you on commission?'

'I am,' lied Eddie.

'I can give you a loan of a few bob, if you want. I know meself what it's like when you're taking out a young one.'

Frankie's stomach was no better. In fact it was worse. There was never a day now when he didn't feel bad. There was blood in the toilet all the time and he smelt terrible.

'You're like a fucking sewer,' Dickie Delaney told him loudly, as usual in front of a crowd of others. Dickie, who ran his own productions, was trying to replace him, Frankie was sure of it, but so far he had been unsuccessful. The panto season meant there was plenty of work available and Dickie had such a bad reputation in the profession for the mean wages he paid and the bad way he behaved to his company that, though he had approached a few other comics, there were no takers. Still, when jobs became a bit thinner on the ground, he'd find someone. The pros might feel sorry for you and tell you that Dickie was a little prick, but at the end of the day, if it was a question of working or not they'd always take the job.

As he got sicker Frankie's secret passion for Kay grew. He would watch her surreptitiously all the time, be in the wings when she was singing, find excuses to go into her dressing room. It was as if the sickness had triggered off something he thought was long dead, a flame of sexual desire which he was sure had burned itself out with his youth. He dreamed of embracing her, of taking her into his bed, of being younger, more handsome, more available, dreams that when he was being honest with himself he knew were a fool's. With a sure feminine instinct she knew all about it and even encouraged it. She always had a word for the little sad-looking man. She would joke, squeeze his arm, entrance him with her smile. 'Here comes me boy-friend,' she'd tell the others, laughing, and he would reply, laughing too: 'You don't know what you're missing.'

Everyone knew she was engaged to Eddie, but at a time and in a place where engagements often went on for years, no one thought further about it. Despite his fantasies about Kay, Frankie liked the young man. In some strange way he felt part of the romance.

'Would the loan of a fiver be any good to you with the Christmas coming up?' he asked.

'Oh God! Thank you very much. You're a decent man.'

'It's a loan, now.'

'I know, of course. I'll pay you back as quick as I can.' He hadn't the faintest idea when. All he knew or cared was that now he could get her something for Christmas.

He saw an item in the *Evening Mail* that Christmas was a popular time to get engaged and that one well-known jewellery firm had sold over a hundred rings in the past week. He went into town, to the Happy Ring House in O'Connell Street. He reckoned he could spend up to three pounds, leaving the other two to take her out over the Christmas. He thought he'd surprise her. They had rings for that price, all right, but they were rotten mean-looking little things. He couldn't give Kay the likes of one of those. He'd seen the engagement ring one of the girls at the Coliseum got, a great big rock of a thing. She was marrying some businessman. Instead he bought her a brooch, marcasite, shiny stuff, silvery. It was a bird with a long tail and it cost two pounds ten, which would leave him an extra ten bob to spend on her. They wrapped it in paper and gave him a little cardboard box with it.

She thanked him a little too carefully, with not quite enough enthusiasm. He knew she was disappointed. She had half hoped for a ring.

'Do you not like it? They said we could change it if you didn't like it.'

'It's dinky, I love it.'

'I wanted to get you a ring, but I couldn't get one good enough.'

'I don't want a ring, yet.' Nor did she, really. If she wore his ring she'd have to bring him home and tell her family that they were engaged. The thought of facing all the questions about what did he do and where did he come from troubled her still.

He looked at her worried face. 'You don't like it,' he said. 'We'll change it.'

'I adore it, it's beautiful,' she said, pinning it on. 'I'm never going to take it off, not even in bed at night.' She laughed and kissed him.

On Christmas Eve she had a rehearsal in the morning, the last one before they opened the day after Christmas. He was waiting when she danced out the stage door only half an hour late.

'That fat cow Mamie Dwyer,' she laughed. 'You'd think she was Dorothy Lamour or some film star. Giving off about her arrangements and her costumes and her lighting. Stopping every five minutes. You could see Harry Harmond and the boys in the pit were only livid. Everyone wanted to get out as quick as possible, being the day it is, but of course Dickie let her get away with it. He thinks she's a touch of class, you know posh, an *awperah* singer. Where will we go?'

They went to a restaurant, where they did a special Christmas dinner for two shillings. Turkey and ham, trifle and cream and tea or coffee, all included. Then they went back to Curran's for a drink. Everyone was there, Bing Kelly, Frankie Fox, Flynn and O'Brien, Vera, the boys in the band, everyone except Dickie Delaney.

'Dickie hates Christmas, he *hates* it,' said Frankie. 'It's the only day in the year he has to spend with his wife.'

It wasn't all that funny, but they roared with laughter. The jars were going well with them. Eddie would have loved to stay, but the fiction was that he was going to Kingsbridge Station to catch a train home. First, though, he and Kay wanted to be alone. They went back into the Coliseum. It was all closed up for the Christmas, with nobody there except old Jemmy Johnson, the stage doorman. They went down the lane at the back, their arms around each other, and knocked on the door. Jemmy let them in.

'I left something behind in me dressing room,' said Kay.

Jemmy, a man of few words, said nothing, just gave her the dressing room key. He had seen everything, heard everything in the forty odd years he had been there.

Kay led the way, turning on lights. Like all old empty theatres, it seemed huge, pregnant, full of just inaudible echoes.

'They say it's haunted,' she said. 'Number twelve dressing room, up at the very top. Footsteps come up to the door and there's a knock, sometimes, and when you open it there's nobody there.'

'I don't believe in ghosts,' said Eddie.

'There's something in it,' said Kay, 'it happened to too many people for it to be just a story. They say, too, in the middle of the night you can see a man in an old raincoat, sitting up there all by himself in the middle of the gods.'

Eddie laughed but felt a prickle on his spine. It wasn't unpleasant.

Kay unlocked the door of the dressing room and turned on the light. Costumes hung on a rack, sticks of make-up and powder puffs sat on the table in front of the long mirror which ran across the room. The theatre smells seemed staler and colder than usual. She turned and put her arms around him. He held her with all his strength and they kissed, long, long, long. She broke away gently and unbuttoned his coat, his jacket, his trousers, stroking him. Then she undressed herself. He had never seen a woman naked before. There was a broken-down old couch in the room, with the stuffing coming out of it. She threw an old coat onto it and lay down.

'Come here,' she said.

That night they made love with a passion neither had ever experienced before. When they were dressing they heard footsteps, coming slowly down the corridor outside.

'Are yiz going to be there all day?' asked a voice.

'Sorry, Jemmy, just coming,' said Kay. 'Janey, I thought it was the ghost,' she said to Eddie, laughing.

She offered to come down to the station with him, but he refused. 'No,' he said, 'go back to the others in the pub, there's no point going all the way down to Kingsbridge and then having to come back on your own.'

'I wish you weren't going.'

'So do I. I'll be back the day after tomorrow.'

'I'll miss you so much.'

'I love you, I love you.'

Lovers' words, lovers' phrases, that mean so little except to those who speak them. He left her back into the pub. They were all flying by now, singing, shouting, laughing, though Vera looked at Kay's flushed cheeks knowingly. He kissed her goodbye shyly in front of them all and left. 'Happy Christmas, Eddie!' they chorused. He took the tram back to Miss Keating's and sat in his room in the cold empty house.

On Christmas morning he lay in and went to late mass, fearful that he might be seen by someone who knew him. He needn't have worried, for virtually everyone was either away or had gone to an earlier service. In fact, the church was nearly empty. He knelt down beside a wizened little woman with a short leg, Miss Johnson of the Society for the Abolition of Evil Literature, had he known it, who was attending her third mass of the day. When the time came for holy communion he remembered for the first time that he hadn't been to confession for Christmas. Besides, his love-making with Kay disqualified him from going to the altar. While the rest of the congregation went up to receive the sacrament he stayed in his place, feeling that people were looking at him, wondering what terrible sins he had committed that he couldn't even go to the rails on Christmas Day.

He still believed in his religion, as did all his family except his Uncle Pat, who constantly lambasted the Church. He had been excommunicated during the civil war for taking the republican side. 'Maynooth was always on the side of the English,' he would say. 'Never trust the boyos in black.'

'It was through our priests, through their persecution and

martyrdom, that we kept the faith in Penal Times,' Eddie's mother would reply. 'Faith of our Fathers living still, in spite of dungeon, fire and sword.'

'And that's an English hymn!' Pat said triumphantly, as if it clinched the argument. Anything that the hated Sassenach was associated with could only be bad; he had drummed that into Eddie since he was a small boy. He was an angry man who had lived in constant pain since, as a young man, he had taken a bullet in the back during an ambush in the Black and Tan times. He walked with a stick and, to ease his suffering, drank more whiskey than he should, which made him even more angry.

His life was given to Ireland, an abstraction that he never doubted for one moment. But it was also a catalogue of betrayals, by the men who had gone to fight Britain's war in France, by the Treaty and its aftermath, by Partition, by the decision of de Valera to enter the Dáil – all of them, as he saw it, the result of English cunning, English duplicity. He was too much an invalid to take a very active part in the councils of the IRA, the only true keeper of the flame, but his support for it never wavered, through all the disasters and splits of the years.

To Eddie his uncle was an authentic hero, someone looked up to by everyone in the neighbourhood, someone who had suffered, almost died, for Irish freedom. From an early age the older man had filled him with stories, told him of the glories ahead when a united Ireland was finally achieved. Through him he had met other old men, other heroes, then younger wild-eyed ones who spoke with anger and passion of the way ahead. He had never for a moment doubted that he would end up one of them. To die for Ireland, what higher destiny could any of them have?

He went back after mass to the dreary lodging house. In the kitchen Miss Keating had left a couple of spoonfuls of tea, a small jug of milk, two dank slices of cold ham, half a loaf of bread and a tiny pat of butter. He went to the scullery to see if he could find anything else there, but the door to it had been locked. He made himself a cup of tea and had a slice of bread and butter, mindful of the fact that his meagre rations had to last him for twenty-four hours.

The day stretched in front of him endlessly. He wandered round the empty house and found that Miss Keating had locked virtually every room in it. Only the dining-room was open. In it he found a couple of old newspapers and a romantic novel by Annie M. P. Smithson. Best of all, though, there was a fireplace there and a radio. When he switched it on mass was being broadcast. There was no fuel for the fire, except for a few half burned logs and some small pieces of turf. He went out into the garden and in the shed down at the bottom he found a wooden box which he broke up for firewood. He thought of lighting a fire there and then but realised he'd have more need of it that night. He went back out into the garden and wandered round listlessly, looking at trees and bushes as if they might hold something, anything of interest.

'Hello, Eddie.'

It was Conor, looking over the wall. He was pink with excitement and wore a cowboy suit, hat, waistcoat and imitation leather chaps on his legs. Round his waist was a belt and holster and in his hands two toy six-guns, which fired rolls of caps.

'I see Santa came,' smiled Eddie.

'Yes. And I got a box of soldiers, a book and a toy plane from my brother and sister and an annual from my uncle.'

'Great stuff. Are you still using the airgun?'

'Yes.' He looked around to make sure nobody had overheard. 'But look, I got these,' and he showed the toy guns.

'Smashing. They're just like the ones you'd see in cowboy pictures.'

'Hello there.' It was Conor's Uncle Seán who had joined them. He was the friendliest of men, someone who sooner or later struck up a conversation with everyone he met.

'What do you think of Gene Autrey here?' he asked Eddie.

'Hopalong Cassidy,' Conor corrected him.

'He's a right desperado,' said Eddie.

They chatted on about this and that, the war, rationing, Conor's uncle's life in the army, with its manoeuvres and marches.

'What time are you having your dinner?' asked Seán.

'Not till about five,' lied Eddie. 'I'm going out to friends.'

'Excuse me asking, you're not on your own in there, are you?' asked Seán.

'Yes, the others have all gone, either down the country or to other families here in Dublin.'

'Well, come in and have a drink.'

'Ah no, I wouldn't like to be a trouble.'

'Sure what trouble is a drink? Come on, come on, hop over the wall there. Sure we can't have you all by yourself on Christmas Day.'

He found himself standing shyly, holding a glass of stout in his hand, in the Kennedys' sitting room. It was everything Miss Keating's cold, bare house was not. Mrs Kennedy had saved up fuel for Christmas Day and a roasting fire danced up the chimney of the big sitting-room with its deep comfortable chairs and sofa. Mrs Kennedy and Maeve were introduced and then, glasses of sherry in their hands, departed for the kitchen, where they were preparing the dinner, Kitty having gone off home the day before.

The men, Seán, Eddie and Barry, stood roasting their bottoms against the fire and drinking their stout, while Conor marched his new soldiers against his old ones on the carpet, and delicious smells started to come up from the kitchen below. The talk turned to their respective families and who might be mutual acquaintances. Eddie thought of making up a family but decided that, rather than risk being caught out, it was probably wiser on this occasion to tell the truth. As usual in Ireland they knew someone who knew someone and it wasn't long before Seán had his identity pinned down.

'So Pat O'Sullivan would be your uncle then?' he asked.

'Yes, have you heard of him?'

'Oh yes, sure everyone has,' said Seán. 'He was a great man in the Troubles, wasn't he?'

'A fierce IRA family, the whole seed and breed of them,' he told the rest of them after Eddie had departed. 'I wouldn't be surprised if your man was up to his oxters in it, too.'

After a second bottle of stout Eddie went back to Miss Keating's. It seemed doubly depressing after the warmth and good humour of the next-door house. He tried to read the novel but found it dreary. Again he wandered around the place, and then went for a long walk. The streets were utterly deserted. The only person he met was a man walking his dog, who barely acknowledged his greeting.

When he got back, darkness was beginning to fall and he could see the lights shining brightly in the house next door. He ate the rest of the bread and the ham, washing it down with the last of the tea. Afterwards he still felt hungry. He wondered for the umpteenth time what Kay was doing, went to the dining-room and lit himself a small fire which barely heated the room. Going back to his bedroom he took the blankets, brought them down beside the smouldering grate and turned on the wireless.

'Germany calling.' Lord Haw Haw, in his strangely implausible version of a posh English accent, was wishing the Tommies a happy Christmas, while telling them that their wives at home were sleeping with black American soldiers. The British Forces Service had a series of variety shows, the best thing all night. A dramatisation of *A Christmas Carol* was on the Irish pro-gramme, then the Colmcille Céili Band and a Christmas message from the Taoiseach, to which he didn't listen.

At eleven o'clock he crawled upstairs and got into bed with his socks still on, his feet were so cold. He lay awake for a long time, thinking about America, about Kay, and about the task ahead of him. Maybe it would never happen, maybe somehow they'd be able to get away out of the country. Finally he fell asleep.

Next day he walked all the way to Kay's house, arriving in the late morning. She answered his knock on the door herself, her face radiant, kissing him lightly. The little house was decor-ated with paper chains and there was a Christmas tree with glittery foil and balloons on it.

He was ushered into the parlour, which was jammed with people, early and all as it was. 'We always have a crowd in early on Stephen's Day before I go to the show,' Kay explained.

He was introduced to uncles and aunts, neighbours and

friends, while what seemed like hordes of small boys and girls ran around his feet, laughing and making a din.

Kay's mother looked like an older version of herself. She was motherly, gentle, but watchful. He felt she was running the rule over him.

'How do you do, Mr O'Sullivan,' she said formally.

Her father was balding, in charge, no-nonsense.

'How're you?' he said when he was introduced. 'You'll have a scoop.'

Eddie demurred.

'Of course you will. Here, get that inside you.' He produced a whiskey bottle with something of a flourish, for it had been hard to come by, and poured a generous measure.

'Glory be to God, Larry, do you want him to be on his ear?' asked his wife.

'On his ear what?' said Kay's father scornfully. 'One little drop of whiskey! Ah Mary!' he said without a pause, as a fat, good-looking woman came into the room. 'How are you, me darling? This is our neighbour and very good friend Mary Mooney. Mary this is Eddie O'Sullivan, a friend of Kay's.'

'Oh, we've heard all about him, haven't we? Indeed we have!' said Mary twinkling at him. 'He's very good-looking,' she said to Kay, as if Eddie wasn't there and he felt himself blushing.

There was tea and the remains of the whiskey and bottles of stout for the men and minerals for the women and children. Then there was a sing-song. Kay's father produced a mouth organ and played and her mother sang 'I Dream of Jeannie with the Light Brown Hair' in a sweet soprano voice. Mary Mooney sang, not very well, 'My Gal's a High-born Lady'.

Kay's little sisters got fits of the giggles during this and there were fierce commands to shush from their father. Finally Kay herself was persuaded to sing, though she was saving her voice for the show. She gave them 'Sweet Embraceable You' and, in the confines of the room, she sounded in a different class to any of the others.

'Beautiful, she has a great talent,' said Mary Mooney as the applause rang out. 'But sure of course I don't have to be telling you that,' she added, digging Eddie in the ribs with her elbow. 'And such a beautiful girl,' she said to Kay's mother. 'She could have any fella she wanted, *any*!' this last in a piercing stage whisper.

Then it was time for Kay to go to work and Eddie with her. They made their farewells and headed off, but before they went down the road he led her down the lane at the side of the house and put his arms around her.

'Kay and Eddie is kissin' in the lane! Kay and Eddie is kissin' in the lane! I seen them! I seen them!' shouted one of the little sisters who had been looking out an upstairs window.

'Shut your trap, you!' said Kay's father, roughly.

'He seems a nice enough young chap, for a country fella,' said Mary Mooney dubiously.

*

That night the pantomime was a bit ropey. The Christmas break and Dickie's meanness meant it all looked a bit rushed. Mamie Dwyer was definitely too old to be playing Cinderella. She looked ridiculous and, though she could still sing well, it wasn't the sort of stuff the Coliseum audience really wanted, opera and so on. They applauded the first aria politely enough, but by the second you could notice them getting impatient and some of the gurriers in the gods started to whistle and shout the third time round. Even Dickie thought that maybe he should have offered her Principal Boy, though again, the bitch would probably have refused to do the show altogether then.

Still, it would all settle down after a few performances and Kay's number went well. It must be obvious to everyone that she should have been given the main part, she thought. Next year it would be different.

Next year! What would it hold? Where would they be? Both Kay and Eddie knew, on her part instinctively, that something would change, something momentous was on the way before Christmas would come around again.

*

On New Year's Eve a caller for Eddie came to Miss Keating's front door, a stranger, a tall angular man in a mackintosh, who spoke in an odd manner with an English accent.

'Hello, friend,' he said in an unfriendly manner. 'I've a message for you from Mr McCaigue.'

'Where is McCaigue?' asked Eddie.

'Seek not to know that which is hidden, friend.'

'Eh?' asked Eddie.

'The message is that the operation is on, three nights from now. Have your weapon ready and in full working order.'

'How do I know this isn't some trick? Who are you anyway?'

'O ye of little faith. You're to meet outside your local picture house at seven o'clock. Just be ready, friend.' With that, he was gone.

The night before the meeting was due to take place Eddie left

Kay home and, as usual, said good night to her in the lane behind her house.

'I have to go away for a few days,' he told her.

'What?'

'It's the job. They want me to go down the country for a few days.'

'Oh, no.'

'It's only for a few days. It won't be long.'

'I'll miss you so much.'

'I know. 'Tis rotten.'

'When'll you be back?'

'I don't know. In a week or so.'

'I'll count the days till you return.'

It was a line she had heard in a film. They kissed and she noticed with surprise that there were tears in his eyes.

The words tumbled out of him. 'I want to marry. I want to marry you and leave here. Go to America and start again. Say a prayer for me that everything will be all right.'

'Of course it'll be all right. Why wouldn't it be all right?'

'Yes, of course it will. Just say a prayer that the job works out.'

It was as close as he had ever come to telling her what he was going to do, but at the last moment he pulled back. He didn't want to involve her. Somehow it might endanger her, he told himself, but subconsciously the real reason was that he feared it might put her off him, loosen the bond between them.

'I'll see you in a few days, love.'

She looked after him, worried, as he strode away down the street.

PART TWO

NEW YEAR 1942

8

Eddie ran and ran until he could run no more. Down the empty streets, clattering along past dimly lit suburban houses, his footsteps echoing in the quiet night. People saw him, but he was hardly aware of them. They were a blur, featureless faces with open mouths. There was a throbbing in his head, the jarring of his feet pounding heavily on the concrete.

Somewhere along the way he noticed that he was carrying something in his hand, something heavy. It was the revolver which he had fired at Sergeant O'Grady. Without breaking stride he tried to stick it in his trench coat pocket, but it wouldn't go. Once, twice, three times, hardly knowing what he was doing. Then he got it in, a bulky object that weighed down the coat on one side. Still he ran, ran, ran, his terror driving him on far beyond the point at which he would usually have had to stop running. The rain began to fall, heavily, relentlessly. His breath started to come painfully, in gulping sobs, but still fear drove him on. Where he was going, what he was doing, he didn't know. Then, when finally he felt he could go no further, and had slowed to a jog, then to a walk, he rounded a corner and found himself on a main road. A tram, heading for town, was clattering towards a stop where a couple of people waited. Forcing himself forward with a last effort, he sprinted and managed to jump aboard just as it was moving off.

He collapsed into a seat, head between his legs, sides pumping. Glancing up, he slowly became aware that people were looking at him. He had lost his cap, and was dripping from the rain, wild-eyed, and still helplessly gulping for breath. As the tram moved off he started to shake uncontrollably.

'Are you all right, son?' asked the conductor.

He could only nod wordlessly. He searched in his pocket for a few coins.

'The . . . the . . .' He had to stop for breath again. 'The Pillar,' he said, not even knowing if they were going in that direction. He hunched himself miserably in his seat, pretending to look out the window, his shoulders heaving. Once more he started to tremble. The conductor exchanged a wordless glance with a woman passenger.

Street lights went past in a wet blur. When the tram arrived at its terminus he sat on after everybody had left, still gazing unseeing out of the steamed-up window.

'This is it, this is the Pillar,' said the conductor's voice.

He stumbled off the tram and stood, unmoving, in the street. People hurried past, trying to get out of the rain, but still he did not stir. His hair was sodden, water ran down the sides of his ears. He was stunned. Something terrible had happened, but his mind could not grasp what it was. Amidst his confusion an idea presented itself. He would go into the Coliseum and see Kay. But then it came back to him with horror – McCaigue, the shots, the dying man. Like a waking sleeper he looked up, half expecting the whole street to be watching him, but the few people who were around were too busy escaping the wet to pay much attention to anyone else.

He realised he must go somewhere, do something, before he was spotted, and all he could think of was the pub where he had first met McCaigue. It was almost empty. A couple of what looked like students were sitting over pints, and one of those dejected-looking solitary drinkers one sees so often in bars sat smoking in front of a glass of whiskey and looking emptily into the mirror behind the counter, his shoulders slumped.

Eddie sat himself at a table against one of the walls. He made no effort to order a drink. The two barmen on duty – one of them the one who had first given him the message about meeting McCaigue – eyed him nervously. They knew trouble when they saw it. Eddie gazed at the floor, trying to shut out the pictures that were going through his mind. As the warmth of the pub seeped through to him, he gradually realised how soaked he was. Getting up, he pulled off his sodden raincoat. The gun fell with a clatter out of his pocket. The students looked round and saw it before he threw the coat over it.

The barman who knew him came over with a whiskey.

'Get out,' he said.

'What?' asked Eddie stupidly.

'Drink that up and get out. This is no place to be. 'Tis being watched.'

He gulped back the whiskey and, for a moment, felt better for its warmth. Then he got up and left. The two students gazed at him, wide-eyed. The solitary drinker ignored him.

It was only when he was out on the pavement again that he realised it.

'Christ, my bike!' he said aloud, as the memory came back to him of it lying on the ground, its wheels turning, after he had knocked it over in his flight. He caught another tram, back to Miss Keating's.

*

The rain slackened and then stopped, leaving the air raw and damp. The street where Detective Sergeant O'Grady had lived had been cordoned off by the police. Small knots of people, kept back by uniformed gardaí, stood at either end, peering towards the dead man's house. Every window was lit there, but there was little to see, except the comings and goings of a number of large men, plain clothes detectives. The body had been moved from the pavement and the onlookers were kept too far away to make out the chalk marks which indicated where it had lain.

'What's up?' a newcomer asked.

'A murder,' he was told. 'Down there, that house with the lights on.'

'I hear tell his throat was cut,' said a woman. 'God rest him. The savages that's going these days.'

'Maybe it was the IRA,' said a small man in a cap.

'Not at all. The IRA would never cut a person's throat,' said a taller man.

'Wouldn't they?' said the smaller man. 'Them fellas would do anything.'

The other glared at him. But an argument and maybe worse was forestalled by the policeman on duty beside them.

'Move along now, move along,' he said. 'There's nothing to see here. Have yiz nothing better to do with yourselves?'

The small group dispersed reluctantly.

Inside the house O'Grady's wife sat gazing emptily into the fire, her face white, her eyes empty and swollen from crying. A police doctor had given her a draught to calm her, a sister who lived nearby had been called and was making tea for the men who filled the house. Seán, the dead man's son, stood helplessly beside his mother. He was still in the sweater he had pulled on over his pyjamas, which were too small for him. His bare shins stuck out from the bottom of the legs, ending in unlaced shoes, hastily stuck on his feet. He felt nothing apart from a faint unease that he had no feelings of grief or even anger.

A priest who had been summoned to give the last rites to the murdered man sat beside his mother, patting her hand and murmuring to her.

'He's in heaven now, with God and His Holy Mother. That's for sure,' he said.

'Thank you, Father,' she said, as if he had done her a favour. 'He was a good man.'

'He was, he was I'm sure,' said the priest, who had not known him. Mrs O'Grady touched her eyes with the handkerchief she held. Already she was growing into her role as a widow.

A tall man, one of the many tall men who seemed to fill the house, came up to the boy.

'I'm Superintendent O'Shea,' he said, 'I'm very sorry for your trouble, Seán.'

Seán bobbed his head awkwardly, too shy to reply.

'We'll get them, we'll bloody well get them if 'tis the last thing we do,' said a younger detective, his face red with anger. 'You can be sure of that, Seán, and when we do get them . . .'

'Yes, all right, Clancy,' said O'Shea.

'He was a great man, a great man, your father,' said Clancy.

'Yes,' said O'Shea who, in common with many who had worked with him, had disliked the murdered man.

'I think we should say the rosary now, for the soul of the departed,' said the priest.

People were summoned from the kitchen and everyone in the

little parlour knelt down. Seán's mother gestured to him to place himself beside her. In the general shuffling around O'Shea left the room and went out of the house, where another pair of detectives were standing, smoking.

'Well?' he asked.

'Two of them,' said the older of the pair, a man with a scarlet birthmark that covered one cheek. 'One small and dark, the other tall and fair.'

'McCaigue?'

'Sounds like him.'

'And the other?'

'Not sure. They're testing the bike for prints.'

'Why did he leave it?'

The other shrugged. 'Sounds like he panicked. Ran off down that way. We've had a load of reports of people who saw him galloping down the streets with the gun still in his hand.'

'A young fella,' said the other detective. 'Inexperienced.'

'Sounds like it,' said O'Shea. 'Shouldn't be too hard to identify him. Get a look-out put on any trains or buses leaving town tomorrow.'

A large car pulled into the road.

'Oh Jaysus, the Minister,' said O'Shea.

The Minister for Justice got out of the front seat of the car, where he had been sitting beside his driver.

'Super,' he greeted O'Shea.

'Minister.'

'Another bad business.'

'Yes, sir.'

'Any progress?'

'Yes, sir. There seem to have been two men involved. We expect to make an early arrest.'

'Good. Keep me informed.' He went into the house.

*

Eddie lay on the bed in his cheerless room and wept. He wept for the man he had killed, for himself and, most of all, for Kay. The events of the night returned to his mind again and again, but somehow he could not fully grasp them. He tried to remember the details but it was all a confusion of shots, of running, of the dead man's staring face, of tram journeys and the pub, in no sequence, but repeating itself again and again.

At one point he fell into an uneasy sleep but woke after half an hour, his teeth chattering. Rising, he realised that he was still in his wet clothes and pulled them off, throwing them in a heap on the floor. He pulled on pyjamas and got back into the bed, but the sheets were freezing and his feet like blocks of ice.

How long he lay there he did not know, in his wakeful nightmare. He thought of Kay and then again of what he had done and despair filled him. He would be caught, it would be the end of him and of all his dreams. He grasped at straws. Surely the Movement would hide him, get him away to America where, in time, she would join him. She would understand, would forgive him. She loved him, she had told him so. Love would conquer all, it always did.

Then reality flooded in again with all its horrors. America was so far away. How could you get there with this war going on? They'd surely get him before it ended. He knew the S-Branch would double, triple their efforts when one of their own had been killed. He thought of all the Boys who had been locked up or shot in the streets or executed. Martyrs for Ireland. What would Kay think if she found out, when she found out, that he was a murderer? But, hold on now, he wasn't a murderer. He was a soldier, doing a soldier's work in a war. She would recognise that. She loved him. She'd said so herself. When would he see her? He'd go to the theatre the next day. No, he couldn't do that, he'd be spotted for sure. What should he do next? What? Lie low, lie low. Exhaustion overcame him and he drifted off from a world of waking nightmares to a world of sleeping ones.

In his dreams the dead policeman, with blood pouring from his mouth, was beating, beating on the road where he lay. Coming up out of his sleep he realised that someone was knocking on his door. He heard a voice.

'Wake up! Wake up!' More knocking, soft but insistent, followed.

Dragging himself from the bed, he stumbled over and opened the door. It was Miss Keating. Clad in a dressing gown with her hair in a net, she held a candle in her hand. There was greasy stuff on her face, some sort of cream. By the flickering light she looked old, grotesque and angry.

'What is it?' he asked.

'There's someone for you. Downstairs.'

'Who?'

'Shhh!' she hissed. 'Be quiet! Hurry on!'

He looked around, saw his raincoat on the floor and pulled it on over his pyjamas. It was still damp and cold. It seemed to have the smell of death about it. He followed her down the dark stairs and into the dark parlour. A black shape rose from a chair as the candle half lit the room. It was the man with the strange, English accent, who had given him the message to meet McCaigue outside the cinema. His hawk-like face was half shadowed in the gloom and a thin scraggy neck stuck out from a dark overcoat with hunched shoulders, giving him the look of a vulture.

'Well, friend,' he said.

'I want him out, out of here!' whispered Miss Keating furiously to him.

'All right, all right, madam,' said the stranger.

'I said I'd take him in for a bit, Harold, while he was on the run, but there was nothing about this, nothing about him plugging a policeman.'

'Calm down now, calm down, be of good cheer,' he said soothingly.

'Get rid of him,' she repeated. 'Get rid of him out of here, now!'

'No one knows he's here, no one knows about this house.'

'Suppose someone talks? Suppose one of the other lodgers twigs who he is?'

'No one will do that.'

'How do you know?' Her face, even in the candlelight, was pink with rage. 'Get him out, or there'll be trouble.'

'All right, all right.' He turned to Eddie. 'You're going to have to leave, friend. Flee out of the land of Egypt.'

'When?'

'Now.'

'*Now?*' Eddie was appalled.

'If it gets out he's in this house, I could end up in jail,' said Miss Keating. 'I'm not going to carry the blame for this. It's got nothing, nothing at all to do with me!'

'Have no fear, madam, he's going.' He turned again to Eddie.

'You're going to have to get out of town, friend. Things are going to be hotter than Hades for the next few weeks.'

'But . . . where to? Where am I to go?'

'Down the country, a little rural holiday.'

'How can I go down the country now, in the middle of the night?'

'Bike. A little cycling tour. Look, every train, every bus out of Dublin will be watched tomorrow, and the roads too. Get on your bike. Put twenty miles between yourself and town before the morning. Then, when you have toiled all the night, hide up for the day. You'll be able to finish your journey tomorrow.'

'My bike, I lost it,' said Eddie shamefacedly.

'I know, I know,' said the stranger. 'I've got a replacement with me.' He looked at Eddie sardonically. 'Pretty clumsy, pretty sloppy. In fact you didn't exactly cover yourself in glory, did you, friend?'

'It wasn't my fault,' said Eddie hotly.

'No? Well, so many people saw you that you might as well have taken an ad in the paper. You can be sure the guardians of the peace know all about you by now. Hide us from the face of him that sitteth upon the throne and from the wrath of the Lamb, for the great day of his wrath is come.'

'Stop hanging around,' hissed Miss Keating furiously. 'Get him out, get him out!'

'What the hell do you think I'm doing?' he said, losing his calm for a moment. 'How often do I have to tell you? Now, pray, do not annoy me further.'

'I have friends,' said Miss Keating, her voice rising in anger. 'I have friends in the Army Council, I have friends in . . .'

'Shhh!' he said, silencing her.

'There are a lot of very important people I know,' she continued in a whisper.

'My dear madam, I suggest you retire to your slumbers. He'll be far away by the time you get up again.'

'He'd better be!' she said, leaving almost reluctantly. 'And I don't want to see hide nor hair of him ever again,' she added as a parting shot. She closed the door and the candlelight vanished. They heard her tiptoeing up the stairs.

The two men stood silently in the room, their eyes getting used to the dark.

'Here's what you do,' said the stranger. 'You take the main Cork/Limerick road. Do you know how to get to that?'

'Yes.'

'Go down beyond Naas, that'll take you all night. When dawn comes find somewhere to hole up.'

'Where?'

'How do I know? A barn or an outhouse or something. You've been trained, haven't you?'

'Yes.' Eddie thought of nights he had spent in the open country, but they had always been with others and had ended eating or drinking in somebody's warm, dry house.

'On the second night you go on till you're past Newbridge and Kildare. Mind yourself on the Curragh, there isn't much cover. Five miles after Kildare you'll see a turn to the left, where there's an old dead tree. Now, look at this.'

He went over to the switch and turned on the light. Though Miss Keating favoured low-watt bulbs that left every room gloomy and underlit, it seemed dazzling after the darkness. The stranger took a piece of paper from his pocket, a map. Eddie noticed that, this time, the overcoat he was wearing was a fine, warm, belted one and that he had on a pair of expensive-looking leather gloves, which he took off carefully, finger by finger.

'Now pay attention to this, friend. This is the way you go, remember it.' He gave him detailed instructions, which involved back roads and laneways, few of them marked on the map. There would be no signposts either, for these had been removed because of the war.

'Now I'll repeat that,' he said when he had finished and went painstakingly through the directions again. 'Now you repeat it to me.'

Eddie repeated what he had been told with hardly a pause.

'Good,' said the stranger, surprised that he had got it right so quickly. 'Good, there's hope for you yet, friend. Come on.' He turned out the light, went out into the hall and opened the front door gently.

'There's the bike,' he said. Eddie recognised it as McCaigue's. 'Here,' he went on and handed him a brown paper parcel. 'Some sustenance, a few sandwiches and a drop of the water of life.' It was a lemonade bottle half full of whiskey. 'Have you any money?'

'No.'

The stranger sighed. 'Surprise, surprise,' he said. 'Here, for use in emergencies only.' He counted out five single pounds.

'Now, I don't have to tell you, or perhaps I do. When you get to that address, you stay there. You don't put your nose out of the door, no matter for what reason, until you are ordered to do so. Is that clear?'

'Yes.'

'Be out of here in half an hour if you're going to get far before daylight. Wrap up well, it's cold.'

'Thank you. God bless you.'

'God has nothing to do with it, friend, it's all luck. Anyway, the fates or whatever be with you. Be careful.'

He went down the steps, pulling on his expensive gloves as he went, looked carefully up and down the street and was gone.

Eddie went back to his room. The first thing he thought of was his gun. He wanted no further part of it, no more shootouts if the police caught up with him, no more bloodshed. He took it and went quietly out into the back garden, meaning to bury it again, deep and for ever. But in the dank chill of the garden he realised it would take too long and make so much noise it might wake somebody. He went into the shed at the bottom and, fumbling in the darkness, placed it behind some old cans of paint that stood on a shelf. It would be safe enough there, he thought, nobody ever went into the place.

He went back to his room and started to dress again. His clothes were still damp from the soaking he had got and he had few spares. He changed what he could and put the rest into the cheap, small suitcase he kept under the bed.

Tiptoeing back down the stairs, he heard a voice and froze. But it was only someone crying out something in their slumber. The old house creaked and groaned, too, as if it also was in a troubled sleep, but he heard nobody else. Letting himself out gently, he went down the steps from the front door to the bicycle. Under her soft satin eiderdown, Miss Keating heard the door close softly and grimly turned on her side.

*

Through the sleeping suburbs he cycled. The wind cut through his still damp coat and his feet, pedalling along, at first ached with the cold, then went numb. It was a long hard journey he had ahead of him, but he was young and strong. He pushed the bicycle along faster in an effort to warm himself. The street lamps had been turned off and there was no sign of life anywhere, no sound except the whisper of the wind. The houses he passed were dark, too, except for one lighted window, where somebody sick or maybe insomniac passed the long hours until dawn. Who could know what went on in other people's lives? Once, in the distance, he thought he heard a car engine. He strained his ears, ready to jump off and hide himself it if came nearer, but it never did.

Dublin was not a large city and before he had cycled very far the suburbs started to thin out. Rows of semi-detacheds became interspersed with empty fields, then changed to single houses with farm implements lying beside them or small county council cottages. Soon he was in open countryside and, as he reached it, the clouds parted and a white, cold moon shed a dim light on the land. Almost at once it started to freeze.

The countryside was dead, whitening with frost. It was as if it had been scorched by a fire of winter so that everything that lived had been burned out of existence. The trees were skeletal, their branches tormented, stiff and brittle, as if they had turned and writhed while they sought to escape the cauterising chill. The high hedges seemed black and ominous, gathering into them the shadows of the wan moonlight. The grass lay in sodden tussocks, lumpy and hard. It seemed as if it would break into pieces if you walked upon it. Small puddles on the road were opaque, grey and slippery. Going over one of them he felt the wheel slide from beneath him and only with an effort kept his balance.

Going through a hollow in the road he found himself in a patch of fog, his head sticking above it as he sat on the bicycle. Across the fields occasionally he could see other patches, writhing and turning, thinning and thickening and putting out long tendrils.

It was the landscape of the dead, the home of those ghosts he had so often heard described during his country upbringing. It was on roads like this and at times like this that men had met the headless horseman or that strange huge man in black with two red, burning eyes, the devil himself. Here the banshee sang her fatal songs, or the spirits of tragic lovers, suicides and foully murdered children roamed diaphanously, seeking justice and revenge through the desolate landscape.

He found himself looking nervously back over his shoulder, listening for sounds that were not there. Ghosts and ghouls had never troubled him, but when he thought of the dead policeman and how it was said that the spirits of those who had died violently roamed the nights he felt a crawling on the back of his neck.

The cold bit at him and his teeth were chattering violently. Dismounting, he put down the bicycle and stamped his numb feet on the road, blowing into his white, aching hands. With difficulty he opened the package he had been given and took a slug from the bottle with the whiskey in it. The warmth of the spirit made him cough, but he felt the better of it and, mounting the bike again, pushed on.

After some hours of cycling he came to the town of Naas. He remembered being there when, as a boy, a local priest had given him a lift to Dublin for an All-Ireland hurling final. Most of the journey had been unpleasant, a constant attempt not to let the car sickness he felt cause him to throw up. But, when they had stopped in Naas and gone into a hotel there, they had had cold salmon, bread and butter and tea and he had thought it the most delicious meal he had ever eaten.

Now, he thought of cycling down the wide main street, but the first glimmers of dawn were already in the sky, so he took a side road instead. It took him the best part of half an hour to relocate the main road on the other side of town and, by then, it was near full daylight. In the fields he could see groups of cattle, huddled together beneath the hedges for shelter. The cold was almost unbearable, made worse by a keen wind that seemed to slice through him.

He cycled on, looking for shelter. A farmer passed him, going in the opposite direction in a pony and trap. He greeted him with a wag of the head, but seemed unsurprised by this lone cyclist at the dawn of day.

A hundred yards off the main road he saw a farm, its outhouses huddled round a yard. He turned down and approached it cautiously. No dog barked, which was unusual, nor did there seem to be any sign of life. Whoever lived there was still asleep. Leaving his bicycle behind a hedge, he climbed over a gate and went into a large barn, packed with hay almost up to the high roof, the sort of place in which he had often played as a child, jumping twenty feet from the top into a soft pile on the ground. Climbing carefully, he pulled himself up to just under the roof and burrowed down in the soft dry stuff. To be out of the biting wind was a relief in itself, the dry, cushioning hay, with its pleasant grassy, dusty smell enveloped him as he drank the rest of his whiskey and gobbled the ham sandwich he had been given. He was still frozen, but gradually exhaustion and the comfort of the nest he had made settled over him and he fell into a fitful sleep. It was there, some hours later, that the farmer's wife discovered him, alerted by his rambling and moaning as he slept. She called her husband and the pair of them went back to the barn.

'Mister! Mister!' The words came to Eddie out of a maze of troubled dreams. 'You! Come down out of there.'

Awake now, he looked down over the edge of the hay cliff. An elderly man and woman were looking up at him.

'Come down outa that!' said the farmer. 'What the hell do you think you're doin' there?'

Bleary-eyed, he slid down the hay, bringing a fair quantity of it with him. He looked feverish, shaking, troubled.

'What the hell do you think you're doin' there?' repeated the farmer. They found it hard to place him. His clothes were too good for a travelling man and, anyway, they had found his bicycle and tinkers didn't go round by bike.

'I'm sorry if I disturbed it,' he said, knowing how farmers objected to the carefully raked, stacked hay being churned around. 'I, I was cycling from Dublin and I was just looking for somewhere to get a bit of a rest.'

'Well, you could have asked,' said the farmer crossly, but not unkindly.

'Where are you goin'?' asked his wife.

'Down south . . . Tipp.'

'Jay, that's a long cycle,' said the farmer. They paused, looking at each other awkwardly.

'I'll be off so,' said Eddie. 'Thanks for the shelter.'

'Don't be messin' up a body's hay again,' said the farmer.

He and his wife watched as the young man turned to go. He looked young, sick and troubled.

'Would you like a cup of tay?' asked the woman.

'That'd be grand.'

There was an iron range in the kitchen which gave a welcome heat. There was a flagged floor, cooking utensils, a dresser with delph on it. The sort of place where he had grown up. They sat him down beside the range and he felt the heat going through him. With a mug of tea the farmer's wife cut two thick slices from a round of home-made bread and plastered it with country butter. He wolfed it down.

'Could you not have got the train?' asked the farmer.

'I had no money for the fare.'

''Tis starting to rain again,' said the woman, looking out the window. 'You'd better stay a while till it blows over. Your clothes are wet, you don't want to get drenched a second time.'

She made him take off his jacket and shirt and hung them beside the hot range, while he clasped a rough blanket round his shoulders. He sat there, gazing into nothing as they went about their daily tasks and the rain poured down for hour after hour. They said little to each other. By early afternoon it was dark again.

'You can't go out in that again,' said the farmer. 'You can stay the night, if you want, here in the kitchen.'

'I'm beholden to you, sir.'

They watched him circumspectly as he sat hour after hour beside the range. They tried to engage him in conversation, but he answered in monosyllables and after a while they gave up. Sometimes his head was in his hands, once or twice he would give a low whimper, at another time his face, twisted in anguish, was wet with tears. He tried to work things out but seemed unable to do so. It was as if his brain had gone permanently numb. What was he to do? Where could he turn?

At one point he thought he might head for home, his Uncle Pat would tell him how to cope with it. But immediately he realised that that wouldn't work. His own house and his uncle's would both be watched. Anyway, what would his uncle tell him? Obey orders, be true to the cause. Another time he thought he would give himself up, but he knew only too well what that would mean. Suppose he went back to Dublin and told Kay everything. Maybe she could hide him. But where? He knew the plan was hopeless and he feared, too, what she might say when she heard that he had killed a man. No, surely she would understand.

At the end of all his agonising he could think of nothing better to do than to carry on as he had been ordered. Perhaps, after a time, things would quieten down. Perhaps the trail would go cold and the police would never know that he was involved. But even as he grasped at the hope he knew in his heart that it was futile.

'He's in some kind of trouble,' the old farmer told his wife. 'On the run or something. Best say nothing about it.' Nor did they, then or thereafter, being quiet, close people who kept themselves to themselves and wanted nothing that would bring them unduly to the attention of the outside world.

'You'll be off in the morning so,' he said to Eddie as, oil lamp in hand, he prepared to turn in for the night.

Eddie raised his miserable face. 'Yes,' he said, 'and thank you. I wish . . . I wish I had something I could give you . . .' The words trailed away.

'No matter,' said the other, embarrassed at the suggestion and turned to go.

'Good night,' said his wife. 'Say a prayer.'

In the morning, when they got up, he was gone.

He had prayed, prayed more fervently than ever before in his life, prayed that God would get him out of it somehow, then prayed for forgiveness, for the soul of the dead man, though he knew there would be those who said that he had committed no sin, that the killing was part of a just war. He was sorry, just the same, and made an act of contrition, but at the heart of it all was the feeling that he was only contrite for himself, in the hope that somehow or other he would escape, that he could start again with Kay.

He remembered what he had been taught about a perfect act of contrition, being sorry for what you had done because it offended God who is so good to us, not for any personal reason. That was the only way you could get divine forgiveness without going to confession, where an imperfect act of contrition, coupled with a firm purpose of amendment, was enough to clear you. He had always found a perfect act of contrition an impossible idea, something that was all right for priests and holy people. For himself it was enough to be sorry, if only for selfish or worldly reasons, to tell it in confession and receive absolution. But, without a perfect act of contrition or confession, you couldn't wipe the slate clean, could you? And if you were to die perhaps an imperfect contrition would not be enough.

He thought of a story he had heard about a man who had been found to be an informer. They had taken him out, while he cried and screamed that he was in a state of mortal sin and must see a priest. They had shot him just the same. Eddie was in a state of mortal sin himself. Apart from the shooting, he had committed the sin of fornication and had not confessed it. If the Special Branch caught up with him they might shoot him first and ask questions after . . .

Some hours after darkness, when the house was dark and silent, he put on his trench coat again, let himself out quietly and, mounting his bicycle, headed off into the night. The rain had stopped again and he made good time, refreshed by the day he had spent sitting out of the weather. He went through the town of Newbridge, taking a chance this time by not making a detour. The streets were empty and then he was heading across the treeless plain of the Curragh, acutely aware that there was little cover if he was spotted.

Some distance away he could see lights coming from the army base. There, too, was the camp where many IRA men and sympathisers had been locked up for the duration by the de Valera government. His Uncle Pat was to have been among them, but had been let go on grounds of age and ill health. He wished he could be among them – at least he'd be out of it then.

Now the town of Kildare loomed ahead. He knew there was an army barracks there, also, on the main road with sentries at its gates round the clock, so again he was forced to take a turning. By the time he had circumvented the town and found his way back onto his route, the night was coming to an end. He pushed on hard, fear giving him an extra edge of strength. He looked for the dead tree, the turn-off point from the main road, but could not find it. Had he overrun it? He expected a car to appear with police or soldiers in it at any moment. Then, when he was on the point of going back to search for the turning again, he saw the tree, exactly as the man with the English accent had described it. With relief he turned into the side-road. High hedges rose on either side of the narrow way, little more than a lane. Dung-stained cows gazed at him curiously over ramshackle gates. He felt safer, less exposed.

The search for the safe house was difficult and took a long time. The roads were small and winding, the turns all looked like each other, so that by the time he reached it, it was nearly midday. He came at it through a wood, walking along a rough dirt track with his bicycle, which had punctured shortly before. The small farmhouse stood gaunt and grey on a small rise, its black lower-storey windows half covered by torn, filthy curtains. A cart with a wheel missing leant drunkenly in front of it. The surrounding land was weedy, neglected looking.

Eddie went round to the back. A bent grey-haired man was feeding a few chickens from a bucket. Land of old men. The owner of the place looked up, cold-eyed, as the young man approached.

'I was sent . . . from Dublin,' said Eddie.

'Were you follyed?'

'No, no one saw me,' lied Eddie, deciding to say nothing about the couple who had given him shelter.

'Are you sure?'

'Yes.' They eyed each other uncertainly. 'Eddie O'Sullivan,' said Eddie, holding out his hand.

The other took his hand out of the bucket of slops from which he was feeding the chickens and, without bothering to wipe it, shook Eddie's hand limply.

'Come in,' he said, and Eddie noticed that he walked with a limp.

Eddie looked around him with dismay. The house was as

uncared for inside as out. It reeked of damp and worse. Musty
paper was peeling from the walls, an ancient sink, stained with
God alone knew what, stood to one side, but there were no
taps. A filthy bucket stood beneath, brimming with potato peel-
ings, scraps of bread and tea slops. Beside it was another bucket,
half full of water. On a wooden table stood half a loaf of bread,
a plate of cold cooked potatoes that were going green and an
oil lamp, which provided the only lighting. A cold fireplace,
which had not been cleaned for weeks, spilled ashes onto the
stone floor. Everywhere there was dirt and cold.

'You can sleep in there,' said the old man.

He went into the next room, which was equally cold and
damp. There was an iron bedstead in a corner, with a lumpy
mattress, also stained, and a couple of filthy-looking blankets
thrown over it. He laid his bag on the floor, sat on the bed and
put his head between his hands.

9

The life of the city went on. The great brewery sent its rich malt smell across the poor streets. Sometimes the knacker's yard gave off an evil stench of boiled bones and hides, or if you went near the markets it could be a whiff of the country, horses and hay and feedstuffs. The ramshackle old houses, some even still in the Flemish style of the eighteenth century, looked as if they could not long survive – nor could they.

Despite the march of armies and a world thrown into chaos, Dublin changed little. The poor remained poor, the middle class settled, comfortable, untroubled. It was a conservative society in which hierarchies were marked and unchanging. People's lives were set out for them from birth and, apart from a few dreamers, poets or would-be revolutionaries, they felt secure and certain things would not alter. Why would they, war or no war? Life could be coarse, narrow and ungracious, but you knew who were and where you were going.

*

O'Shea sat at his desk. He was a bulky man in his forties, quick-witted, humorous and with the rare combination of imagination and diligence. In addition, his thinking was not clouded by any personal grudges or hatreds of those whom he was investigating, as was that of many of his fellow-policemen. He had a distinguished record of getting his men. But progress was slow on this one.

He worked, dispiritedly, at a number of files. Known subversives, suspected sympathisers, reports from the RUC in the North, with whom there was mutual, wary, secret co-operation – all the minutiae of police work. His thoughts, though, were still on the shooting of O'Grady. Three weeks and bugger all.

His gloomy ruminations were interrupted by the arrival of Callinan, a young detective garda.

'Well, Jim?' asked O'Shea.

'Nothing,' said the younger man. 'We raided Pat O'Sullivan's. Nothing there except a load of abuse.'

'What else did you expect? Jaysus, if I'd a quid for every time that fella's place has been searched I could retire in the morning. You could be sure the nephew wasn't going to be there, wherever he is. Any sign of him anywhere else in that neck of the woods?'

'We tried all the usual spots, asked all the usual people. He's not there, I'd swear it.'

'Well, keep an eye on it. Sooner or later, if we don't get him first, Master Eddie will want to head home.'

'You're certain 'twas him?'

'Not a doubt in the world. Half of Dublin saw him running round with the gat in his hand. The prints on the bike, too, match the ones we got from the bank job in Tipperary town last year. We knew he was mixed up in that.'

'Nothing here in town?' asked Callinan.

'Not a sausage. He was seen in that pub on the quays soon after the job, and that's the last sign of him. We have the word out to all the usual informants, but none of them have come up with a styme. He's in a safe house somewhere, if he's still in Dublin.'

'I still think he must be. How could he have got out with everywhere watched?'

'We're not that good,' said O'Shea, smiling. 'There's still plenty of ways of moving around, plenty of people ready to help the bastards.'

'What now, then?'

'Same as ever. Keep at it, keep at it, Jim. Sooner or later, sooner or later, something will break.'

'Patience is a virtue,' said Callinan.

O'Shea sighed. 'I wish you'd tell them that upstairs. They're starting to get edgy.'

'We'll get him, don't worry,' said Callinan, leaving.

'Who's worried?' said a worried O'Shea after him.

*

Conor played rugby with the under-tens. He played it passionately, full out, running after every ball, never staying in his position. He loved it and he day-dreamed about scoring the winning try for school, province and, after the war, even for Ireland. But the sad fact was that he was not much good at it. Though tall for his age, he was neither strong nor fast and, for all his resolve, timidity gripped him at all the wrong moments on the field. Not like Skinny Duggan who, despite his nickname, was like a small bull, and who swept would-be tacklers aside like flies and could out-run and out-kick anybody of his age in the school. But it was more than your life would be worth to let him hear you calling him Skinny, a nickname he hated.

Conor still played in his back garden, despite the bitter east wind that was knifing through the city, but the airgun remained hidden in the cupboard in Barry's room. He had the toy guns from the cowboy set he had got for Christmas, but was sometimes tempted to take down the forbidden weapon again and practise shooting at jam jars or at stray cats. But Eddie never seemed to be in the garden now and, anyway, he was afraid of being found out by his mother or by Kitty, who would surely spill the beans if she saw him with it.

The year had turned by now and, almost imperceptibly, the evenings were getting longer. One raw day, despite the cold, Conor had gone out into the back garden to play with his cowboy six-shooters. At first he had had rolls of caps, which made a satisfying bang, but these were all used up now and anyway one of the guns was broken, its trigger slack and its stock starting to come adrift from the rest.

The garden was damp and dead. The vegetable beds were empty except for a few mouldy-looking cabbages, the trees had not yet started to put out leaves. Conor pretended he was the US cavalry, charging a band of Indians. He lined up his troops on either side of him, the way you'd see them coming over the top of the hill in the cowboy films. The horses started at a walk, then broke into a canter. He blew an imaginary bugle and shouted 'Charge!' firing his guns as he galloped forward, but the chill dispirited him and his imagination failed to take flight. He picked up a stone disconsolately and threw it at nothing in particular, then looked over the wall into the garden next door. It was as empty as his own, but in one of the beds he saw a small rubber ball which he had accidentally kicked over some time before and never recovered. It had lain, hidden under the leaves in the potato patch for months, but was now revealed on the bare earth.

There was a foothold in the shoulder-high brick wall between the gardens and he pulled himself up, his legs frozen as he sat on the top in his short trousers. Cautiously he looked back up towards the houses, but there was no sign of life anywhere. He jumped down into Miss Keating's and got his ball.

Standing in the strange place, everything looked familiar, but from a different perspective. With his usual curiosity he started to poke around, taking care not to venture too near Miss Keating's house. But there was nothing to be seen, it was as bare and unwelcoming as his own garden, a place of dead mouldering leaves, a gravel path and rank weeds. He recovered the ball, threw it over the wall and was about to climb back when he saw the shed at the end of Keating's. Without much expectation of finding anything, he decided to take a look.

The door was half off its hinges but easily pushed open. There wasn't much to see inside: a rake, a spade, an old lawn-mower, rusty and obviously not used for years, and a wooden crate that had once held bottles of Guinness. On a shelf stood a row of dusty old paint pots and a dog-eared book. He stood on the beer crate to get a better look at it, but it was just an ancient seed catalogue, mouldy and musty-smelling from the damp.

Then he noticed it, a parcel of something behind one of the pots. Stretching, he could just get his fingers to it. Slowly pulling it to the edge of the shelf, he took it down. It was heavy, wrapped in some sort of oily stuff, then tied with a piece of string. He paused, knowing it was something he shouldn't meddle with, but curiosity won through. With difficulty he managed to get the string off and unwrapped the webbing.

He was thrilled. It was a real gun, a revolver like you'd see in the pictures, heavy, menacingly graceful, with an oily glint.

He'd often tried to draw such guns among the scribbles and doodlings he did in the back pages of his school exercise books. He lifted it up, looking along the sights as Eddie had once shown him, pretending to fire it. He peered out through a crack in the half open door, there was still nobody about. He knew he shouldn't do it, that he'd get into trouble if he was discovered. But temptation entered his soul, to take the gun, to play with it just for a while. Then he could leave it back where he had found it.

He crept out of the tool shed cautiously, put the gun on the wall and scrambled over, scuffing his knees in his hurry to get back. Nothing moved in the gardens, no one looked out of any of the tall houses of the terrace which backed on them.

Inside the house, his mother was writing to her brother.

Dear Jim,

I don't know how to thank you for your cheque. Once again you have come to the rescue. You're so good. I know it can't be easy for you, you have your own family to take care of and times can't be great for business. Be assured I am resolved to pay you back somehow, no matter how long it takes.

It was then she heard the shot, a thin crack that might have passed unnoticed had the afternoon not been so quiet. Frowning, she went to the window and looked out.

'Oh my God!' she said.

Conor stood, frozen, in the garden, startled by the bang and the recoil when, only half meaning to, he had pulled the trigger. He still held the revolver in his hand. Looking up to the house, he saw the white face of his mother upstairs. She tried to pull up the window, but it was stuck. She rat-tat-tatted furiously on a pane, holding up the palm of her hand in a sign to stay where he was, not to move. She ran down the stairs and out to the back, but Kitty was ahead of her. The two women stopped in front of the boy.

'What's that?' his mother shouted to Conor foolishly, for it was all too obviously a revolver. He burst into tears.

'Where did you get it? Where did you get it?' In her shock she was still shouting. He said nothing.

'Better go in, ma'am,' said Kitty gently, taking the gun from him, gently, fearfully, as if it might explode in her hand. Putting her other arm round his shoulders, she led him back into the house. They went into the dining-room, where Kitty put the revolver on the table. It lay there, looking bigger and more sinister than ever, alien, a mystery object. It seemed to have a presence of its own, a history, though they couldn't know what it could be, but something hidden, evil even.

Laura Kennedy was calmer now, back in her house, where she had become used to being in charge. 'Now, dear, what happened?'

He gulped, the tears still streaming down his face. He looked small and very young. 'It . . . it just went off in my hand.'

'Where did you get it? You could have killed yourself.'

'I . . .' (gulp) 'I didn't mean to . . .'

'Yes, all right, love,' said his mother.

''Tis all right, pet,' added Kitty.

'Did you find it somewhere?'

'In next door. In the next garden.'

'In Miss Keating's?'

'Yes, in the shed. I went in after a ball, I didn't mean to . . .'

The two women exchanged a glance.

'What should we do, ma'am?' asked Kitty. 'Should we give it to Miss Keating?'

'No, I don't think so. God knows how it got there, or who's mixed up in it.'

'Will I put it back in the shed then?'

'No,' said Laura, 'they might see you from the house. Someone in there could have put it there, one of the lodgers.'

Conor gave a succession of silent sobs. He was getting over his shock, but was still frightened by the solemnity of the adults.

'What'll we do?' repeated Kitty. 'Should we tell the guards?'

'I'll have to think about it.'

She took the gun carefully, went to a sideboard and opened a drawer. Still afraid of it, she put it in, closed and locked the drawer and put the key in a pocket of the apron she was wearing.

'Now,' she said, turning to the two others, 'listen to me carefully. This is very, *very* important. Tell nobody, I mean nobody, about this. Do you hear me now, Conor?'

'Yes, Mummy,' he replied in a small voice.

'I don't know where this thing came from, but there are people around, bad people, Conor, and if they knew we had this gun, or even knew about it, we could be in very big trouble.'

He looked at her, wide-eyed.

'So you see you must tell no one about it, till I decide what to do. No one, not your friends at school, not even Barry and Maeve, no one. And you too, of course, Kitty.'

Kitty, she knew, would stay silent. She was discretion itself. But Conor was only a little boy. When the first shock had worn off, he would be tempted to talk about what was, after all, a Great Adventure.

'Now, Conor,' she said, 'you've been a very, very bold boy.' The tears welled up in his eyes again. 'You could have killed yourself, you could have killed someone else. I'm not going to say any more about it for now. If your father were here you'd get a good spanking.'

'I'm sorry,' he sobbed.

'It's no good saying you're sorry. Do you promise not to mention this to a soul? Say "I promise".'

'I promise,' said Conor.

'Now if you say one word . . . one word, I'll, I'll . . .' Her voice trailed away. 'Bring him down and give him a drink of milk, please, Kitty,' she said.

When they had gone, she sat down at the table. Who could she talk to? What should she do? Her husband would have known. She put a trembling hand to her forehead.

That night, when Conor was asleep and all the others had gone out, she went to the drawer again and opened it. Almost to her surprise, the revolver was still there. It was as if it was a mythic object that had come, unwelcome, into their lives and that she half expected would vanish by some magic as suddenly as it had arrived, leaving no trace behind it. But there it was, dark, bulky, still pregnant with menace. She closed and locked the drawer again, picked up the telephone and, with a beating heart, rang the local police station.

'I want to report a, a gun,' she said.

'How do you mean, report?' said a voice at the other end.

'It was . . . it was found,' she said.

'Just a minute,' said the voice.

She waited nervously.

'Hello.' Another voice, older she reckoned.

'You're reporting finding a firearm?'

'Yes, a revolver.'

'What kind of revolver?'

'I don't know what kind. It's, it's a big one, black.' She sounded stupid, she thought. A typical silly woman, they'd say.

'Could I have your name and address, please?' asked the voice, impassively.

She gave them.

'And how did this firearm come into your possession, ma'am?' The voice, with its country accent, sounded like a comic policeman in a sketch by Jimmy O'Dea.

'My son, my young son found it in the next-door garden when he went in after a ball.'

'What house would that garden belong to?'

'Number thirty-four.' The Kennedys lived in number thirty-two.

'Right,' said the voice, sounding unconcerned. 'We'll send someone along to see about it.'

She was surprised how quickly they called, little more than an hour later. There were two of them, a massive young man with pink cheeks and an older one with a grave, humorous face. Instinctively, she liked him.

'Mrs Kennedy?' said the older man. 'Gardaí. Superintendent O'Shea, and this is Detective Callinan. May we come in?'

They entered the hall, looking about them curiously.

'Is there anyone else home?' asked O'Shea.

'No, the maid and my two elder children are out. There's just my little boy. He's asleep upstairs.'

'Is he the one that found the gun?'

'Yes.'

'Could we see it, please?' asked O'Shea.

She led them into the dining-room and unlocked the drawer of the sideboard. They looked at it impassively. Then Callinan took it out carefully by the barrel and placed it in a large envelope. She noticed he wore gloves.

'Who else knows about this, I mean in this house?'

'Just myself and the maid, Kitty Maher is her name, and of course Conor, my little boy that found it.'

Callinan was writing in a little notebook, painstakingly. 'You mentioned two older children. How about them?'

'They're students in UCD. They don't know. I thought it better to tell as few people as possible.'

'Good woman,' said O'Shea. 'Now, tell us once more how the little boy came to find the gun.'

She went through it all again. They listened silently, the only sounds being the scratching as Callinan took down what she said, using a pencil, and a sympathetic clicking of the tongue by O'Shea when she described the shot going off and the fright she had got. When she had finished he nodded his head and paused for a moment.

'Tell us,' he said, 'who lives in the house next door?'

'Well,' said Laura, 'there's Miss Keating.'

'Miss Nora Keating?'

'Yes, do you know her?'

'No, just checking. That was the name you gave when you

phoned in.' Later, when she thought about it, she was pretty sure she hadn't given the name on the phone.

'Any idea who else lives in that house?' asked O'Shea in a tone of voice that gave the impression it was really of little account.

'Well . . . I'm not sure. Miss Keating and a maid . . . and there are lodgers, maybe four or five of them. One of them is an actor or something, I think, I'm not sure about the others . . . Oh yes!' She remembered. 'My brother asked one of them in here for a drink on Christmas Day, he was all alone in the house for the morning. A young fellow, fair hair, I can't remember his name.'

The two detectives remained impassive but exchanged the faintest flicker of a glance.

'Thank you, Mrs Kennedy, you've been very helpful,' said O'Shea.

'We may have to talk to the boy,' said Callinan.

She was alarmed. 'He's only nine years old. I know it was very naughty of him but . . .'

'No, no, don't worry,' said O'Shea. 'Just routine, we probably won't have to do it at all, don't worry yourself. Now, I don't have to tell you how important it is that that no one talks about this. It's vital to our investigations that it doesn't get out.'

'Could you tell me what it's all about?' she asked.

'Probably nothing at all, just routine. We'll take some tests on this gun and then we'll know more.'

'If you see anything let us know, ma'am,' said Callinan.

'See what?'

'Anything. Anything out of the ordinary. Anyone calling next door that seems . . . out of the ordinary,' said O'Shea. 'Here,' he took a leaf from Callinan's notebook and wrote on it. 'Here's my number. You can leave a message if I'm not there.'

They let themselves out carefully, looking up and down the street first, and went back to their car. They had parked it a few streets away; cars were so rare nowadays that they would draw immediate attention to their drivers.

'Well, well, Nora Keating,' said O'Shea with a grin as they drove back to the depot.

'Who is she?' asked Callinan.

'An old republican. She was engaged once to Phil Hurley.'

'That was killed be the Tans?'

'Yes, she was involved with the diehards during the civil war times too.'

'Why didn't we have her watched then?'

'That was twenty years ago. As far as we knew she hasn't had anything to do with politics since.' He chuckled. 'She had the name of being a bit of a good thing.'

Callinan's eyes widened.

'They say she had a fling with Cormac Duddy,' O'Shea went on. Duddy was a politician who had been in and out of the cabinet.

'But, but he's a married man with kids,' spluttered Callinan. No matter how long he was in the force he never ceased to be amazed at human depravity, particularly of a sexual nature.

O'Shea burst out laughing. 'Ah sure, God love your innocence, Jim,' he said.

They drove on a while.

'Will we raid the house?' asked Callinan.

'We don't even know yet if O'Sullivan is there,' said O'Shea. 'The first thing we've got to do is find out. We'll put a watch on the place. Find out, too, who the other lodgers are. We should be able to get some information there. And, it goes without saying, keep it quiet.'

10

She was pregnant, she was sure of it. She was three weeks overdue and Eddie had vanished. After a week it had been a faint worry, after two it had been bad, now she felt frantic. No one knew, so far, though she could see Vera giving her the eye. Old shrewdy Vera, she didn't miss a trick. She'd know just from looking at you, a change of colour in the face, the faintest shadow under the eyes.

Jesus, Mary and Joseph, what was she going to do? It was the ultimate nightmare, the worst thing that could happen a girl. Unmarried and up the spout and the fella done a bunk. But he hadn't done a bunk, had he? Not, anyway, because she was pregnant, for he didn't know that. But supposing he was tired of her, even not knowing about the other? Would he come back then and do the decent thing?

Where was he, where was he anyway? Not so much as a note to her, no word at all. The bastard! No, he wasn't that type. There were plenty who were, who'd have their fun and then leave you. But not Eddie. If Eddie knew . . .

She wandered the streets in a daze. She looked in shop windows without seeing their contents. She went up to the Phoenix Park one day, but it kept reminding her of Eddie. She forgot to eat meals or, when they were put in front of her, pushed away the plates after a few bites. She smoked cigarettes, though she had given them up years ago after she had been told they might damage her voice. She did the show automatically, hardly thinking of what she was at, though she was grateful for anything that would take her mind off things, even for a couple of hours.

She found it hard to sleep and would drop off, exhausted, in the small hours of the morning. When she awoke there would be a moment when she didn't know where she was, but then she'd remember and despair would cover her like a blanket. One morning her young sister heard her crying in the bed.

'What are you crying for, Kay?' she said.

'You mind your own business,' said Kay, and hid her head under the pillow.

'We don't see that boyfriend of yours around any more, ha ha,' said Dickie Delaney. 'Has he given you the push?'

'Maybe I gave him the push,' she replied, but he just laughed his nasty little laugh again.

Could he have found another girl? She felt a violent twinge of jealousy for her absent and totally imaginary rival. No, no, he had told her so often how much he loved her. He had made all the running. He was very sincere, everyone said that he was daft about her. Maybe he'd got scared with all the talk about getting married. Sometimes that made men shy away. But he was the one that had brought it up in the first place, wasn't it? Or was it? Everything was confused. She couldn't remember who had actually said what or when any more.

Maybe he'd had an accident, something that meant he was laid up or in hospital. Surely he'd have got word to her, though, if that was the case. Supposing he was dead? No, that couldn't be it, could it? No, she'd have heard. Why hadn't he at least written?

Maybe she could get in touch with him through the firm he

worked for, what's this they were called? Mooney's, that was it. Maybe she could reach him through them. There was something funny, but, about that job of his. He never had a bob and the samples he had given her just looked like any bars of chocolate you could buy in a shop. He never seemed to have any trouble getting time off to meet her too, even in the morning. Maybe he only had some tiny little messenger boy job, maybe he didn't have a job at all, maybe that was why the idea of getting married had scared him off. He'd been lying to her all the time and he couldn't support a wife. But that couldn't be, either. Sure if he'd no job couldn't he go into the army, the same as loads of fellas she knew had done? Or there were jobs going for the unemployed cutting turf for the government. He'd get something for that anyway.

If only she could talk to him. But where was he? Wait a minute! Frankie would know, Frankie Fox. Weren't they in the same digs? Wasn't he the one had brung him along to the show in the first place?

She'd ask. No, she didn't want everyone in the Coliseum knowing she was looking, searching for Eddie. But she'd have to. It was the only way she might be able to reach him and give him the news about the baby. He'd have to marry her then, whether he wanted to or not. Anyway, he *would* want to, he loved her, he'd said so. She remembered all the kisses, his arms round her. 'Gor, I'm mad about you,' he'd said. 'I'm in love with you.'

So her mind went, round and round in circles. Finally she decided she'd ask Frankie. He was a decent skin, he'd keep his mouth shut and, in his funny way, though he was ancient, he fancied her. But she kept putting it off and putting it off, and all the time she became more certain about her pregnancy.

The matter was finally resolved one day in the dressing room. She'd come in early, to get away from home, and Vera found her, puking in the wash-hand basin.

Kay looked up from the basin, her face wet with tears from the exertion of vomiting. 'I must have ate something funny,' she said.

'You're in the club, isn't that right?' said Vera.

Then it all came out in a torrent of crying and words. It was even a relief to tell everything, after the weeks of tortured secrecy.

'The bastard,' said Vera, 'the fucking bastard!'

'No,' said Kay, 'no he's not. He doesn't know, he doesn't know I'm pregnant.'

'Huh!' snorted Vera derisively.

'He doesn't. He went away before I knew meself. He loves me!'

'He does in his eye. Where's he been all these weeks then?'

'I don't know. But he couldn't possibly know about me. If he found out he'd come back. He would!'

'Men,' said Vera. 'They're all the same.'

They looked at each other, hopelessly.

'What are you going to do?' asked Vera.

'I don't know.'

'Do your mammy and daddy know?'

'Are you kidding? Jaysus, they'd kill me.'

'Have you been to a doctor?'

'No.'

'You'd better go. Go up to the Rotunda.'

'Oh God! I thought . . . I thought maybe I'd ask Frankie Fox if he could get some word to Eddie.'

'Yes, ask Frankie. What have you got to lose? Ask Frankie.'

'And Vera,' begged Kay, 'please don't tell anyone.'

'Of course not!' said Vera, who couldn't keep a secret if you paid her.

*

Corrigan was feeling pleased with himself. Things were better now, though the previous week had been a trial. After a night of 'bad thoughts' he had gone to confession on Wednesday, but by Saturday he had had to go again. Well, he couldn't take the risk of walking round in a state of mortal sin, could he? Supposing he was run down by a bus? He'd go straight to hell for all eternity.

So, he had made his way to Father O'Mahony once again, with a sinking heart. Father O'Mahony had the name of being 'easy' in the confessional. There was always a good crowd waiting outside his box, not like Father Glynn, the other curate, who, it was said, ate the face off people and gave them enormous penances. But, for all Father O'Mahony's lenience, two confessions within a week might try his patience. Corrigan had waited outside his box, trying to concentrate on his prayers, but noting nervously that those in front of him in the queue seemed to be taking for ever inside.

Eventually it had been his turn. He had gone in and knelt in the near darkness while, just out of earshot, the mumbled confession of the penitent on the other side went on and on. Eventually it ended and the grille in front of him slid open to half reveal the dim features of Father O'Mahony.

'Bless me, Father, for I have sinned,' said Corrigan. 'It's three days since my last confession.'

An involuntary groan escaped from the priest. It had been a long, tiring day with many confessions, and these even more tedious than usual. Try as he might, his thoughts were turning more and more to his supper, which was overdue. The thought of a lengthy session with one of those scrupulous penitents suddenly seemed too much.

To Corrigan, however, the sound from the priest denoted, not impatience, but a gasp of horror at the wickedness of someone who would need to go to confession twice in a week.

Father O'Mahony sighed. 'Yes, my child?' he asked.

Stammering and stuttering Corrigan told his sins. He used euphemisms, 'bad thoughts', 'impure actions by myself'.

The priest sat there, fighting not to think his own thoughts, which ran more to bacon, egg and sausage, home-made brown bread and good strong tea – the parish housekeeper was a provider famous through the diocese. He pulled himself up with a jerk; he hadn't been listening at all.

'What?' he asked.

Corrigan froze in mid-sentence. Had he unknowingly revealed something particularly terrible?

'I . . . I was inattentive at my prayers,' he said. It was his habit to get the worst sins over first, then throw in a few minor transgressions as a sort of buttress before the priest had his say.

But all Father O'Mahony said was: 'For your penance, say three Hail Marys. Now make a good act of contrition: "Oh my God, I am heartily sorry".'

Three Hail Marys! His first reaction was to feel cheated. That was the sort of penance children got for telling lies or being disobedient to their parents. Then the thought occurred to him that in some way the priest was giving up on him, that he was such a hopeless sinner that even his confessor couldn't be bothered lecturing him. For his part, Father O'Mahony, to whom the confession of masturbation was as common as daily shaving, wondered briefly if he'd been a bit short with the sinner, then decided it was of little account, knowing as he did in his heart that Corrigan, whom he had recognised, would be back again very soon with the same old story.

That had been a week ago, but it had been a good seven days for Corrigan. He had not fallen once, fighting off all temptations. The curtness of the priest had, somehow, shocked him and kept him free from sin.

He was on his way home from a meeting of the Society for the Abolition of Evil Literature and that, too, had been a success. Mrs McGuire had had a triumph. Her complaint about the corset ads had fallen on fertile ground. The archbishop himself had been furious, she had learned, and fired off a broadside at the bad taste and immodesty of one of the city's leading Catholic firms. The corsets had vanished from the evening papers and would not be seen again. Flushed with success, the society had decided to keep a permanent watch on all newspapers and magazines in future.

As he walked homewards Corrigan permitted himself to hum a little bit of 'The Garden Where the Praties Grow', a song of his mother's. Two tall men, one middle-aged, one in his twenties, started to walk beside him.

'Mr Corrigan?' asked the elder.

'Yes,' said Corrigan, surprised. His circle of acquaintances was not large.

'I wonder if we could have a word with you?'

Corrigan looked at them suspiciously. Could these be a pair of those con men of whom he had heard, who tried to wangle money out of strangers? They waylaid you in the streets with stories of bad luck, or schemes involving the making of easy fortunes, and diddled you out of every penny you possessed.

'Afraid I'm in a bit of a hurry,' he murmured.

'This won't take a minute,' said the younger. 'A police matter.'

Corrigan looked at them wide-eyed.

'Superintendent O'Shea, and this is Detective Garda Callinan.' They were passing a pub. 'Let's go in here, will we?'

Corrigan let himself be steered in by a hand on his elbow. Pubs were places he hardly ever visited. Like so many others, this one was dark and smelled of beer and tobacco.

'Will you have something?' asked O'Shea.

'I don't drink.'

'A mineral then?'

The big young policeman went to the bar, while the other two sat at a filthy table, covered in tobacco ash and the sticky rings left by glasses. Corrigan wrinkled his nostrils in disgust at the place.

Callinan came back holding the drinks in his massive hands – two bottles of stout and three glasses, one of which contained a fizzing reddish-orange lemonade that had never seen a lemon.

O'Shea seemed more friendly. 'We had to approach you like this,' he said. ''Tis a confidential matter.'

Corrigan examined his conscience. Among his sins there were none that would bring him to the attention of the police. Could someone in the job be on some kind of black-market fiddle?

'Is it anything to do with the Department?' he asked.

'No, no. 'Tis to do with security.'

'What has that to do with me?'

'You're in digs with a Miss Nora Keating, isn't that right?' asked Callinan.

'Yes.'

'Who else is in that house?'

'Me, a man called John Dolan in the civil service like myself, that fella Frankie Fox . . .'

'The comedian, yes. And . . .?'

'A young fella, O'Sullivan.'

He knew then, of course. He knew what they wanted. It was an IRA matter, it had to be. He had suspected Eddie from the start. His sympathies were all too obvious. Not that he disapproved – on the contrary. The IRA might overstep the mark sometimes, but they stood for the right things, a united Ireland, free and Catholic. They were anti-British and who could blame them for that?

'Eddie O'Sullivan, would that be?' asked O'Shea casually.

'Yes, why?'

''Tis a police matter.' O'Shea poured his bottle of stout with great care down the inside of his glass. 'Is he there now?'

'No, he's been away for the last few weeks. He's a traveller, a commercial traveller.'

'Is he now?' Callinan drank deeply, leaving a line of white foam on his upper lip, which he wiped away with the back of his hand.

'We'd like a word with Mr O'Sullivan,' said O'Shea.

'I told you, he isn't there.'

'That's what I want to talk to you about.' Corrigan felt

uncomfortable under the stare of the policeman. 'This, of course, is confidential.'

'Yes,' said Corrigan uncomfortably.

'Highly confidential. It wouldn't do anybody any good if this conversation got out, you know what I mean?'

Corrigan said nothing. There was nothing to say.

'You heard of the O'Grady murder?' Callinan went on.

'The guard that was shot dead at New Year?' Yes, he had read something about it in the paper. It was something to which he had not paid a great deal of attention, part of that shadowy world of killings and counter-killings, raids, imprisonments and trials, that went on between the police and the IRA. Not anything he thought about very much, it didn't affect him. It was regrettable, probably, but not something you could really disapprove of, like a crime or sexual misconduct. It was hard to work out the rights and wrongs of it, there were things to be said for both sides, it was better avoided.

'We need to know about O'Sullivan's movements,' said O'Shea.

'I told you, he's not there.'

'Yes, but if he comes back, or if you hear anything about him, anything at all, we'd be glad to know.'

'It's got nothing to do with me.'

Nor had it. Why should he be involved? It wasn't that he was a republican, except in the widest sense. He knew some families that were involved, of course, who didn't? But he didn't mix with them. Still, why should he be tainted with the name of informer, the lowest of the low, the ones who throughout history, again and again, had sold out the cause of Irish freedom?

'I'm no informer,' he blurted out.

'All we're asking,' said Callinan, 'is that you keep in touch with us.' He seemed annoyed.

'I'm no informer,' he said again.

'You're an employee of the state.'

'What?'

'In the Department of Supplies. A civil servant, aren't you?'

'Yes, but . . .'

'I wonder what your superiors would think, what your minister would think, if they heard you were unwilling to co-operate with the gardaí on a serious matter involving the shooting dead of a police officer?' said Callinan.

All his cowardice welled up. He had heard of people who had black marks against them, whose promotion was unaccountably blocked, who were transferred into dead-end jobs and to places in the back of beyond. He had even heard of people being dismissed altogether. He thought of his secure career being disrupted, maybe of being out of a job altogether at this stage of his life. It would kill his mother. To be a civil servant, or a teacher, or a guard, those were the best things anyone of his class could aspire to, next to being a priest. He lifted up the lemonade and drank, to give himself more time to think.

'It'll be completely confidential,' said O'Shea, in a more friendly manner. 'No one need ever know you helped us.'

'But . . . but what do you want me to do?' he asked.

'We told you. If O'Sullivan turns up again, and I'd be very surprised if he does, tell us at once. Also if anybody unusual, anybody at all, visits the house.'

'How will I let you know?'

'You could call at your local police station,' said Callinan.

'No, no,' said O'Shea. 'No need to do that. Here, just ring

this number.' He took an empty cigarette packet that had been left on the table and, fishing an expensive-looking fountain pen from his pocket, wrote on it. 'Just ring this number. Any time, day or night.'

'But do it at once,' said Callinan. 'Don't wait around.'

Corrigan put the cigarette packet in his pocket. 'Did he . . . was it he killed that policeman?' he asked.

O'Shea shrugged. 'Who knows? We just want to question him.'

'To help us with our inquiries,' added Callinan.

'Just one other thing,' added O'Shea. 'No one is to know. Do you have a girl?'

Corrigan shook his head.

'No one,' said O'Shea. 'Not your friends, your parents, your family, no one.'

'If word got out it could be very serious for you,' said Callinan.

'Do you understand?' asked O'Shea.

Again he nodded without saying anything. He knew all too well what could happen to informers. He remembered that fella, back in Fenian times, what's this his name was? The authorities had got him away safely to Australia, so they thought, but he was followed and they shot him dead on the ship. He went back to the digs, his heart pounding.

*

Kay hadn't seen much of Frankie lately. Dickie Delaney was giving him less and less to do in the shows each week since he'd tried to stick in the spot for himself. He spent most of the time skulking up in his dressing room, only coming down when he had to go on stage. She waited for him one night after the final curtain, though, and caught him on the stairs on his way out.

Even in her own misery she couldn't help noticing how awful he looked. She always thought of him as an ould fella, but now he appeared positively ancient. He seemed to have shrunk, bent almost double with slumped shoulders and a complexion the colour of porridge.

'Frankie,' she said.

'Oh hello, Kay.' He didn't attempt the usual quip or bit of gallantry about what a glamour girl she was.

'Have you a second?' she asked. Bing Kelly came down the stairs on his way out and passed them.

'Adios, amigos,' he said, 'keep the faith.'

'Good night,' said Kay and then, to Frankie, 'Could I talk to you somewhere, private, like?'

'What's up?' asked Frankie and then he noticed the tears brimming up in her eyes. 'Let's go into number four,' he said, leading her to an empty dressing room.

Number four hadn't been used for some time. There was some problem about the floor. They stood facing each other in the empty room, nothing in it but broken bare boards and stained mirrors and the smell of damp.

'It's about Eddie,' she stammered. 'Have you seen him?'

'Not since, not since he went away. Has he not been in touch with you?'

'No.' She started to cry.

'Ah come on now. Maybe ... I mean he's probably been down the country, travelling. Has he not been in touch with you at all?' he repeated.

She shook her head, wordlessly.

''Tis probably, 'tis probably . . .' He searched for a reason. 'He's very busy, likely.' Even as he said it he knew it sounded lame.

'Is he due back? Did you hear, is he due back in town?'

'I'm sure he is, don't worry now.' He patted her shoulder awkwardly. 'And you know what they say – never run after a bus or a man, there'll always be another one along, ha ha.'

She didn't even try to laugh. 'Could you find out is he coming back?'

'Sure.'

Miss Keating dismissed the question out of hand when he asked her next day.

'Mr O'Sullivan? He's gone, he's moved.'

'Where to?'

'I haven't the faintest idea,' she said and swept out of the room.

When he told Kay the next day she collapsed into tears.

'Aisy on, aisy on,' he said, trying to comfort her.

'You don't get it, I'm . . . you know,' she said.

'You mean . . . having a . . . Oh Jaysus, I'm sorry. Are you sure?'

'Of course I'm feckin' sure.' She wiped her nose. 'He doesn't know, Eddie doesn't know. If I could only see him, if I could only tell him. Look.' She took out a letter. 'I've written this. If you could get it to him some way. If anyone knows where he is, anyone.'

Frankie took the envelope. It was violet-coloured and smelt of perfume. 'I don't know,' he said doubtfully. 'I'll try.'

Back again to Miss Keating. 'I told you,' she said coldly, 'I don't know where he's gone.'

'I have a letter for him. It's very important.'

'I can't help that.'

'Did he not leave a forwarding address?'

'I told you. No.'

But Frankie saw something in her eyes, the ould bitch.

'It'd be worth money, a good sum of money, if'n someone could trace him.'

'I said I don't know where he is.'

'But if you, if someone, could make enquiries, like, it'd be worth five quid.'

Greed fought with discretion within her and, as usual, greed won.

'Well,' she said. 'I could make enquiries. I could get somebody to make enquiries, someone who could do with the money,' she lied.

'Hold on,' he said. He went up to his room and rummaged under the mattress until he felt the lump of his wallet. He took it out and abstracted five pounds from the wad of notes, then put the rest back carefully. As he did so a searing pain shot through his stomach.

'Oh Jaysus!' he groaned, sitting on the edge of the bed and bending double. 'Oh!'

He passed wind and it wasn't quite so bad. Sweating from the pain he shuffled his way downstairs again.

Miss Keating was waiting at the bottom. He handed over Kay's envelope first. She took the highly coloured cheap-smelling object with distaste, holding it between thumb and forefinger as if it was some dirty, sex-soiled thing. Eddie's name was written on it in a childish hand.

'Is it from some girl?' she asked.

'It's from a friend.'

She knew straight away. It was some girl of his. Likely as not he'd got her in the family way, otherwise she wouldn't be offering so much money to have it delivered.

'And there's another five as soon as she knows it's got to him,' said Frankie.

Again Miss Keating paused. She had fully intended to take the letter, read it and then tear it up. But here was the chance of a very substantial sum of money. It meant taking a risk, of course, of making contact again with someone she had decided she would remove totally from her life in future. If she was found out passing him letters there could be very nasty repercussions from the Movement, not to mention the police. Someone that was on the run for a killing. Still, what of it? The risk was small enough, just get the letter to him, make sure he had it and then collect the second fiver. She knew people, people who, for two quid, would do a lot worse than delivering a letter.

For his part, Frankie wondered at himself. Five quid! What sort of an eejit am I at all? Throwing around money like that, you'd think I'd won the sweep. Oh well, what the hell, the poor kid, and what would the cash be doing anyway, only lying under the mattress in his room?

'Have you got the money?' asked Miss Keating.

He paid it over. A big five-pound note. She took it, her eyes glittering at the feel of it and at the thought of all the other notes which she knew were hidden in his room. But first of all, she thought, two pounds was too much. She'd get the letter to O'Sullivan for a quid. Seeing the risk she was taking, why waste good money?

*

Conor was bursting with his secret. A real gun, found by him and he had shot it! But there was no one to talk to about it. 'Any word about the gun?' he had asked his mother, trying to make it sound casual.

'No,' she had replied shortly, 'the police have taken it. I hope you haven't told anyone about it?'

Even Kitty refused to discuss it. ''Tis better left alone,' she said. 'It was probably just left there by somebody legally. There's probably some perfectly good explanation. Anyway, the guards will find out. I hope you haven't been blabbing about it to your pals.'

'I certainly have not!' said Conor indignantly, as if the very idea was out of the question, but of course he had.

One day at school, in the yard during lunch break, he had been unable to contain himself any more. Clancy had been going on and on about *The Corsican Brothers*, starring Douglas Fairbanks Junior, a film that was full of 'massive fencing' that Clancy demonstrated with his ruler.

'There's these two twins,' he told Conor, 'and when one gets stabbed, the other one feels the pain in the same part of his body, even though he's hundreds of miles away.' He clasped his side in agony and staggered round the yard. 'Have you not seen it?' he asked incredulously.

'Yeah, well I found a real gun,' said Conor, who'd had enough of talking about pictures which he hadn't seen.

'Get off!' said Clancy incredulously.

'I did. I found it in a shed in the next-door garden.'

'Who do you think you're codding?'

'I did so find it.'

'Where is it then? Let's see it.'

'They took it away, the guards took it away.' He decided to gild the lily a bit. 'They say it was used in a stick-up of a bank.'

'It was in me granny!' jeered Clancy.

'It was so. It might even have been used in a murder.' He knew that every detail, true or false, made it sound more implausible. 'In fact it could have been used in several murders. When I found it, I fired it. It jumped in my hand. I shot a bird out of a tree.'

Clancy just looked at him pityingly and made a few rapier passes. Then he ran Conor through with his ruler.

'Little boys shouldn't tell fibs,' he said.

Conor thought of jumping on him and pinning him to the ground. There weren't many boys of his own age he could do that to, but Clancy was a bit of a softy. He was forestalled, though, by Skinny Duggan, who hove into sight with his acolytes in attendance.

'Hey, Clancy,' he said, 'got anything to eat?' As he spoke, he got Clancy's arm and twisted it behind his back.

'Ow! Cut it out, Skinny!' shouted Clancy.

'What did you call me?' asked Skinny menacingly.

'Nothing, let go my arm.'

'What did you call me?'

'Nothing. Duggan. Let go, you're hurting me.'

Father Curran, who was taking yard that day, was walking towards them. Skinny let go the arm.

'You just watch yourself,' he told Clancy.

'Yeah, watch yourself,' said his sidekick, Brennan.

Going home that afternoon, Conor felt relieved that Clancy had not believed his story. Imagine if it got back to his mother? He was lucky already, he knew, to have got off so lightly for having taken the gun.

It was starting to get dark by the time he got home. It was a part of the day he liked, the light not quite gone, the rattle of the trams, the golden light from the shop windows spilling onto the pavement, the promise of home, his mother, Kitty, bread and milk, a fire. He dawdled along, trying to avoid walking on the cracks in the pavement. As he was about to turn in the gate, his eye caught the old, abandoned house across the road. It was as it always was, an unkempt patch of garden overrun with weeds and waste paper, damp grey walls, a hall door so weather-beaten that it had lost whatever colour it once had, black eyeless windows, two with broken glass.

Startled, he looked again, closer. Behind the grey wisp of filthy net curtain that hung behind one of the windows something moved. Yes, a figure, something! Again he looked, but it was gone. He felt the hair prickle on the back of his neck and rushed into his own house.

Kitty was in the kitchen. 'Hello, pet,' she said.

'Kitty, Kitty, I saw it!'

'Saw what?'

'It, the ghost.'

'What ghost?'

'In the house across the street. It was a man. He was there for a minute and then he vanished.'

'Ah no, you only imagined it.'

'I saw him, I promise.'

'There's no ghost there.'

'You told me yourself there was.'

'I was only joking.'

*

In the house across the street the detective assigned to watch Miss Keating's looked at his watch for the umpteenth time. Only ten minutes had passed since he had last done so. Was there anything in life more boring than these surveillance jobs? he thought. Hour after hour and bugger all to do. Since they'd started to watch the house no one had come or gone except for that fella who turned out to be the local butcher. He'd had a big parcel, presumably of meat, and the fact that he was delivering it himself, instead of a messenger boy, would lead you to believe there was some kind of rationing fiddle going on. That would be my deduction anyway, the detective told himself. But that was no business of the Special Branch. Good luck to whoever it was if they could get away with a few extra rations, sure wasn't everyone doing it that could?

Unaware of the sensation he had caused with Conor, who would spend another sleepless night because of him, the silent watcher rubbed his hands together vigorously in an effort to stay warm, and thought gloomily that it would be another two hours before he would be relieved.

11

Eddie sat on the edge of his lumpy bed, gazing at the wall. The days went by interminably. Crotty, the old farmer, went about his business, which was little enough at that time of the year. He would milk his few cows and then bring the milk in a churn to the creamery a few miles away. When he came back he would walk around his meagre fields in a desultory way, feed his few scrawny chickens and that seemed to conclude the day's business. He had an overgrown potato patch behind the house, where he got the spuds which were his staple diet. Once a week he would go into a nearby small town to collect the dole and would return with what he called 'a few groceries', a loaf of bread, some tea and sometimes a small piece of bacon and a copy of the *Irish Press*.

The short days were hardly over before he was kneeling by his ashy, smoky fire muttering lengthy prayers to himself. Then he would shuffle off to the byre outside, for he suffered from arthritis in his hips, and relieve himself, apparently with some pain, for Eddie could hear him groaning to himself, 'Jaysus, oh Jaysus!' as he did so. Then he would take the oil lamp that lit the room dimly and head off to bed without a word, leaving the young man alone with only the dull flicker of the fire for lighting.

The weeks went by like years. There was nothing to do, nowhere to go. One day, no longer able to bear the boredom, he had headed off on a long walk. The countryside was bare, deserted, there was hardly so much as a bird to be seen. The fields were empty and weedy, the trees stood silent in dark, sombre clumps. His feet rang out on the frosty roads, his breath made clouds in the chilly air, he longed for the warmth of companionship. Yet, to be moving, stretching his limbs, was better than sitting endlessly in that squalid house. Again and again he thought about the shooting, but repetition had dulled the pain somewhat. For the umpteenth time he considered heading for home, but it seemed, if anything, even harder to do. How would he get across country in wartime like this, when there was hardly a bus or a train running and no cars at all from which he could cadge a lift? He could cycle, of course, but he would be more conspicuous that way and, as soon as he neared his home territory, the guards would surely get wind of him.

Easier to get back to Dublin and Kay . . . Kay! What would she be thinking? No word from him now for nearly a month. She'd think he'd dumped her. Maybe she'd dumped him by now. A beautiful girl like that, fellas would be after her, fellas coming into that theatre every night. He had decided to write to her, but when he'd asked Crotty for a pen and paper the old man had just said:

'No. No letters.'

'Why?'

'That's what they said, no letters. The censors is opening everything now. They'd be traced, you'd be found.'

Everything was subject to censorship, in case it might in some way reflect on Irish neutrality.

''Tis important.'

'You can tell me and I'll get word to the Boys.'

''Tisn't that. 'Tis personal, like.'

But Crotty had just repeated: 'No letters. And don't be goin' out walkin' nayther. The word will go round if there's a stranger spotted here. You'll get me into trouble.'

He scoured the newspapers, when they came, for word of the shooting, but there seemed to be nothing. The reports of it had appeared in the days immediately after it had happened, when he had been unable to see a paper and now, with no word of a breakthrough in police investigations, it had vanished from the press as if it had never happened. Meanwhile, for lack of anything else to do, he read every paper he could find, old and new, when he could get one, from cover to cover.

He felt a twinge when he read the theatre and cinema advertisements. There was the Coliseum, '*Serenade to Laughter* with Dickie Delaney and all your old favourites', but there was no mention of Kay. 'Film: *Frisco Lil*,' the ad went on. 'Girl versus gangsters with Irene Harvey and Kent Taylor. Book for Sunday night.' Sunday night was the big one, when there were full houses and touts sold tickets in the street outside at black-market prices.

In his mind's eye he saw Kay singing 'Sweet Embraceable You', or maybe something jazzy, doing an Andrews Sisters with a couple of girls from the chorus, 'Boogie Woogie Bugle Boy of Company C' or the like. He saw her afterwards, too, in Curran's, surrounded by admirers. They'd be buying her drink and plying her with compliments, telling her what a smasher she was, how they were mad about her, and asking her on dates, dancing or maybe to some really posh place like the Dolphin or the Gresham Hotel. He could see her smiling at them, laughing at their jokes, dazzled by their sophistication. They would be suave characters with moustaches and loads of money, smoking cigarettes in holders. She could even be doing a line with one of them already, and why not, seeing as how he'd vanished without trace? Pull yourself together, he told himself.

Then came the letter. Crotty came back from his messages in town one week with it.

'Here,' he said roughly, 'this is for you.'

'How did it get here?'

'Mind your own business.'

At first he thought it was from the IRA, orders to move on or some sort of information about what was happening, but then he saw the violet envelope and his name on it and knew instantly it was from Kay. His heart leaped as it had not done since the shooting. He took it and went out of the house, wanting to be alone while he read it.

Outside, he looked at the envelope again, hesitating to open it, savouring it, delaying the pleasure. The envelope, he noticed, was stained as if it had got wet. He sniffed at it and imagined a faint perfume off it, a scent of Kay. He tore it open. The writing was childish and badly formed.

Dear Eddie,
    This is to tell you that I am pregnint. I was not sure first of all then I went to the doctors and he said it is true. He said to tell my mam and da but I am afraid. I don't know what to do. Please come back. I miss you I love you, please.
    Kay

The ink had run in places, where she had been crying. At the bottom, as an afterthought she had put S.W.A.L.K. – sealed with a loving kiss – the way schoolgirls do.

It was a blow to equal the killing of the policeman. His head reeled. He walked away from the house, away, away as fast as he could. Pregnant! He had got her pregnant! Shame and horror filled him at his wickedness. What could he do? How could he get to her? She was going to have a baby, his baby. It couldn't be! He shook his head in disbelief, then knew it was all too true. Jesus Christ! Jesus Christ! He was a bastard, that's what he was, the sort that got a girl pregnant, that had his way with her, committed mortal sins and then got her pregnant. He thought of stories of local unmarried girls who'd got in the family way when he was at home. They'd vanish, packed off to England, he supposed, or to some convent where they took in that sort of woman.

He thought of the jokes, the snide remarks behind the backs of their families. She was always a good thing, a hot coort, the young fellas would say, a trollop, the older ones would call her. It's no surprise to me, they'd say, she got what was coming to her. And the man. Oh, 'twas so-and-so, they'd say. She threw herself at him, or That fella's no better than an animal. Yet they'd never turn their backs on him, the way they would on a girl, because anyway you could never be completely certain who was the father if he didn't own up and marry her. Girls should know that men can't help themselves, 'tis the way they're made. That's why girls have to be extra careful, not inflame them, never let them go too far.

He walked and walked until the rain came down again and he had to turn back. When he went into the house Crotty was sitting beside the fire, looking at him.

'Bad news?' he asked, without sympathy in his voice. Eddie just nodded noncommittally. 'Somebody dead?' Crotty went on.

'No,' said Eddie, 'no,' and went to sit in his grim bedroom.

*

'Have a gin,' said Vera. 'It'll give you a bit of spunk.'

'I can't tell them,' said Kay.

'Course you can. It won't be so bad, your ma and da are decent people. Now, swally that.'

She told them that night, after she came in. Her mother was doing some ironing, her father was reading the *Evening Mail*. She'd rehearsed it.

'I've something to tell yiz,' she said, 'some news.'

Her mother knew straight away. 'What?' she asked anxiously.

'I'm going to have a baby,' said Kay.

Her father put down the paper. 'What? You're what?' he said slowly.

'A baby.'

'Oh my God,' said her mother. 'Are you sure?'

'Yes, I was at the hospital.'

'Oh my God!' Her mother started to cry.

'And who's the father? Is it that bollocks? That country bollocks?' Her father's voice was starting to rise.

'Larry!' Her mother was trying to quieten him.

'Well, have you lost your tongue?'

'Larry, you'll wake the children.'

'I don't give a shite! Well, who's the father?'

'Yes, it's him, it's Eddie,' said Kay.

'Eddie! Eddie! Jaysus, I'll bate his fucking brains out.'

'Is he, is he going to marry you?' said her mother.

'I, I don't know.' She was crying now, too.

'Well, maybe you should think of asking him,' said her father with heavy sarcasm. 'Have you asked him?'

'I don't know where he is.' Her voice was almost a whisper.

'You don't know where he is, you don't know where he is. Great!' said her father. 'What do you mean, you don't know where he is?'

'He, he went down the country on a job.'

'Down the country, where down the country?'

'I don't know.'

'Has he written to you?' asked her mother.

'No.'

'How long is he gone?'

'About, about six or seven weeks.'

'Oh Jesus, he's done a bunk,' said her mother.

'He didn't know about it, about me, about the baby.'

'Huh!' said her father disbelievingly.

'He didn't, he didn't know a thing. He'd come back, he'd come back if he knew. I know he would.'

'Jaysus! That I'd live to see the day,' said her father. 'A daughter of mine carrying on the like of that.' He glared at her mother. 'I told you not to be always pushin' her into doin' that singin' and play-acting. The women in them theayters, they're all hoors!'

A heavy silence fell.

'How could you?' said her mother. 'How could you? We always brung you up carefully. There was never anything like that in this family.'

Kay said nothing; there was nothing to say.

'You realise you've ruined your life,' her mother went on.

'No decent man will look at you after this. You've ruined your family.'

Silence again.

'Could you not get in touch with him and tell him? Maybe he'd marry you. Maybe if you reached him he'd agree to do the right thing.'

'I wrote to him,' said Kay.

'And?'

'There's been no answer . . . so far anyway.'

'The no-good bastard,' said her mother, and because she never used bad language it sounded twice as bad. 'No, listen, could your father write to him? Maybe if your father had a word with him.'

'What good would that do?' said Kay.

It was too much for her father. He threw his paper on the ground and jumped up. 'You little tart!' he said, 'you bloody little . . . little tart.' He drew back his fist and rushed at her but tripped on the surround of the fire and, grabbing to save himself from falling, knocked his hand against the edge of the fireplace, bruising it.

'Oh Jaysus, it's broken,' he roared, sucking his skinned knuckles.

'Let me see it, Larry,' said his wife.

'I'm all right, let me alone.' He roared again at Kay. 'Get out, get out you! Get out of this house and don't come back. Get out, you bloody prostitute! Jaysus,' he said as an aside to his wife, 'what'll we say to the neighbours?' He noticed Kay was still there. 'Did you not hear me?' he shouted. 'Get out of this house before I bate the shite out of you!' He was crying now, too.

Kay turned and ran. As she passed through the little hall she was half aware of two of her younger sisters, awakened by the noise, standing gaping on the stairs in their nighties.

She ran into the street. Luckily, there was a bus passing, going through town on its way back to the garage for the night. She got off in O'Connell Street and made her way to Vera's flat, not knowing what she would do if her pal wasn't there. But, by the mercy of God, she was.

'He threw me out!' she said through her tears. 'Me da threw me out into the street.'

'You poor kid,' said Vera. 'Sure, you can stay here till things is sorted out.'

'I don't even have any clothes,' said Kay, realising it for the first time.

'Not to worry, you can borrow mine. Here, you can bed down on the sofa there.'

Vera's flat was actually one room. You washed in the sink and shared a lavatory one flight down with the rest of the house. The sofa was tiny and lumpy but by pulling up her knees Kay could just about lie down on it, with a couple of coats on top of her. She cried herself to sleep.

A couple of days passed. Then, one evening when she went to the theatre, there was a note for her at the stage door. It was from her mother, saying to come and collect her stuff from the house next morning, when her father would be out at work. Nothing more than that.

She went along. Her mother had the stuff in a suitcase.

'Ma,' she said.

'I don't want to talk about it,' said her mother.

'Ma, please.'

'If your father hears about you being here he'll kill me.'

'Ma, it wasn't my fault.'

'Don't say that, don't say that. It *was* your fault. No one made you get pregnant. He didn't force you, he didn't rape you, did he?' She had no reply. 'I was thinking we could go and talk to Sister Carmel. She'd know, she'd know places where you could go.'

'Oh Ma.'

'What else are you going to do? You know what I'm praying? I'm praying every morning and every night that you'll lose it. God forgive you, you've broken me heart.' She started to cry.

Kay took the bag and went out the front door. As she carried it down the path she saw Mary Mooney standing in her little front garden next door, looking at her. Their neighbour said nothing, just turned her back and went into her house. She knew.

Kay was in despair.

'Listen,' said Vera, 'you're not the first girl got in trouble and you won't be the last.'

'I won't go to them nuns,' said Kay, 'I won't. Cold bitches. They lock you up there with street women and the like, doing laundry and praying, morning, noon and night, to make up for your sins. Some of them is there for years. I seen them, looking out the gate of the Magdalene house. Half cracked, some of them, dribbling and giggling daft ones.' Despite herself she started to laugh. 'Could you imagine me there? I'm not going.'

'There is another way,' said Vera.

'What other way?'

'You could get rid of it.'

'What?'

'There's people that'll arrange it.'

'I couldn't.'

'It needn't be that bad. All you need is some money.'

'No, I couldn't! Anyway, where would I get money?'

'You could borrow it.'

'Where?'

'There's places. Money lenders.'

'I couldn't. It's murder, you could be hanged for that. I wouldn't kill my own child.'

'Please yourself.'

'I couldn't do that.'

'What'll you do then?'

'Eddie will come back.'

Vera just looked at her disbelievingly.

'You'll see, he'll come back.'

'He will, when the moon turns blue,' said Vera.

Next day Vera said to her: 'Now don't get cross. I had a word with someone about, about you. He says he might be able to help.'

'Help, how?'

'To get rid of it.'

'I can't, I told you I won't do that. No!'

'Well, if you change your mind, this person can help. No one need ever know. You can tell your ma and da you lost the baby.'

For three days she held out. She even went to confession and, trembling, told her story, though she said nothing about what Vera had said. The priest was compassionate. Was it with a married man? No. God saw everything and forgave everything to those who came to Him, he told her. Go forth and sin no more, he told her and he would pray for her and for the young man that he would see the error of his ways and marry her. But what would she do, where could she go?

Go to the nuns, he had said. They would take care of everything, if the young man could not be found or would not do his duty. They would arrange for the baby to be adopted into a good Catholic family. She would spend some time with them, making reparation for her sin, then they would find her a job, probably, maybe working for some good family.

A maid in some house! Her!

She didn't know which way to turn. That night during the show one of the Coliseum Girls said to her: 'I'm sorry for your trouble, love,' as if someone in her family had died. 'What are you talking about?' she replied, but, obviously, the whole place knew about it. Tommy and May Flynn were very cold with her. Everyone knew they were very holy. She might have known Vera wouldn't keep her mouth shut.

After the show she said to her friend; 'Who's the person that said they could arrange you-know-what?'

'Are you going to give it a go?' asked Vera.

'I don't know.'

'Why not talk to him anyways. What's the harm in that?'

'Who is it?'

'Dickie Delaney.'

'Oh Jaysus!'

'Now don't get on your high horse. He's been very decent about it.'

'Dickie? Decent?'

'Yes he has. Says to come and talk to him, that he might be able to put you in touch with someone. And when I mentioned about the money, he said he was sure he could fix something up for you.'

That night, after the show, she knocked on the door of the number one dressing room. Dickie had his name on it, with a glittery star Frankie Fox said he'd stolen off a tree at Christmas. He was seated in front of the mirror, taking off his make-up. He wore trousers and a vest and he smelt of sweat.

'Well,' he said with his little laugh, 'I hear you're in the pudding club, ha, ha, ha,' and he patted her stomach slowly. Tears formed in her eyes. He put his arm round her shoulders. She hated the way he did it.

'Don't worry, darling,' he said, 'I wish I'd a quid for every girl I've seen has got a little bun in the oven. Any sign of the daddy?'

She shook her head.

'Fucker!' said Dickie. 'I never knew what you seen in him. Country gobshite up to his ears in the IRA.'

'What?'

'Did you not know? Oh yeah, I had him spotted from the word go as one of the laddos. "A Nation Once Again" and they think they can do what they like. Oh yeah, I know the type. I'm surprised you didn't twig.'

Her head was spinning. She couldn't take in this new information.

'So you want to get rid of it, is that it?'

'I, I'm not sure.'

'Not sure? What are you coming here to me for then? Not sure! Do you realise the risks I'd be taking helping you? A man in my position. I could end up in jail for aiding and abetting an abortion, and me not even the father!'

'I'm sorry.'

'Listen, don't be blubbing. It's all right, it's okay,' and again he squeezed her shoulder. 'Here, I've a little present for you.'

He took a bunch of keys off the dressing table, went over to a cupboard in the wall and opened it. Kay got a glimpse of packets of stuff, cigarettes and chocolate. From a box he took out a pair of stockings.

'These are for you,' he said. 'American nylons, best quality. A friend of mine in the North gets them for me. You couldn't get these anywhere down here, know what I mean?' He winked. 'Oh, they'll be lovely on you, very sheer,' and this time he ran his hand down her thigh. 'You have lovely legs, you should only wear the best.'

Kay stepped back. 'The operation,' she said. 'Who'd be doing it?'

'A woman I know, a nurse, very experienced. Oh, you'll be in good hands there. Some of the ones that does it is only butchers, but you'll be safe there. Of course this is private, it has to go no further than this room. This'll be our little secret, do you understand that clearly?'

'Yes. How . . . how much would it be?'

'Don't you worry about that. I'll make you a little loan. We'll stop a bit out of your wages every week. No, no,' he said, holding up his hands magnanimously, 'don't thank me, I wouldn't like to see a lovely little piece like yourself in trouble.'

'You're, you're very good,' she said haltingly, though she didn't think so really.

He smiled at her. 'And you'll be good to me too, won't you, darling?' he said. 'I always thought you were a smasher, right from the time I brung you in to the show. I watch you from the side sometimes, you didn't know that, did you? I like you, I like the way you move, know what I mean, ha ha.'

'I've got to go,' said Kay.

'Don't go.' He put on an American accent: 'Listen, kid, you and me could be an item.'

Kay pulled herself free. 'I've got to go,' she stammered. 'I, I think I'm going to be sick.'

Dickie shrugged. 'Please yourself,' he said. He went over to the mirror and started to sleek down his hair with two silver-backed brushes. He looked worried. Was that a bald patch starting to develop?

*

Eddie was going back to Dublin. It took him two days to decide. First of all he had asked Crotty to post a letter for him to Kay, but again he was refused. He considered going into the nearest town and doing it himself, but then he thought of being spotted. Anyway, what good would a letter be, even if it got through to her? No, he'd make his way back to the city, find her and they could get married, quietly. They'd go to some priest who'd do it after early mass some morning. Surely they'd find one willing to help out, she being pregnant and all that. Then he'd go on the run again, vanish down the country somewhere.

It would be hard for her, but at least the child would have a father, at least she'd know that he still loved her and would do anything for her. If he could lie low for long enough the heat would be off and, if they didn't know who'd shot O'Grady, he might be able to get back to town permanently, join her and, maybe, get some sort of job. Then, as soon as the war was over, they'd be off to America and a new life.

In the dark of the night, though, as he lay awake on his hard bed, the truth of his predicament came over him like a cold cloud. His mind was churning, he was confused again. He'd lost his head after the shooting, he'd almost certainly been identified, and they would be on the lookout for him. Still, they'd no way of knowing about Miss Keating's, had they? He'd go there and hole up for a few days. She'd never turn away a fellow-republican, would she? Just long enough to see Kay and arrange to wed her. Kay! He couldn't abandon Kay.

*

The night after her encounter with Dickie, Kay was still in bits. Here eyes were swollen from crying and she could hardly get the words of her song out. The audience listened to it in silence and, at the end, someone blew a raspberry to general laughter. No one in the company even mentioned it.

On her way out of the theatre Frankie Fox was waiting for her. 'Listen, kid, come here,' he said and pulled her into number four dressing room again. He seemed to have shrunk even further and his breathing was laboured.

'Vera told me,' he said.

'Told you what?'

'About your parents kicking you out.'

'What business is that of hers, telling everyone about me,' said Kay, with a spark of anger.

'It's all right, it's all right, I won't tell anyone. It'll be all right. It'll be okay when he gets your letter.'

'There's been nothing, has there? No reply at all.'

'Well, not so far,' said Frankie. 'But, sure, you know how it is. Give it a bit more time. He'll answer, I know he will. He's a decent young fella.'

'He's given me up, that's what he's done. He's done a bunk.'

'No, no, not at all.'

'He has, he has!'

'Don't cry, Kay, don't cry, darlin'.'

'What am I going to do?'

'Shh, don't cry.'

'I wish I was dead.'

'There, there, I'll take care of you.'

'Oh Frankie!'

He put his arms around her and she clung to him. He didn't come much above her shoulder. His hair was lank and greasy. He smelt of stale tobacco and something worse, a sour, metallic kind of odour off his breath.

'I'm going crazy, so I am,' she sobbed.

'There, there, don't worry. I'll mind you, I'll see you're all right. Don't cry, me darlin'.'

He felt her body against his and smelt a sweet perfume from her neck. Suddenly he was trying to kiss her, standing on his toes, ridiculously trying to reach her face.

'Kay! Kay, I love you. I'll mind you. I've loved you for ages, you must know that. I'll take care of you, I'm mad about you, darlin'.'

He tried to cling more closely to her, but she wrestled him away in a frenzy.

'No! Get away from me!' she screamed. 'Get away from me, you dirty little bastard. You're filthy, you dirty old . . . old pig! Youse are all the same, get away!'

'Kay, I didn't mean to . . .' But she had run out the door, slamming it after her.

'Oh God, oh God, oh God!' he said to himself in misery and shame. His stomach started to stab at him violently. He wrapped his arms round himself and sank down on the bare boards, groaning. By the time he got home he could hardly stand.

Dolan was in the hall when he got back to the digs. 'Are you all right?' he asked.

'A bit under the weather,' he gasped, whey-faced.

'Do you want a doctor?'

'No, I'll, I'll go in the morning.'

He half dragged himself up the stairs, while Dolan looked worried. In his room he sat on the bed, sweating from the pain. Cold and clammy, he struggled out of his jacket, cramming a handful of his tablets into his mouth. They stuck in his throat, making him cough, which racked him with fresh pains, but he was unable to leave the room and go to the bathroom for a mouthful of water. It was as if there was a leaden ball in his stomach and nothing could move it. With an enormous effort he managed to get his shoes off and, barely managing to pull the blankets over himself, fell into the bed.

One by one the lights went out as the lodgers in Miss Keating's went to bed. The house became silent, except for the creak of old timbers, the drip of a tap or the faint rattle of a pane of glass stirred by the wind. A flurry of rain whispered against the windows, a tree in the garden crackled its bare branches. In his sleep someone mumbled an incoherent sentence, but not loud enough to wake the sleepers. Only Frankie seemed to be awake, cocooned in a web of pain, groaning quietly to himself.

He was not the only one who could not or would not sleep. Someone was listening, someone was alert.

Finally, Frankie fell into a troubled slumber. His dreams were extraordinarily vivid. He was in a theatre, but it was not the Coliseum. He was in the wings with Dickie Delaney, who was threatening him in some way and for some reason he could not understand. Stepping onto the stage, he looked out and found to his surprise that there was only a sprinkling of people there.

He saw his father and mother, his mother, tear-stained, defeated as always, his father sullen. Others were there, too, brothers and sisters and old neighbours. But they were not a welcoming audience. They seemed abstracted, taken up with something other than the show.

Then he saw Mags. She was smiling at him, beckoning him to join her. He tried to get down off the stage to where she was sitting, but there was a huge orchestra pit, black and empty, like an abyss between them. He tried to climb across, but it was too wide, too deep. Dickie Delaney was laughing at him from the wings. Then, somehow, he had got into the stalls and was running through the rows of empty seats towards her. But she was gone! He felt fear, depression. Now he was out in a lane, like the one at the back of the Coliseum. He ran towards where it joined the street, still looking for Mags, but his father was there, drunk and dangerous. His father was taking off his belt, the way he used to when he'd give Frankie a hiding . . .

He woke with a start and immediately the pain hit him agonisingly. Oh Jesus! His scream was half stifled, high-pitched, terrified. Help, he must get help! Somehow, he pushed aside the bedclothes and got out onto the floor. He felt an intense heat inside him, then a gush of liquid, as if a hot-water bottle had burst within his stomach. He took a couple of steps. The room swam around him and he pitched forward face down.

Two storeys downstairs in her bed, Miss Keating faintly heard the thump as he fell and instantly raised her black head, listening. What was it? Normally she would have got up immediately and gone to investigate, but tonight she was not alone. Beside her on the pillow was another, bald head. If she got up, if there was a disturbance, if others awoke, her bedfellow might be discovered and that was not to be contemplated. Better wait till the night had advanced a bit more and then get him out. Her companion slept soundly, breathing evenly as she waited, grimly, in the dark.

The house was silent. But could that be the softest of footsteps she heard? No . . . or was it? She strained her ears, but she could not be sure. Interminably, the hours passed by until the first, very faint glimmerings of day started to creep through the window.

A lone bird, early riser, began to chirrup. Miss Keating drove a sharp elbow into the ribs of her companion, who was snoring lightly.

'Wake up!' she hissed. He groaned. 'Wake up, wake up.'

'What time is it?' asked Byrne the butcher.

'Shhh! Be quiet!' she said. 'Get out, get out of the house!'

'Jaysus, it's still the middle of the night,' he said.

'Will you be quiet? Get out, get the hell out of here,' and using her feet, she started to push him onto the floor.

'All right, all right!' He started to pull on his clothes. Donning a dressing gown, she went cautiously to the door and the pair of them tiptoed down the stairs to the hall. Quietly, she eased open the door and he went out, still pulling his clothes around him to keep out the early chill.

'See you again soon, Nora,' he said.

'Quiet!' she whispered, closing the hall door gently in his face.

She listened. It was the deadest of hours, when the dawn had not yet taken hold and all the world seemed to be still. Up the stairs she crept again, her eyes getting accustomed to the dark by now, past her own room and up again to where Frankie slept in a little attic at the very top of the house. His door was slightly open.

Not bothering to knock, she put her head in. At first she could see nothing, but then she noticed the bulky shape on the floor. Frankie lay where he had fallen, his head to one side, his mouth open and his eyes staring into nothingness.

Silently she knelt beside him, put her ear to his chest, felt his wrist and then his neck for a pulse. There was no question. He was dead.

Again she listened, long and carefully. There was nothing, this time she was sure of it. Carefully she started to search the room. She looked under the mattress, where she had first discovered Frankie's savings – nothing. There was a chest of drawers with a few clothes in it, some old newspapers containing notices of shows which he had been in. Nothing. She went through the dead man's pockets. A few coins, old bus tickets, a wallet with a ten shilling note and an old photograph, scuffed and torn, of some woman. But still nothing. She became angry, she lost her caution, she turned on the dim electric light with no shade that hung from the ceiling and searched the room again. She looked under the bed, but still there was nothing. Rage filled her. Where the hell was the money, what had he done with it, had someone got there before her? She started to pull the bedclothes apart and it was then that she heard Dolan and Corrigan on the stairs. She composed herself.

They came into the room, wearing their overcoats over their pyjamas.

'Is something wrong?' asked Dolan. She nodded her head towards the body on the floor.

'Is he . . .?' asked Corrigan.

'Dead,' said Miss Keating.

'Oh God,' said Corrigan. 'We'd better get a priest.'

'Yes, and a doctor.'

'I heard a noise, it woke me up,' said Miss Keating. 'When I came up I found him there.'

Corrigan knelt down and started to mutter an act of contrition into Frankie's ear: 'O my God I am heartily sorry for having offended Thee and I detest my sins above every other evil . . .'

'Better put him up on the bed,' said Miss Keating.

'No,' said Dolan, 'better leave him there till the police come.'

'The police? But there's no question of violence or anything.'

'No, you could see how sick he was. Still, they need to come when there's been a sudden death.'

Corrigan got to his feet, blessing himself carefully as he did so. 'I'll go down to the church if you go to the police station,' he said to Dolan.

They left the room. Frankie stared on. No one had thought to close his eyes.

On their way out, after dressing themselves, they met Nellie in the hall and told her. She broke into loud lamentations, snuffling and wiping her nose with the back of her hand.

The police came, with a doctor and a priest. It was the local sergeant and there were no questions asked apart from the obvious ones about Frankie. No mention of Eddie, nothing of a dangerous nature.

Miss Keating was relieved, but still resentful about the money. After they had gone she called Nellie, who was still in tears.

'Stop snivelling,' she told the girl. 'Now, have you something to tell me?'

'Wha'?' said Nellie in her stupid way.

'Where is it?'

'Wha'?'

Miss Keating was getting more and more irritated. 'The money, the money, you stupid girl!'

'What money, ma'am?'

'Mr Fox's money. He told me he kept money in his room and it's gone.'

'I know nothing about no money, ma'am.'

'You took it! Do you think you can fool me? You took it.'

'No, ma'am. I swear.'

'Where is it? Is it in your room?' She took Nellie by the shoulders and started to shake her.

Nellie was crying again: 'No, ma'am, no!'

Miss Keating took her by the wrist and half dragged her down the stairs, down to the basement where Nellie had her small, dark room. Furious by now, Miss Keating pulled out Nellie's pitiful possessions, throwing her few grubby clothes on the floor, tearing a pocket of her thin overcoat as she rammed her hand into it, ripping apart an old women's magazine. Nellie bawled lustily. In a frenzy Miss Keating tore the bed clothes off and then hurled the mattress onto the floor.

'I'll get the police, I'll have you jailed!'

'Aw Jaysus, ma'am,' said the terrified girl.

'You can take your things and get out of this house,' she screeched.

Miss Keating was utterly baffled. Nellie could not have taken the money; she would surely have broken down and admitted it if she had. There was no question of calling the police about it. She was lucky enough that they didn't seem to know anything about her providing a safe house for the gunman. Better draw no more attention on herself. She probably couldn't even get rid of Nellie in case she'd blab. Maybe Fox had taken his money away, maybe put it in a bank. But what about the noise she thought she had heard earlier? Had she imagined it?

In her rage and frustration she turned again on Nellie.

'You stupid, stupid little bitch,' she shouted, and hit her hard across the face.

12

There had been a pump clipped onto McCaigue's bike and a puncture repair kit in a small bag on the back of the saddle. To keep himself busy Eddie had mended the tyre one day, taking out the inner tube, pumping it up and finding where the puncture was by placing it in a basin of water and observing where the bubbles came out. Then he had patched it and, finally, polished up the machine with an oily cloth. That night, when Crotty was asleep, he crept downstairs and went to the shed where the bicycle was. The farmer's old sheepdog growled at him, but he knew him by this stage and went silent when Eddie told him to shush now.

Taking out the bike, he walked half a mile down the road, then mounted and was away. With any luck, he'd have fifteen miles behind him before Crotty woke up and was able to pass on word of his having gone. It was a bright night and, though winter still gripped the countryside, there was almost a warmth in the breeze, a hint of spring perhaps, or just one of those soft, mild spells that come for a time in Ireland at an unexpected part of the year.

He cycled on energetically, even with zest, his spirits high. To be away from the gloomy, squalid farm was in itself enough to cheer him, but it was also as if the dangers ahead were almost to be welcomed. The interminable waiting was over and, one way or another, things would be resolved. He felt light-headed, optimistic, fooling himself that fate was on his side. He was less careful than when he had fled from Dublin, continuing to cycle long after daybreak.

In one of the towns through which he passed there was a fair in progress. Crowds of farmers stood around in the dung-deep street with herds of cattle, which they kept in place with sticks, occasionally haggling among themselves over the price of a beast. He hesitated for a moment when he saw a guard, but the policeman was deep in conversation with someone and paid no attention to Eddie.

He went into a public house, jammed with men drinking pints of stout. Nobody paid any attention to him. He enjoyed standing there, drinking the black beer and listening to the talk of crops and prices and farming matters, which he was so used to at home. Afterwards he went into a shop, where he bought himself some bread and a bottle of lemonade, and ate hungrily behind a wall outside the town.

As the afternoon came he felt tired and found an old shed in a field, away from any house. Here he sat down on some straw, propping himself up against the wall, and tried to rest. The place was draughty and damp and uncomfortable and he found it almost impossible to sleep. After a while he did manage a fitful nap, but his mind was full of Kay and the wrong he had done her, mingled again with mental pictures of the dying policeman, his flight from the scene of the shooting and his first, nightmarish cycle through the night away from Dublin.

When he awoke he was shivering and stiff, but the daylight was nearly gone. Stamping and banging his hands against his sides, he got some circulation going, then, mounting his bicycle again, he set off, pedalling hard in an effort to warm himself. He had no light, of course, and coming round a corner found himself nearly forced into the ditch by a lorry piled high with turf that seemed to come from nowhere. Then he was through Naas, cycling up the main street, with lights glowing dimly in the windows. In some houses the curtains had not been drawn and he got brief glimpses of armchairs, sofas, glowing fires and, in one place, a table set for tea. The rooms looked cheerful, warm and spoke of a settled, comfortable world of which he was no longer a part. But he was on the last leg of his journey. He was tired now, but still forced himself to push on and on. A light drizzle started to fall, the sort that almost imperceptibly wets you through, but still he continued, hoping that he would be in time to catch Kay when she left the theatre. Drenched, he drove himself, almost in a frenzy till he reached the city.

*

Kay sat alone at the mirror in her dressing room. She hated the theatre now, but even more she hated going back to the cold comfort of Vera's flat. Vera had a date with some fella, which meant she wouldn't be back till late, if she came back at all. At least that was better than when she brought guys back to the flat, usually with a brown paper parcel containing bottles of stout or sometimes whiskey. They'd be there for hours, half pissed, screeching and laughing at stupid dirty jokes and cuddling up to each other, till she felt her head would burst. Then the noise would get too much and there'd be bangs on the walls or on the ceiling from people being kept awake in the other rooms.

One night a fella had even got into the bed with Vera and she could hear them at it, while she lay on her little sofa with a coat over her head. At least Vera had had the grace to be sorry about that and hadn't let it happen again, though another night a guy had brought a pal, who started getting fresh with Kay and had kicked up blue bloody murder when they told him to go.

Frankie's death had been another blow, just one more in the succession of them that seemed to be raining down on her all the time. Normally it might have saddened her briefly and then she'd have been over it, but now she felt guilty about her last meeting with him. Sure, he'd tried it on with her, but so what? Men, they'd only one thing in their minds ever, as she knew all too well by now. But he had always been nice to her. He had tried to get her letter to Eddie, even if it looked as if he hadn't succeeded, and hadn't he offered to help her that last night they had met? He'd meant it too, you could sense that, it wasn't just that he wanted to have her, like Dickie Delaney.

You couldn't but feel sorry, too, when you thought about the poor little divil, sick and dying and nobody to care about him. She could guess how he had felt. He had been buried in a bleak graveyard, a place with no grass or trees, just bare earth and row after row of gravestones. The little crowd was mainly made up of people from The Business, who looked shabby and faintly grotesque away from their world of lights and costumes and make-up. Bing Kelly was there, wearing an overcoat with an astrakhan collar that had seen better days. The Coliseum Girls all seemed to be wearing too much make-up and shivered in their thin coats. There were some pros from other theatres, too, and a few circus people, a dwarf and a couple dressed in fringed buckskin jackets, boots and cowboy hats. Kay had stood by the grave, shaking with cold, a bit apart from the others, and thought that death maybe wasn't so bad.

Frankie hadn't got a bean when he died. They'd had to get up a whipround in the theatre to bury him; otherwise it would have meant a pauper's grave. Dickie Delaney had given a couple of quid, big deal, and him only rolling in money, as Vera said. There had been short bits in the evening papers about Frankie – 'Death of noted Dublin comedian' – very little really. 'The sudden death has taken place of the comedian Mr Francis (Frankie) Fox at his home. Mr Fox worked in many Dublin theatres, in pantomime and variety, but in recent years was mainly to be seen as a support for Dickie Delaney at the Coliseum, where he was currently appearing in *Winter Wonderland*. He was widely known for his catchphrase, "Where is my hat?"'

Next day a tribute to Frankie, written by Dickie Delaney, appeared in the *Evening Mail*. There was more about Dickie in it than about Frankie, though you would think to read it that they had been like brothers. A heartbroken Dickie described how he had given a grateful Frankie his big chance, nurtured him through many shows and, he subtly hinted, put up with him when thousands wouldn't. He ended with a little rhyme:

> Goodbye, old pal, the lights are dimmed,
> No more we'll act and chat,
> We'll meet again in heaven above,
> Where you have found your hat.

The bollocks hadn't even turned up for Frankie's funeral.

Kay combed her hair listlessly and looked at herself. Was she starting to show? It was only a question of time. She'd wait a bit longer in the dressing room, she thought, to make sure everyone was gone. She never went to Curran's now for a drink after the show. The one night she'd gone there recently she'd felt everyone was talking about her behind her back and, anyway, she'd been sick afterwards.

The theatre seemed to be quiet, everyone was gone now except the doorman, Jemmy Johnson. She could hear him going round the place, with his game leg click-clacking on the stone floors, checking to see that the place was empty and turning off lights. Pulling on her coat, she took a final look at herself in profile in the mirror. Was that a little bump on her tummy? She sighed.

'Good night, Jemmy,' she said as she met him on the stairs.

'Night, Kay, safe home.'

Outside there was a lane that ran along the back of the theatre, dark except for a dim light over the stage door. The rain still came down in a soft drizzle. A bicycle was propped against the wall of a building and a figure stood in a doorway.

'Kay.' At first she didn't hear.

Louder. 'Kay.'

It was Eddie, soaked through, his hair plastered down on his forehead, little rivulets running down the side of his ears.

'Oh sweet Jesus, Eddie!' she cried and ran towards him.

They fell into each other's arms, unheeding of the rain, unheeding of anything but each other. Their words were incoherent, broken. He kissed her again and again, holding her face in his hands.

'I'm so sorry, I'm so sorry, I love you,' he repeated it over and over again.

'It doesn't matter, you're back, you're back,' she said. 'That's all that counts, love, you're back.'

'I never knew, till I got your letter. Did you tell your father and mother?'

'They threw me out, they threw me out on the street. I'm staying with Vera.'

'Oh Jaysus, I'm so sorry.'

'It doesn't matter, you're here now.'

'I'll marry you,' he said. 'I'll fix it. We'll get married as soon as we can.'

'Yes, yes.'

He paused for the first time. 'I have to tell you something, something else . . . Something terrible.'

'What? What's wrong?'

'You know I'm, I'm involved in . . .'

'Yes. They say you're in the IRA?'

'Yes.'

'I don't mind, I knew.'

'It's not just that.' Again he paused and she felt fearful. 'You know that policeman?'

'What policeman?'

'The one that was shot dead, at the New Year?'

'No . . . yes, I think I remember something . . . Oh no, Eddie, Eddie, you didn't . . .?'

'Yes, I didn't mean to. Well, I did, but, if I'd known I'd never have, I, we, we'd never have killed him. I didn't do it. My shot didn't kill him. I don't think I even hit him. Honest.'

'Oh my God. Are you on the run?'

'Yes, I'm sorry. I had to hide outside of Dublin, I'm sorry. They wouldn't let me write. I came back when I got your letter. I don't know if the police twigged on 'twas me. But listen, I'll marry you. We'll get married quietly. Then I'll have to hide away again. If they find me . . .'

'If they find you. Oh!' She gave a cry of pain, her head swam at the thought, she felt sick, she stumbled and he had to catch her.

At that moment the policeman's torch caught them in its beam. All he could see was a pair of dim figures, maybe struggling, one of them a woman who seemed to be falling.

'Hey!' he shouted and started to run towards them.

'I'll see you, I'll see you soon, tomorrow,' said Eddie to Kay. He ran towards his bicycle, jumped onto it and was away, standing on the pedals in his haste, before the policeman was within fifteen yards of them.

'Eddie!' she cried after him, but he was gone.

'Are you all right, miss?' asked the policeman. 'Was he attacking you?'

'No, of course he wasn't,' she said furiously. 'Don't be so thick!'

The policeman looked at her as if he doubted she was telling the truth.

*

Out in the house which Conor thought was haunted, another policeman, one of the detectives who had been assigned to watch Miss Keating's house, pulled his overcoat round him and fought the drowsiness which, despite the cold, threatened to overcome him. Feeling in his pocket for a cigarette, he discovered that he had left the packet at home. He was a heavy smoker and the thought of the whole night stretching in front of him without one made the longing almost unbearable.

The more time went on the worse he felt, and he found himself gazing at his watch. Half an hour to closing time. If he nipped out quickly to the pub just down the road he might, just might, if he was lucky, be able to get himself a few fags and be back within ten minutes. But supposing something happened and he wasn't at his post? He'd be rightly in the manure business then. But sure there hadn't been sight nor sound of anything for weeks and it was late now. He'd be back before anyone would know he was gone. Duty fought with addiction and, as usual, addiction won. He went down the ruined stairs of the abandoned house and let himself out the back way.

His luck was out, as he was to think ruefully later. He had hardly left the room when Eddie came cycling down the street, his cap pulled down in an effort to hide his face. There was nobody about because of the rain. He went in the gate of Miss Keating's and down the steps to the basement door, carrying his bicycle with him.

In the kitchen, Nellie sat half-heartedly rubbing a pot and singing through her teeth without sense or tune. To her relief, Miss Keating had said no more about throwing her out, but the prospect of it still hung over her. She didn't know why they had happened, but she remembered the blow and the threats vividly. At the knock on the door she became instantly alarmed, for she had a colourful imagination. The world, for her, was peopled with thieves, murderers and rapists, all out to have their way with her. She read newspaper reports of crimes avidly, if with difficulty, shocked to the core at the dangers of life, and when she went to the pictures she screamed at the top of her lungs if anything of a horrific or even unexpected nature took place.

The knock was repeated.

'Who is it?' she asked tremulously.

''Tis me, Eddie.'

'Hah?'

'Eddie O'Sullivan. Let me in, Nellie.'

She unlocked the door. 'Jayz, you put the heart crossways in me, Mr Eddie,' she said. 'Listen, you can't bring that bike in here. The mistress says bikes is not to be brung in the house.'

''Tis all right,' said Eddie, 'I'll just leave it here, inside the door.'

'But the missus . . .'

''Tis okay. I'll sort it out with Miss Keating.'

She looked at him questioningly. 'You're wringin'.'

'I'll be fine.'

'You've been away. Frankie said you'd gone for good.'

'Not at all.'

'He's dead.'

'What? Who?'

'Frankie Fox, he's dead.'

'What? What happened?'

'He died,' said Nellie, as if this was explanation enough. 'The missus found him in his room and him dead. Oh Jaysus, Mr Eddie, if you seen him, all white and . . . and white. I was in mortal terror after lookin' at him.'

'When did this happen?' asked Eddie.

'Last . . .' She made a big effort to think. 'Last Tuesday I think it was.'

'Did the police come here?'

'They did. And I never took it. Word of God I never took one thing.'

Eddie hadn't an idea what she was talking about, but it was often thus with Nellie. 'What did the police say?' he asked.

'Wha'?'

'Did the police say anything about, about anything else?'

225

'They never said about anything being taken. I don't think there was anything taken.'

'Did they say anything about me?'

'Who?'

'The police.'

She thought. 'No, nothin', why would they? There's no tay,' she went on.

'It doesn't matter. Listen, is there anyone in my old room?'

'Hah?'

'Is there anyone new staying in the house? Is there anybody in my old room? Sleeping there?'

She considered the question at length. 'There's no one there,' she said after an age.

'Good, I'll just go up there so for the night. No need to disturb anybody, 'tis late.'

At this point Miss Keating, who had heard their voices from upstairs, came down.

'You!' she hissed. 'What are you doing here?'

'I had to come,' said Eddie.

'Get out, get out,' she said. 'I told you not to come back here.'

'I had to, I had to. Just let me stay here, just for a few nights.'

'No! It's out of the question. I told you when . . .' She stopped dead and glared at Nellie who was standing, mouth hanging open, like a spectator at a tennis match, her head turning from one to the other.

'What do you think you're doing?' she asked. 'Get out!'

'But, ma'am . . .' The tiniest flicker of disagreement for once registered faintly.

'Out, out, out!' said Miss Keating in a voice that brooked no more discussion, and the girl slunk away to her room. 'And you too,' she added to Eddie.

'I've nowhere else to go.'

'Well, you should have thought of that before you came back to Dublin. You can't stay here. Fox died, the police were round.'

'Nellie told me. She said they said nothing about me.'

'It doesn't matter. You can't stay here, it's too risky.'

'If I have to go out on the streets, it'll be even more risky. Supposing I'm picked up?'

'That's your hard luck.'

'You'd be implicated.'

Miss Keating's cheeks went pick with rage. 'Are you threatening me?'

'No,' said Eddie. 'All I'm asking is one night. I'll be gone tomorrow, I swear it.'

She hesitated. 'I'll report you to your superiors in the Movement,' she said. 'They know who I am. They listen to me, always!' But he could see she was weakening. She knew there was something in what he said. He'd be better off the streets. If he was picked up God knows what they might force out of him about where he'd been hiding.

'All right,' she said, 'but you'll be out of here tomorrow.'

'God bless you.'

'You can go to your old room. Don't let anyone see you and don't move out of it till I tell you.'

The room was cold, dusty and stuffy at the same time. No one had been in it since he left. Eddie took off his wet trench coat and, finding nothing else to do it with, dried his face and hair on the thin curtains. It was an unwelcoming place but, compared to what he had had to put up with in the past few weeks, at least dry and sheltered. He took off his shoes, hung his wet trousers on the end of the bed and wrapped the pink counterpane round his shoulders. Blessing himself, he knelt down, begged God for forgiveness for his many sins and got between the cold sheets. He thought of Kay and how he would see her the next day. He thought of kissing her and touching her and found himself sexually aroused, which made him feel ashamed of himself. He asked God some way, somehow, to help him and Kay and to deliver them both. Then, exhausted, he fell into an uneasy sleep even as he prayed.

On the floor below, Corrigan had heard the footsteps in the room above him, just as he had heard the voices of Eddie and Miss Keating as he was making his way upstairs to bed. Lying there, he strained his ears but was unable to make out anything, for the usual rhythmic and lusty snoring of Dolan across the room drowned out all other sounds.

When he was certain that the house was still, he got up and took his clothes, which were as always folded with meticulous neatness on a chair beside the bed, and brought them up to the lavatory. There, in the dark, he dressed carefully, socks, underclothes, trousers, shirt and pullover, not forgetting a carefully knotted tie. Then, very quietly, he made his way downstairs, carrying his shoes in his hands. He decided that if he was seen he would plead illness, insomnia, a sudden overpowering need for fresh air, anything in fact. Then he would return to bed and forget his mission. He couldn't be expected to do more than that, he thought; if the word ever got round that he had informed it would be more than his life was worth.

But nobody challenged him. Very carefully he eased open the front door, slid out and made his way down the street. The watching detective, who had returned with two precious Woodbines, bought from a barman for an inordinate sum of money, saw him go, recognised him and wondered. Corrigan walked to the nearest phone kiosk, put in tuppence and called the number the police had given him.

Next door Kitty heard the front door of the neighbouring house close as Corrigan came back, but hardly noticed the sound as she lay in her bed.

*

They came just before the dawn and it was Eddie who heard them first. His sleep had been uneasy and across it he became aware of the crash as they tried to break in the door. It was the smaller one into the basement they were at; the bigger, heavy hall door would take too long to burst open.

In an instant he was awake, pulled on his trousers and was running downstairs, not even pausing to put on his shoes. The thump of burly bodies against the basement door and the sound of it being kicked was wakening the house now, for it was proving to be a stouter obstacle than the police had expected. Taking the stairs three at a time, he hurled himself downwards. Miss Keating, ghastly in her curlers and face cream, came out of her room and he collided with her, his shoulder sending her hurtling back into the landing wall. He reached the hall as the basement door below gave way. Big men burst into the kitchen and started to run for the flight of stairs up to the hall. Nellie, coming out of her room, started to scream and scream, long-drawn howls like an animal in pain. In their room, Dolan jumped up and ran to see what was happening, but Corrigan crouched back, the sheets pulled up to his chin.

Eddie ran down the hall towards the back of the house and flung himself out the back door into the garden at the rear. If he could get over the wall at the end, he thought, there was a lane and he might still be able to get away. But he wasn't a couple of paces down the garden when he saw figures running towards him – the police had sealed off the back, too. Still he charged on, like a trapped rat which can see no way out but attack, straight at the first man. Someone fired a shot in the air, as he hurled himself at the figure, still dim in the early morning light. But he was stopped in his tracks by a huge blow that broke his nose. It was Callinan, O'Shea's assistant, a strong man among strong men, who had struck him. Then the other two were on him and he was hurled to the ground, where they started to kick him vigorously.

'Get up, get up, you bastard!' shouted Callinan, his boot thumping into Eddie's ribs. Another kick struck him on the side of the head, dazing him. A man knelt on his back, pushing his face into the earth and twisting one of his arms back.

'All right, all right, that's enough!' It was O'Shea, running from the house with several more detectives, some of them carrying revolvers.

'Edward O'Sullivan, I arrest you for the murder of Detective Sergeant Paul O'Grady on January the third last.' Eddie was stunned, trying to focus his eyes. Blood poured from his swollen nose, mingling with the dirt on his face, where he had been pushed into the flower bed. His clothes were torn and his bare feet were turning blue with the cold.

'Yes, and anything you say may be used in evidence against you, you bastard,' added Callinan, still blowing hard from the fight. Another detective produced a pair of handcuffs, put one roughly on Eddie's wrist and the other on his own. Eddie was in a daze, he could think of nothing, focus on nothing. His nose was aching as if it would burst, but otherwise he seemed to have no feelings. He had no idea of what to do or say, or what might be going to happen to him next.

Callinan punched the air with his fist. 'We've got him, we've got the bugger!' he said with fierce joy and the others grinned happily. They congratulated themselves. It was a job well done, the result of fine police work. Afterwards, when they talked among themselves about the case, they would make little of the role of luck in their capture – how the gun had turned up – or of the foolishness of Eddie in returning to the place from which he had set out for the shooting. They had watched and waited once they got the breakthrough. They had never been seen, never lost their nerve, even when the comedian fella had died suddenly there and some said they should have raided the place and looked for more clues. Nor would their superiors worry too much about how the murder had been solved. For them it was enough to be able to report success and to have struck another blow against an almost defeated IRA.

Back in the house Miss Keating was roundly abusing a young detective who had been detailed to keep an eye on her. How dare they break in her door? What was going on that they could burst into someone's home brandishing guns in the middle of the night? This wasn't Russia or one of them places. They'd pay for this, not only for the damage they had done, but because she knew people in high places, who would see that they were severely disciplined.

She was only stopped by O'Shea, who told her curtly to get

dressed, that she would have to go to the police station. For what? Aiding and abetting a suspected murderer.

Miss Keating's cheeks went red with rage. Her? Who did they think they were dealing with? She was a respectable woman, she was the friend of cabinet ministers, she had done her bit for Ireland when to do your bit for Ireland involved dangers about which the present, soft generation knew nothing. So passionate was her anger that she almost convinced herself of her innocence.

Dolan and Corrigan, too, were ordered to dress and proceed to the station, as was Nellie. Corrigan feared that the police would show some sign of recognising him, but to his relief they treated him politely, but as if they had never met. They got dressed and assembled in the hall, silent except for the girl, who wept as noisily and as messily as ever.

The breaking in of the door, the shouts and the shot had wakened many on the road and when Eddie was taken out a small crowd had assembled. The Kennedy family and Kitty stood in a group on their front doorstep and, though he had been told to stay indoors, Conor had slipped out too in his dressing gown.

'What's going on?' Barry asked one of the uniformed guards who were keeping an eye on the onlookers.

'Police raid,' said the other. 'The fella that shot the sergeant at the New Year.'

Just then they brought out Eddie, still blood-stained, dirty and barefooted.

'Resisting arrest,' said the policeman with a grin.

As he came out Eddie caught Conor's eye. It was as if he was the first person he had met that day, the first face he could recognise.

'How're you, Conor?' he said and managed a broken grin.

The little boy's jaw dropped and his mother pulled him over to her, putting her arms round him. Eddie winked before he was hustled down the front steps by the detectives and into a waiting car.

13

Kay had hardly slept the night before. Mixed with her joy at the reappearance of Eddie was the terror she felt for him. On the run, for shooting someone dead! She found it almost impossible to believe that her lover, who had always seemed so gentle and shy, could do such a thing, but she had heard it from his own lips. She knew he didn't mean to do it. It must have been some mistake, the gun went off or something.

Next morning, despite herself, she told Vera. It was the last thing she meant to do, but she was desperate to talk to somebody. Her friend went white in the face.

'You mean Eddie did that murder?'

'It wasn't a murder.'

'What was it then?'

'It was a shooting, an IRA thing. It could have been an accident even.'

Vera looked at her dubiously. 'What are you going to do?'

'We're going to get married.'

'Married? How?'

'I don't know, in secret. Eddie'll fix it up some way.'

'Supposing he gets caught?'

'Don't say that! Sure the police don't even know it was him . . . and if you tell one living soul . . .' she went on, already regretting she'd said as much as she had.

'Of course I won't,' said Vera.

'Swear.'

'As God is my judge, I swear.'

'Swear what?'

'That I won't tell a soul about Eddie murdering . . . killing that guy. Jesus,' she went on, 'if he's caught for that he could be hung.'

'Shut up!' said Kay angrily.

She went to the theatre early, half hoping that he might be there waiting for her, but there was no sign of him. She did the early show in a daze, but when she came off he still hadn't turned up, though she'd left word with the doorman to let him wait in one of the disused dressing rooms if he did. He's being cagey, she thought to herself, probably waiting for darkness so he can move around without being spotted.

But when she came off after her number in the early evening show, Vera was waiting for her in the dressing room and one look at her face told her the news was bad.

'What?' she cried.

'I'm sorry,' said Vera.

'What? What?'

'He's been caught,' said Vera. 'It's in the evening paper.'

'On no! Oh Jesus Christ!' She tried to find some glimmer of hope. 'Are you sure it's him?'

'Police earlier today raided a house in connection with the murder of Sergeant Paul O'Grady early in the New Year,' read Vera from a newspaper. 'A man, aged twenty-five, from County Tipperary, is understood to be helping them with their inquiries.'

'It mightn't be him.'

'Kay, love, it's him. Don't kid yourself.'

She collapsed to the floor. Vera bent down and put her arms round her and there they stayed, both in tears, rocking back and forth. All her dreams were dead, the last of her hopes had vanished. One of the Coliseum Girls came in and stopped in alarm at the door.

'What is it? Is the child coming?'

'No,' said Vera, 'it's not that.'

'Youse are wanted for "Run Rabbit Run".'

'Don't be daft. You can see she can't do that.'

'What'll we do?' asked the chorus girl.

'How do I know? Skip the number, tell Dickie to fill in.'

'Jaysus, he'll go mad.'

'See if I care,' said Vera. 'Shh there,' she said to Kay.

The Coliseum Girl went off, to return a moment later with Dickie.

'What's up?' he wanted to know.

'It's her boyfriend,' said Vera.

'Ditched her, has he?'

'No,' said Vera. 'For your information, he's been arrested for shooting that guard at the New Year.'

'He didn't do it,' said Kay, through her tears.

'All right, no panic,' said Dickie. 'I'll fill in.' He turned and went but, as he did so, they heard him say 'the stupid little tart' to the Coliseum Girl.

*

O'Shea was filling up his report of the arrest. He looked up when Callinan came in. 'Well?'

'Nothing yet,' said Callinan, 'but sure we're only starting on him.'

'I wonder how much he has to tell us anyway. Pity about the broken nose, though. They'll claim torture or whatever.'

'Sure we don't need a confession. We have everything. The gun, the prints, the witnesses.'

'Sure, but I'd like to lay my hands on McCaigue, too, if he could lead us to him.'

'He'll be gone North long since.'

'I suppose so. The RUC have no word of him, though.'

'I'll get back to Eddie so,' said Callinan.

'No, wait a bit. Give him a bit of time to think things out. I got a phone call from Dickie Delaney.'

'From who?'

'You know, the comedian.'

'Oh yes. He's a gas ticket.' Callinan grinned as he blew on the skinned knuckles of his right fist.

'Apparently Eddie has a girlfriend in his theatre. I think we'll go and talk to her.'

They came as she was about to go home with Vera. 'Miss Nelligan?'

'Yes?' She turned a tear-swollen face to them.

'Police. Could we have a word with you,' he looked at Vera, 'alone.'

'Eddie O'Sullivan, I believe he's a friend of yours,' said O'Shea.

'We're engaged to be married.' Kay was trying to keep calm.

'Indeed? How long have you been engaged?'

'Since Christmas.'

'You know that he's been charged?'

'I read it in the paper.'

'Murder,' said the younger man, who was rougher and meaner looking.

'I'm sure he didn't do it,' said Kay. That was her story and she was sticking to it.

'Are you now?' sneered Callinan.

'Where would you have been on the night of January third?' asked O'Shea

'Here. We were doing the panto.'

'And O'Sullivan, did you see him that night?'

'Yes. He was here too.'

'What time was that?'

'All night. He was here all night.'

'Who else saw him?'

There was a pause. 'I don't know. He was in the audience and then he came round.'

'Came round?'

'After the show.'

'Then the doorman would have seen him, wouldn't he?'

No reply.

They asked her about Eddie, how they had met, what she knew about his friends and his family. They quizzed her left and right, up and down about his movements. She knew so little it all sounded improbable.

'Listen, Kay,' said Callinan, as if he knew her real well, 'Eddie's charged with murder. If you don't help us you could be up for being an accessory.'

'I've told you all I know,' she said, 'I swear.'

As she left she asked: 'Can I see him? When can I see him?'

'That'd be hard,' said O'Shea.

'Maybe if you could remember some useful details about who he hung round with,' said Callinan.

'You don't understand,' she said, 'I've got to see him.'

'Look, we'll keep in touch with you,' said O'Shea, but he said it with compassion. He looked at the door after she left. 'God love her,' he said.

*

Eddie sat in his bleak cell. Two bloody pieces of gauze still plugged his swollen nose. He ached all over, his arms and ribs a mass of bruises under his clothes. His head throbbed, even his teeth were paining.

It was a nightmare that didn't seem to have an end. He gazed curiously at the graffiti on the wall beside him as if he was seeing it for the first time.

'May Coyne is a hoor . . . fuck her . . . I am innocent . . . tell it to the mareens . . . Oh God, oh God have mercy on me . . . shut up you stupid bastard . . . Billy Quinn, aged 17 years . . .' The usual, banal catalogue of poverty and degradation. Somewhere, in the back of his mind, behind the pain and the confusion, Eddie saw himself as no different to the parade of thieves and sex offenders and the rest who had flowed through the cell over the years like a river of misery. When he was gone from there he'd be replaced by someone else and he in turn and so on, an unending procession of those born to be losers.

He'd been whisked here from his place of capture in a car, handcuffed to a detective on either side, then worked over all day by young brawny men in braces and rolled-up shirtsleeves, their jackets taken off. Questions had been shouted at him, most of which he couldn't understand; once he had been given a cup of watery tea, which was taken off him after a couple of mouthfuls. He had tried to give nothing away, not that he had much to give away, anyhow. Then a doctor had been brought in, who had examined him and said 'He'll get by.' After that he'd been taken up to a room, where he'd been put up before three stony-faced army officers and some barristers, one of whom, some Dublin guy, claimed to represent him. He had refused to recognise the court, as he'd always been instructed to do. There were a handful of bored reporters, who had been summoned from a card game in the corridor outside to hear bail being refused and Eddie being remanded in custody.

Heavy footsteps approached in the echoing corridor outside his cell and the door clanged open. He braced himself for another beating.

*

Kay was on her way to Vera's room, which was in a house within walking distance of the theatre. Her only thought was to get into bed, or rather onto the sofa and cover her head with a blanket or a coat. The business of facing the light of day, of putting on a face before people, of even their sympathy, was becoming unbearable. Somewhere in the darkness she might find sleep and, until then, she could at least shut out the world and curl up in misery like a wounded animal that returns to its lair. What she would do the next day she didn't know; certainly she was not going back to the Coliseum.

'Miss.'

It was a man in an overcoat and a pair of expensive-looking leather gloves. He had glasses and a bony hawk-like face that was a bit like Mr de Valera's, except that he was shorter and spoke in a funny accent, English maybe. He carried a little attaché case.

'Miss Nelligan, could I have a word?'

'Is it police?' asked Kay.

'No, not police. I'm a friend of your friend.'

'What?'

'Mr O'Sullivan, Eddie. I have the honour of his acquaintance.'

'What do you want?'

He looked around furtively. 'Were you followed?'

'I don't know. Look, what's all this about?'

'Come with me,' he said, and when she hesitated he added: 'It's to your own advantage.'

She followed him, though she didn't know why. They went down a side street to where there was a small cafe and went in. He bought her a cup of thin, wartime tea, without asking her what she wanted, and an oily coal-black liquid that purported to be coffee for himself.

'Well,' he said. 'Here's a how-de-do.'

'Who are you?' she asked. 'What do you want with me?'

'I'm a representative, a humble representative of the organisation. The voice of one crying in the wilderness, as it were.'

'What? The IRA, is it?'

'Let's just say something like that. Tell me, have the S-Branch been speaking to you?'

'The guards? Yes.'

'I hope you told them nothing.'

'What would I tell them?'

'You might let slip something inadvertently. Tell them nothing, that's the ticket. Let your lips be sealed.'

She looked at him. He was smiling and she felt her gorge rising. For the first time since the whole business started she felt hard, tough.

'Look, I don't know what your game is,' she said, 'but I want no part of it. None.'

He was instantly conciliatory. 'No, no,' he said, 'don't be cross. He that is slow to answer is better than the mighty. Let me get to the nub.'

With his funny way of talking you wouldn't know what he was on about, she thought.

'Look, we know all about you. We know you're in the family way and that your parents have disowned you. Most regrettable, most regrettable.' He shook his head sorrowfully. 'Now, what I, we, would like to do is take care of you.'

'What do you mean, "take care of me"?'

'We'd like you to go away somewhere, somewhere away from Dublin. We'd fix it. Somewhere you can have the child, arrange for it to be taken care of.'

'An abortion?'

'Certainly not!' He was shocked. 'Good God! What do you take us for? The child would be put up for adoption or into an orphanage.'

'And what about me?'

'You? Well, you couldn't come back here, not for a while, the way things are. An Egyptian exile, you could go down the country. We'd see you had somewhere to stay there.' He stared hard at her. 'Look, you know it's for the best. What else are you going to do about the child anyway? This way you'll have some money, you'll have somewhere to go.'

She tried to think. 'Why do you want to do this?'

'We like to take care of our own.'

'I'm not one of your own.'

'Ah but Eddie is. He's a soldier of the Republic. Like the song: "Soldiers are we, whose lives are pledged to Ireland".'

'What do I care about that?'

'Everyone should care about that.'

'If he wasn't mixed up in that stuff, this would never have happened.'

'True, but he chose to be mixed up of his own accord.'

She gazed into her tea. 'What'll happen him?'

'We must be prepared for the worst, miss.'

(Miss? Why was he calling her that, she wondered.)

'But remember, there can be no higher destiny than to give your life for Ireland.'

'Rubbish!' she said, quite loudly. The waitress who had served them lifted her head. 'That's a load of rubbish!'

'Quiet!' he said. 'People are listening.'

'I don't care, I don't give a . . .'

'There's no need for that,' he interrupted. 'Look, you're upset, I'm trying to help.' He lowered his voice. 'Listen, I've ten pounds here. Take it and go. Go where you want, only get out of this town.'

'And what about Eddie?'

'You can do nothing for Eddie. You can only make it worse for him.'

'I'm staying. I'm sticking by him.'

'What help would that be? Look, to a lot of people he's a hero, one of the chosen ones.'

'Another martyr for old Ireland,' she said bitterly.

'Yes, sneer all you like,' he said passionately. 'They'll blackguard him all they can, and what better way to do it than to parade a pregnant girlfriend? What'll people think about him then?'

'That's it, that's all you care about, isn't it? That he looks good when, when whatever it is happens to him, so youse can parade him as some kind of saint. That's all that matters to you.'

'Ah no,' he protested, 'we want to help, we want you to be taken care of.' He took an envelope from his pocket. 'Take it,' he said. 'It's good money.'

She ignored it. 'Could you get me to see him?' she asked.

He shook his head. 'Can't be done. They have him locked up tight as a drum.'

'Could I get word to him?'

'What word?'

'Send him a letter, like.'

He looked dubious. 'A letter about what?'

'About marrying me. I know he wants to marry me.'

'How can he marry you?'

'From jail. We could get married in the jail.'

Again he looked doubtful. 'I'll see what I can do. Would you go away to have the baby after that?'

'Yes,' she said. 'What else can I do?'

'Maybe he wouldn't want to do it, to get married.'

'Yes he would. Just get the letter to him.'

'All right, I'll try.'

'I'll have the letter for you tonight at the Coliseum.'

'Someone will be there to collect it.'

She got to her feet. Her head felt light and clear. Somewhere within her she was finding something, some strength she never knew was there. If there was a moment when she left her girlhood behind her, this was it. From now on she would be a fighter, harder, more self-aware. The tears seemed to have dried up in her. The grief that she felt would be contained. Without looking back she walked out of the cafe.

He caught the waitress's eye. 'In Rama was there a voice heard,' he said, 'lamentation and weeping and great mourning.' Her jaw dropped in astonishment.

Back in Vera's flat, Kay got out an ink bottle, a pen and some wartime paper, crude and brown with rough bits in it. The nib was scratchy and she got ink on her fingers and a blot on the paper.

> Dear Eddie,
>
> I am very sorry you were caught. A man came to me and said he might get you this. I know you want to marry me. Ask them in the prison will they let us be married for God's sake and the baby. I pray to God and the Blessed Virgin that all will go good for you. I love you and I will always I swear. Ask them can we get married.
>
> Your loving Kay

She sealed it, but put no name on the envelope, and gave it to Vera to bring to the theatre. During the evening show a young fella, a messenger boy, came to the stage door and took it away.

That night, in a room somewhere in the city, the man with the gloves, McCaigue and a third man, read the letter.

'God help her,' said McCaigue.

'God help her, what?' said the third man, who was younger than the others. 'Bitch! She deserves everything she gets.'

'Charity,' said McCaigue.

The young man got angrier. 'I'll keep my charity for someone more deserving, thank you. Corrupting a decent fella like O'Sullivan with her carrying-on. Those show people are no better than barnyard animals.'

'Maybe it wouldn't be so bad if they got married,' said McCaigue. 'You know, like Plunkett in 1916 that married Grace Gifford on the night before he was shot. It'd get a lot of sympathy for him.'

'No,' said the man with the gloves. 'Grace Gifford wasn't pregnant. He'd get precious little sympathy if that came out, and it would come out. The S-Branch would make sure of that.'

'I dunno,' said the third man.

'No,' said Gloves. 'Let things take their course. There'll be protest meetings and demands for his reprieve when he's sentenced. That's where we'll get the sympathy. The girl will take the money, we'll hear no more from her.'

'God help them both,' said McCaigue.

'I'll tear up this so, will I?' asked the third man, picking up the letter.

'No,' said Gloves, 'we'll send it to him, in an amended version. For the letter killeth but the spirit giveth life.'

'What?'

'Second Corinthians, chapter three, verse five.'

'Jaysus, you and your bible quotations,' said McCaigue.

'The advantages of a Protestant education,' said Gloves.

*

When Eddie was handed the letter, by a warder who had been paid for his trouble, the colour of the paper had changed. He recognised the writing as Kay's, for it had been skilfully forged and, indeed, the words were hers for the most part. But all mention of marriage had gone from it and, instead, she told him that she was going away to England to have the child.

His eyes filled with tears as he read the letter and he kissed it fervently.

'Will there be a reply?' asked the warder, who had been watching him with curiosity.

'Could you get something to her?' asked Eddie.

'It'd cost me me job if it got out that I'd helped you,' said the warder. 'I'd need, you know, a few bob.'

'I have nothing.'

'No, but your pals, the ones who paid to get this in . . .'

'I'm sure they'd pay you again, well.'

The warder looked around furtively, then produced a crumpled piece of paper and a pencil butt from his pocket. 'Be quick about it,' he said, 'and if anyone finds it, it's got nothing to do with me. Understood?'

'Understood.'

My darling Kay,

I pray to God this will reach you before you go away to England. I love you and always will, no matter what should befall. Come to the prison, tell them about the baby and say we wish to marry. I am more than willing to give my life for Ireland and for the Cause I believe in, that one day our beloved country may strike off the tyrant's chains and be free, but I want you and the baby to carry my name always. Please come. If not, we will meet again for certain in a Better Place some day. With all my love may God go with you,

Eddie

The warder took off his cap (he had a cigarette behind his

ear, Eddie noticed) put the letter in it and put the cap back on his head. Eddie rolled up the one from Kay, as he supposed, into a small ball which he placed in the toe of his shoe.

Dear Kay, [said the letter which she received]

It has come to my notice that it is being said that I am to be the father of your child. I do not know who is trying to blacken my name by this dastardly lie. I cannot believe it could be you. As you know, I never in any way behaved in an improper manner to you and I beg you to tell the truth to all about this. I am more than willing to give my life for Ireland and for the Cause I believe in. Do not let the shoneens and despoilers of the nation's liberty slander me in the hour of my greatest glory. Soon the Irish people and our beloved land will be united. My only regret is that I will not be with them on that glorious day when we are A Nation Once Again. Tell them the truth about my innocence, carry on the good fight and God Bless Ireland.

Signed Volunteer Edward O'Sullivan,

South Tipperary Brigade, Óglaigh na hÉireann

Kay's face went white with anger. 'He never wrote this. Eddie never wrote this in a fit,' she said.

The man with the gloves spread his hands out as if helpless. 'That's his letter. Don't you recognise his handwriting?'

She realised that she had never seen anything written by him. 'He didn't, he didn't write it!' she said.

'Shhh! Quiet!' he said. 'It was smuggled out of Mountjoy yesterday.'

'You know perfectly well that he's the father,' she said. 'You said it yourself.'

'I was *told* he was the father,' he said. 'it's not the same thing. Now I know differently.'

'He is the father, he is the father. Everyone knows he is!'

'Quiet, people are listening.' They were standing on a street corner and, to be sure, heads were turning.

'Do you believe me?'

'I have to believe what our own man wrote.'

She started to scream. 'You bastard, you bloody swine!'

He pushed her roughly into a doorway. 'For God's sake be quiet,' he said.

But she still went on screaming. 'He never wrote this letter. It's not by him. Fuck you! You fucking bastard with your lies and your . . .' She burst into sobs. A passing woman made a move as if to join them.

'It's all right,' he said, 'just a bit of hysteria, she'll be fine.' The woman looked doubtful, but moved on.

He placed his gloved hands on her shoulders but instantly withdrew them, for he was a man who found physical contact difficult. 'Calm down, please,' he said. 'Look, it's all most unfortunate. The best thing you can do is go away to England and have your baby. Here, I still have the money, take it.' He handed the envelope towards her.

'Stuff it! Stuff your money, you liar! I wouldn't touch it, I wouldn't touch your dirty money,' and she ran away from him down the street.

He started to go after her, then stopped. Ten pounds was a tidy sum and there was so much could be done with it. There were no funds left to help those who had been deported from England at the start of the war, or the dependants of those interned in the Curragh. There were no funds left to carry on the armed struggle. It was madness to give ten pounds to some girl who was having a baby.

He shrugged and turned on his heel, muttering to himself: 'Wherefore do ye spend money for that which is not bread? and your labour for that which satisfieth not.'

It was only when she got back to the room that Kay began to wonder how she would manage.

*

They had another whipround in the Coliseum, same as they'd had to bury Frankie Fox, this time to send Kay to England. The result was a disappointment to Vera, who had organised it. It wasn't that people were unwilling to give, so they said, but it was a bad time of year with Christmas not long over and the hard times that was in it. Most of them gave something, but very little, just a bob or two. Dickie Delaney, the miserable little skinflint, promised something but then never stumped up and, when Vera took him on about it, turned abusive and threatened to fire her.

Tommy and May Flynn refused to give anything at all, saying Kay had made her bed, let her lie in it. But Tommy came round later and slipped Vera two pounds, which she knew he couldn't afford.

'I'm sorry. It'd be more but we've got to batten down the hatches,' he said. 'Dickie is letting us go at the end of the month and there's nothing doing anywhere else just now. We're hoping we might get something with a circus. Only don't say anything to May about this. She'd have me guts for garters if she knew. She's very holy.'

Vera had got the address of a theatrical digs in Manchester

that Kay could go to. Harry Harmond, the conductor, had written and the landlady had agreed to take her in. Everyone said the landlady was a decent woman, but Kay looked at the few pounds in her fist with a sinking heart. How could she pay the rent for any length of time, let alone keep the baby? Yet keep it she was fiercely determined to do, more than ever. No one was going take it from her, no one was going to force her to hand it over to some orphanage, not her parents, her friends, the IRA or anyone else.

She knew well enough already the stigma of an illegitimate child, but if she could get some theatre work, at least the people there would be more understanding, less inclined to look down their noses at her. What's more, in a strange land she could be more anonymous, less likely to be gossiped about and pointed out.

Eddie, though she didn't fully admit it to herself, was dead for her. She still loved him and suffered the pain of what had happened, but there was nothing more she could do about him, she felt. Somehow, she realised, she had to close the door on all that had gone before. What lay ahead of him was too awful to contemplate. It would be better for her and for the child to be far away from it all.

But how? The money would hardly do more than pay her fare. She would have the baby, but then? Even if she didn't get into a show at once, there were plenty of jobs for women over there, people said, in factories and the like. But until she was right after the baby how could she live? And after that where would she live, who would mind the child while she worked? Again she looked at the miserable few banknotes that had been collected.

Then, a few days before she was due to go, a man came to the front door of Vera's place. Another man. He looked vaguely familiar, but she couldn't remember where, if ever, they had met.

'Miss Nelligan?'

She had come to hate these unexpected encounters. Men with questions, men bearing letters, men with plans for her, but always men bearing bad tidings. 'What do you want? Is it police?'

'No,' he said hastily, 'no, no, nothing like that.'

He was bald, middle-aged with a kind face and seemed shy. But that meant nothing, nothing at all.

'Are you from the other lot?'

'What?'

'You know what I mean, the *Boys*,' she said sarcastically.

'Good God no, not at all.'

'What do you want then? How did you find me?'

'I went to the Coliseum. I talked to a friend of yours, a blonde girl. She gave me this address, she told me you're going away to England. Thank God I found you before then.' He tried not to look at her too closely; her pregnancy was becoming obvious.

'Who are you from?'

'From? No one . . . well, I suppose from Frankie Fox, in a manner of speaking.'

'What? What do you mean Frankie? Frankie's dead.'

'Yes, I was in the same digs as him.'

'Well?' She was still suspicious, though in spite of herself she was interested.

'He was sick, sicker than we realised.'

'Yes.'

'One night he came to me. He looked awful, I think he knew

he hadn't long, though nothing would persuade him to go to a doctor. He asked me if I'd mind this.'

Dolan took a bulky brown envelope from his raincoat pocket. 'I think it's money, he said he wouldn't trust a bank. He said, I remember it: "If anything happens to me I want you to give it to Kay Nelligan, the singer from the Coliseum. Her name is written on it." You remember, I met you once before, after the show?'

Kay took the envelope in her hands, but didn't attempt to open it.

'I said: "For God's sake, get some treatment for yourself," and he said "Yes, yes," but I knew he wouldn't,' said Dolan.

'Why didn't he give me this himself?'

'I asked him that, too. He said: "It's only if something happens me." But, says I: "You hardly know me." "I'm sure I can trust you," he said. "There isn't many in the business I'm in that wouldn't pocket it for themselves, given the chance. Anyway," he says, "it's just a precaution, as the bishop said to the actress."'

Dolan looked puzzled. ' "As the bishop said to the actress." That perplexed me. What was that meant to mean? One of his jokes I suppose. Three days later he was dead . . .' He paused awkwardly. 'I'm very sorry,' he said, 'about Eddie O'Sullivan and, and everything . . .'

'Yes.'

There was another awkward silence between them, neither knowing what further to say.

'Well,' said Dolan, 'I'd better be off so.'

'No,' said Kay, 'wait.'

She tore open the envelope. It was packed with bank notes.

'God save us,' said Dolan, 'there must be more than two hundred quid there.'

There was a grubby note too, written with indelible pencil, the kind that left a purple stain on your lips and your fingers. Frankie had scrawled:

Dear Kay,
This is for you to take care of yourself. Remember me and don't do anything I would not do, God Bless.
Frankie.

She had to bite her lip to stop the tears flowing. Wordlessly she gave the note to Dolan.

'He was a decent man, a good man,' he said after he'd read it. 'Well, he's in heaven now, I'm sure of that.'

They looked at each other, then he put out his hand. 'Goodbye, miss,' he said. 'Be careful of that money and mind yourself now.'

'I will,' she said, shaking his hand. 'Goodbye.'

He turned and walked away down the street. It was only after he was gone that she realised that she hadn't thanked him, or even asked him his name.

*

Four days passed. Trailing a plume of black smoke, the ship headed out towards the grey, warship-infested sea. Down the river it went, leaving a white wake, past the grimy empty warehouses, the gas holders, the poor riverside pubs and the wet, cobblestoned streets with their slum houses that led off from the quays.

Kay stood on deck, looking back on the city, growing dark

in the twilight, old, battered, its ancient houses here and there, relics of old decency. It looked tired, worn out with too much history and too much suffering. Out the boat carried her, out into a bigger world. The buildings fell away, the ship ran beside a long sea wall, ending in a red and white lighthouse. Behind it, across a strand, the lights of the suburbs were beginning to twinkle. Beyond the wall the waves rolled large.

She thought of all that had gone before and wondered, now without fear, about all that was to come. She thought of Eddie, of Frankie and all the others, living and dead. The waves slapped against the sides and she felt no anger, only an acceptance of what lay ahead. She looked back for a last look – she would not see that sight again. Time moved on a notch. The child moved within her. It was a blessing.

EPILOGUE

I

A month after Kay left, Eddie was tried. Refusing to recognise the court, he was unable to call witnesses or to give evidence. Passing sentence the judge said: 'The court finds you, Edward O'Sullivan, guilty of the charge, and the order and sentence of this military court is that you suffer death by shooting . . .'

The case was reported, briefly, on the inner pages of the papers, for wartime censorship made sure that everything to do with terrorist activities was played down. Nevertheless a protest meeting in the Mansion House about the sentence was well attended by, among others, a couple of TDs, a senior barrister and a rising novelist, whose latest work had just been banned as 'tending to deprave and corrupt'. The meeting had no effect, however, for the government declined to commute the death sentence.

On the night before Eddie was to die a rosary vigil was held outside the General Post Office. Those present prayed for the repose of his soul, as it went to join the gallant dead who had given their lives for Ireland. They prayed, too, that God might open the hearts of those who were sending an innocent man to his death. They gossiped as well about a girl he loved and was engaged to marry, but none of them knew who she was or where she might be found. As they knelt on the wet pavement, most passers-by crossed the road or went into the roadway so that they would not have to walk past them.

Eddie spent his last night in the company of two warders, assigned to keep him safe from violence until it was time for him to be shot. They were awkwardly good-humoured during the night, offering him tea and cigarettes, and talking about football, films and anything but the subject that was nearest everybody's mind.

His only request had been that, at the time of his execution, he could keep on his person what he supposed to be Kay's last letter, which had been found during a search. At first this had been refused but then, when the prison chaplain had had a word with the archbishop's palace, the decision had been reversed. The note was harmless enough, it was decided, and providing no word of it reached the outside world, he could carry it with him to his death.

The chaplain, who had befriended him and prayed with him, also got word to him about Kay's departure to England.

'Sure it's probably for the best, Eddie,' said the chaplain. 'She'll have a chance to start afresh there and make a new life for herself.'

Eddie said nothing, nodding his head and looking at the floor so the tears in his eyes could not be seen.

Now that everything was decided there was no more anger, only sympathy for him. To the other prisoners, criminal as well as political, he was a hero, though an unseen one, for he was kept well away from them. Before he was taken from his cell, he made his confession to the chaplain and took holy communion. Then he shook hands with his warders and went to his death looking pale and impossibly young.

The prison was hushed as he was brought to a distant yard, blindfolded, and placed against a wall. A squad of soldiers, most of them as youthful as himself, took aim. There was a barked command in Irish and a volley rang out. Silently he fell, as if in a swoon. The officer in command stepped forward and delivered a *coup de grâce*, a single shot through the heart. The forged note was in Eddie's pocket, but when his body was returned to his family it had been removed.

Wrapped in a tricolour, his coffin was brought back to his home in the country and given a full republican burial. A large crowd turned out, men marched in step on either side of it and his Uncle Pat insisted on limping at the front of the procession. Like most of those present he was a veteran of many such occasions. At the graveside a fiery orator, drawing heavily on the speeches of Robert Emmett and Padraic Pearse for inspiration, called down the spirits of the republican dead and told the listeners that Eddie's memory would live as long as time itself.

Within a week he was utterly forgotten, except by Kay, his family and a handful of people who could recite the lists of the national martyrs. Within a year he was no more than a footnote in a few rarely read books, subsumed into the general body of the sacred dead.

Six months later McCaigue was lured into a trap by the Special Branch and killed in a shoot-out. The fact that there had been only one shot and that it was in the back of his head caused some disquiet, but all attempts at an official inquiry came to nothing.

II

Fifteen years came and went and the war became a memory. In a pleasant, leafy suburb of an English city a postman delivered a letter to Kay from a woman in Belfast.

> Some time before his death, my late brother, Liam McCaigue, who was murdered by Free State police in Dublin during the war years, left me a number of papers. He said to me that a wrong had been done to you when one of the Boys back then had been under sentence of death. That he had tried to send you the enclosed letter from prison but that you had never got it and another one was sent you in its place. I don't know why this was done.
>
> I have had the real letter for many years, not knowing who you were, but then I saw you on the television series and realised it must be for you it was intended. I pray that it may, in some way, undo the wrong that was done. Say a prayer for the soul of my brother, as I will for this young man that sent the letter.

Kay sat on the side of her bed and read the letter from Eddie, now faded with age. Dry-eyed she read it twice, then stayed for a long, long time, utterly still, long after darkness fell. Finally, she started as if to tear it in two, then stopped and put it in a larger envelope, which she hid under some clothes in a drawer. Her children would discover it there after her death.